Rebecca's Hand Shook At the Enormous Responsibility She Had Undertaken. . . .

Knowing that she held the stranger's life on the tip of her trigger finger, she wanted to know very badly who he was and where he had come from.

"Look at me."

As though reading her thoughts, his head rose slowly on his shoulders until he stared proudly forward. Lost in his piercing gaze, Reb momentarily surrendered to the stranger's power, willingly giving to him a part of herself never before offered to anyone. In that fleeting instant she experienced a feeling of intense belonging so unique that it took her by surprise.

"I will never belong to any man, including you," she whispered, "who does not also belong to me."

Dear Reader,

We, the editors of Tapestry Romances, are committed to bringing you two outstanding original romantic historical novels each and every month.

From Kentucky in the 1850s to the court of Louis XIII, from the deck of a pirate ship within sight of Gibraltar to a mining camp high in the Sierra Nevadas, our heroines experience life and love, romance and adventure.

Our aim is to give you the kind of historical romances that you want to read. We would enjoy hearing your thoughts about this book and all future Tapestry Romances. Please write to us at the address below.

The Editors
Tapestry Romances
POCKET BOOKS
1230 Avenue of the Americas
Box TAP
New York, N.Y. 10020

A Loving Defiance

Joan Johnston

A TAPESTRY BOOK
PUBLISHED BY POCKET BOOKS NEW YORK

This novel is a work of historical fiction. Names, characters, places and incidents relating to non-historical figures are either the product of the author's imagination or are used fictitiously. Any resemblance of such non-historical incidents, places or figures to actual events or locales or persons, living or dead, is entirely coincidental.

An *Original* publication of TAPESTRY BOOKS

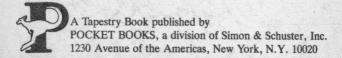

A Tapestry Book published by
POCKET BOOKS, a division of Simon & Schuster, Inc.
1230 Avenue of the Americas, New York, N.Y. 10020

Copyright © 1985 by Joan Mertens Johnston
Cover artwork copyright © 1985 Harry Bennett

ISBN: 0-671-54426-8

First Tapestry Books printing February, 1985

10 9 8 7 6 5 4 3 2 1

Printed in the U.S.A.

For Hugh

Chapter One

Laramie Mountains
April 1865

REB HUNTER KNEED HER BAY MARE, BRANDY, AND
when the animal grunted, she tightened the cinch on
the saddle one more notch. She led her horse out of
the barn and hitched her to the rail in front of the log
ranch house. One of the few things Reb enjoyed
about being a rancher's daughter was owning her own
cowhorse. She gave the horse's silky jowls a comforting pat and darted inside. Brandy snorted twice at
being left standing in the cold, the foggy air billowing
from her nostrils like smoke from some mythical
dragon.

"Where do you think you're going?"

Reb closed the door behind her and stood, feet
apart, facing her father. Matt Hunter leaned against
the heavy pine trestle table that dominated the room.
Steam rose from the mug of coffee cupped in his
hands. Behind him Reb could see her younger sister,

1

Dillon, working on some flapjacks at the iron stove and trying not to appear to be eavesdropping.

"Where I go every spring at this time—to take supplies to Blue in the mountains," Reb replied quietly.

"I can't spare your brother to go with you this year. Spotted Tail's Brulé Sioux tribe is under guard at Ft. Laramie on their way to a reservation they don't want any part of, and Standing Buffalo's band of Brulé renegades are raising hell. I have to get the roundup finished before that powder keg blows up," he said brusquely.

Reb raised her chin an inch and crossed her arms under her breasts. "Fine then. Adam can stay here and help you. I'll go by myself."

"No Reb, it's too dangerous. You saw what happened to the Morgan family."

Reb's face paled. One of the many groups of settlers that passed by on their way to the promised land, the Morgan family had stayed overnight at the ranch before continuing their trip north to the Oregon Trail. After dinner Reb had held the little blond girl in her lap and the towheaded boy had played with her younger brother, Jesse. Even now, the picture of what had been left of the mutilated couple and their two children when she and Adam had discovered them an hour north of the house made her sick. Reb swallowed back her nausea at the memory of those bloody, hairless heads.

"That was March. This is April, almost May. I'll be careful," she managed to say.

Matt rose to his feet. Tall and attractively lean, the golden-haired man hardly seemed old enough to be father to five children, the eldest of whom was twenty-two. But there was no question he was the figure of authority in the house and expected obedience.

"Rebecca, don't argue with me. I said no."

Calling her by her full name was a sure sign of his distemper, a reminder that she was a seventeen-year-old girl and there were limits to what she could do. The setdown was not surprising, just frustrating. She had been prepared for her father's attempt to keep her from making the journey. In the past he had found other excuses. One year it had been a threatening blizzard; another, she had just gotten over a bad cold. Each year she had overcome his objections and made the trip. This year there was a difference, however. She no longer had a strong ally to support her. Perhaps invoking her ally's name would be enough. It would have to be.

"If Mama were alive, she'd let me go. I know it!" Reb said defiantly.

It was Matt's turn to pale. His topaz eyes fixed on the empty chair where Rachel should be sitting. In six months the loss hadn't gotten any easier to bear. Reb was right, of course. If Rachel were alive, she would insist Reb be allowed to make her yearly pilgrimage to see the mountain man who had been like a second father to her, and to please Rachel he would have agreed.

For most of his adult life, Matt had trapped beaver with his friend Blue in the Laramie Mountains. Six years ago they'd parted ways. Matt's eyes narrowed and his jaw tightened in anger until a muscle in his cheek jerked. He'd trusted Blue, and had been enraged at the discovery that his best friend had deceived him. In his first fury at that betrayal, he'd almost killed Blue, who would not fight back when

3

Matt attacked him with a knife, stabbing Blue in the ribs. Rachel had grabbed his arm then, begging him to spare Blue's life. That had only infuriated him more, and it was not until she reminded him what Blue meant to Reb that Matt dropped his knife, and turned his back forever on his friend.

Matt had left the mountains and moved his family down to this road ranch along the Overland Trail that was one of the many way stations where the Overland Stage changed horses while its passengers enjoyed a meal. Over the years he'd established a good-sized herd of cattle so that he operated more as a ranch now, with the station a service he continued to provide. Through it all, Matt had hidden his bitterness and anger from his children.

He regretted that decision now. He couldn't explain to his daughter why he didn't want her to go near the mountain man, especially now that Rachel was dead and could not answer the questions that were sure to arise. The Indians provided a valid reason to forbid the sojourn without any other explanation, so he turned away from Reb without answering her charge.

"It's time for breakfast. Call your brothers," he said, dismissing her.

Reb hadn't given up, but she had planned to eat before she left anyway. Hiding her exasperation, she moved to the front door and called Adam from the barn, then called Garth and Jesse from their wing of the house.

Dillon flashed her sister a conspiratorial grin that crinkled her green eyes at the corners, and then flipped her auburn curls back from a breathtakingly creamy complexion.

"You could help by setting the table," Dillon suggested. When Reb passed her at the stove Dillon

4

murmured so their father couldn't hear, "I'm surprised you gave in so easily. Or did you?"

Reb just grunted and pulled some dishes from the cupboard. If she had been more desirous of male attention she might have been jealous of her sister's beauty. Her own short black locks and mahogany brown eyes did not seem to have the same effect on men. She had no way of knowing it was not her looks or her exceptional height that discouraged male attention, but her distant manner. In fact, she had the same flawless complexion as her sister, if you didn't count the freckles. Her straight, boyishly cut hair fell onto her brow haphazardly and hid the beautiful arched brows that framed her large, expressive eyes. An aquiline nose, high cheekbones and a stubborn mouth and chin completed the picture.

When Reb finished setting the table with the good china, she poured herself a cup of coffee and seated herself at her place to the left of her father. He didn't seem to notice when they were joined by two of her brothers.

When it appeared Jesse's fidgeting might break her father's reverie, Reb shot a warning glance at Garth, who, at twenty and the second son, was least like his sire. He silently nodded his head in understanding and immediately proceeded to distract the youngster. Garth's quiet demeanor, dark hair and penetrating black eyes evidenced their grandmother's Indian heritage. Shorter than Matt, Garth made up in wiry strength what he lacked in size. Garth also lacked the flamboyant sense of humor Matt seemed to have handed down intact to Adam, his first-born.

The tension dissipated when Adam burst into the house, rubbing his hands together and blowing on them to warm them. As he passed by his youngest brother's chair he placed his frigid fingers on Jesse's ears.

"Hey, stop that!"

Adam tousled Jesse's hair in conciliation, then plopped into his chair next to the youth.

Jesse was a miniature physical copy of Adam, and it appeared from his gangly limbs that he would grow to equal his brother's six-foot size. Both had Matt's sandy blond hair and their mother's green eyes.

"Jacks coming up," Dillon announced. She handed the plate of flapjacks to her father and joined the rest of the family at the table, where they joined hands in the traditional short grace Matt still said in deference to Rachel.

"I've got the mules packed," Adam said, pouring honey on his pancakes.

"Well, you can unpack them," Matt snapped. He threw Reb an aggrieved stare.

"What's going on?" Adam asked, looking from Reb to Matt and back again. "I thought you told me Dad was letting us go."

"He didn't say anything about not going until just now," Reb defended. "How was I supposed to know he would go back on the promise he made when Mama was alive?"

"This has nothing to do with my promise to your mother," Matt said heatedly, knowing as he spoke that it had everything to do with just that—the promise Rachel had forced him to make and the sanctity of which she had protected all these years—that Reb be allowed to visit Blue each spring. He rationalized that it was a promise to Rachel, but did not say that aloud. Instead he growled, "I am trying to keep you from ending up with your scalp hanging from some Sioux lodgepole! Standing Buffalo and his braves are on the prowl and there's no reason for you to expose yourself to that danger just to deliver some supplies to Blue!"

"I'm not afraid of any Buffalo Man . . ."

"Standing Buffalo!" Matt and Adam said together.

"Standing Buffalo," Reb repeated irritably. "For that matter, I can just as easily be attacked when I'm searching for cattle in some gully during the roundup. That's no good reason to keep me here. You promised Mama when we moved down from the mountains that I could visit Blue every spring. Well, it's spring and even though Mama's not here to help I'm going to hold you to your promise," she grated out.

Reb pushed her chair back and stood at her place, fists balled at her sides. "Unless you plan to keep me tied up or locked in my room, you can't stop me," she said through clenched teeth. "If you do lock me up I'll never forgive you," she added in a harsh whisper. "Don't you understand? I *need* to go."

Her brothers and sister shifted uncomfortably at the melodramatic scene, but no one joined in the private battle of wills.

Reb was as close to pleading for permission as her pride would allow her to go. She let her stricken eyes rest for a moment on her father's stony visage. She didn't know how to explain in words the sense of freedom she found in the Rocky Mountains, isolated from civilization of any kind. Not that their road ranch was a hub of society, but they were visited frequently by travelers on the Overland Stage and by those pioneers headed for the Oregon Trail to the north. And, too, Matt's previous trapping partnership with Blue had made his ranch a haven for those mountain men who, every so often, craved the sound of a human voice.

7

Reb loved to sit by their campfires at night and listen to their stories of survival in the wilderness. She vicariously lived each of their adventures and yearned for the one week of each year that she and Adam took off for Blue's cabin on their own. She refused to be cheated of the time in the mountains she'd enjoyed every year since she had turned eleven.

"At least eat your breakfast before you leave," came a calm voice from the shadows in the corner.

Reb turned to where her grandmother, the Old One, sat in her willow rocker. The perfectly straight white hair, framing her face in two braids that hung forward nearly to her waist, proclaimed that the Old One possessed Indian blood, but not even she herself could say how much, or what kinds. Her flesh seemed to have shrunk over the years so it was stretched taut over her facial bones like a pelt staked out on a willow hoop to dry. Reb had found the Old One's dark black eyes to be wells of wisdom, always providing the cup of promised knowledge. So, as in the past, she let them sway her now.

"You're right," she agreed. "I would only get hungry on the trail." She sat down and picked up her fork, although her trembling hand revealed the tension in her lithe young body.

The sound of the Old One's rocker creaking on the wooden floor filled the silence that had settled on the table. Occasionally a pewter fork would scrape against a china plate, but they ate without speaking.

The Old One felt the charge of lightning in the room waiting to strike. It was bound to come to this, she thought. Maybe if she and Rachel had not been so much at loggerheads . . . but they'd been as different and as evenly matched as two adversaries could be, and Reb had been caught between them.

The Old One had warned Matt against marrying the green-eyed woman with milk-white skin and auburn hair because she had never expected Rachel to fit in to the wilderness life her son led. Who would have believed that the daughter of a Philadelphia historian traveling with the first party of missionaries and settlers along the Oregon Trail would have adapted so well to the hardships endured by a trapper's wife?

But the Old One had to admit she had. Oh, Rachel had clung tenaciously to selected values of the civilization she'd left behind, all right, but she'd been intelligent and realistic enough to reject others and adopt the wisdom of mountain customs instead. The bony point of their contention rested on the fact that Rachel never compromised in her belief that the mountains couldn't remain isolated for long.

She could remember the lecture Rachel gave to the children more than once. "When civilized society finally arrives in the West, as it will in your lifetimes," Rachel had preached, "you'll need certain talents not only to survive, but to excel."

The Old One had scoffed at Rachel's ideas, equally sure, as her Indian forebears had been, that the white man was only passing through. She couldn't swallow the possibility that her daughter-in-law might be right without a lump in her throat, and had looked for ways to thwart Rachel's efforts to prepare her children for "civilized society." Reb had been by far the best tool for that job.

While Rachel instructed Reb on how to read and write, using everything from Shakespeare to obscure philosophies provided by her father, held regular dancing lessons and observed strict etiquette at the table, the Old One made sure Matt instructed Reb on how to shoot straight, trail game and trap beaver. When Rachel insisted a dress was proper attire for Reb in and around the cabin, the Old One was equally adamant that buckskin shirt and leggings be donned for Reb's forays into the mountains.

She gladly would have made the same arguments on Dillon's behalf, but Dillon, two years younger than Reb, had different priorities in life. Attracting a man was more important to her than dressing like one. She chuckled to herself at Dillon's one-track mind. No, Reb had definitely been the better tool with which to antagonize her foe.

The Old One had more than once encouraged Matt to let the child try her wings merely as a goad to Rachel, who didn't approve of Reb's increasing deviation from the accepted feminine role. Reb was adept at the things her mother taught her, but she enjoyed doing the things her father taught her more. As the Old One watched Reb meet and conquer every challenge, she developed a curiosity to see for herself how far the girl could go.

Unfortunately, time had proven that Rachel was right and she was wrong. The Overland Stage ran a regular route through the territory now, and a telegraph line sang along the plains. There was even serious talk of a railroad coming across the country.

The Old One understood Reb's fear that the wilderness she loved was escaping her grasp because she felt the same fear herself. That understanding made her decide to support her granddaughter's wishes in spite of the pain she knew it would cause her son for Reb to seek out Blue. How strange that in this first confrontation between father and daughter without Rachel there to act as mediator, she should find herself taking the side her daughter-in-law would have argued. She consoled herself with the thought that what Rachel had really cared about was that Blue see Reb. The Old One wanted Reb to see the mountains.

Her thoughts were interrupted when Dillon had the temerity to speak to her rebellious sister.

"I don't see why you want to go up there. Except for Blue there's not another man around for fifty miles."

The reactions to that statement were as varied as the personalities at the table, but Adam's hoot of laughter irked Reb onto her feet.

"I'm going to see Blue and I'm staying the week," she decreed. "Adam is welcome to join me, if you can spare him." Reb left the table abruptly and stalked outside to await her brother.

Adam turned to his father with a quizzical look, awaiting his decision.

Under his breath Matt swore. "Damn!" Reb had more than a little of her mother in her.

A firm, soft voice broke in to soothe his consternation.

"The danger is not greater than in the past, only of a different nature. She's a woman, not a child. You trained her yourself. She's a better shot than any man you know and cool-headed. She's Adam's match at reading signs. Let her go."

Matt considered his mother's words carefully. He was not so ignorant of Reb's nature as to think he would be successful in keeping her confined against her will. Nor could he blame her for missing the mountains when he missed them himself. If she were a man he'd know how to handle her. If she acted more a woman he would not have felt so at sea. But Reb was something in between—a woman who knew everything Matt could teach her about being a successful

mountain man. He refused to let the bitter gall that
rose when he thought about Reb with Blue make him
alienate his daughter any further. This year he would
let her go, but he knew he had to find some way to end
these hellish confrontations each spring. Maybe he
could send Reb away to one of the finishing schools
her mother had suggested for the two girls shortly
before the accident. Settling on this possible solution
to an apparently insoluble problem, he turned to
Adam.

"Your brothers and I are going to start the roundup. I'm not so sure General Dodge's attempt to put
the Brulés on a reservation won't backfire and I want
Garth to get the cattle back on the range before the
repercussions start. Go ahead and go, but keep your
eyes open and get back here as quickly as you can. We
can use the help. Come on, boys," he called to Garth
and Jesse. "We'll see you at dinner, Dillon."

Reb eyed her father warily as he stepped onto the
porch. When he reached his arms out to her, however, she stepped into them and laid her head against his
buckskin shirt, drinking in the familiar earthy smell of
him.

"Be careful," her father whispered in her ear as he
held her close.

"I will." She hugged him tightly.

Matt stepped away and headed for the corral.

"Are you going to bring me a baby bear this time?"
the irrepressible Jesse asked Reb on his way by.

"Let's hope not," Garth said. He pushed the
eight-year-old toward the corral, then paused to
search deep into Reb's eyes. She automatically lowered her gaze to protect her private self.

"Have a good trip. Keep your eyes open, and don't

do anything you'll regret later." Garth kissed her lightly on the cheek and headed after Jesse.

Reb was still musing over Garth's admonition when Adam came to the porch with his arm on Dillon's shoulder. Dillon hugged herself to stay warm in the frilly, bright yellow cotton dress that was flattering, but too light for the cold snap they were having.

Adam pressed a kiss to her forehead. "So long, little sister. Don't let any beaus get too friendly while I'm not here to protect you."

Dillon giggled and gave Adam a hug. "No one you wouldn't approve of, anyway," she reassured. "So long, Adam. So long, Reb. Take care."

Adam and Reb mounted and he pulled the pack mules loaded with supplies behind him as they rode toward the sun-rimmed Laramie Mountains.

Reb longingly eyed the broken ridges silhouetted in an orange daybreak. "If I were a man, I'd live in the mountains and never leave."

"But you're not," Adam reminded. "You're only a girl. So dream, dear sister, of something more practical, if you please."

"Well, it doesn't please!" Reb shot Adam an impish grin and urged her mare into a canter. "This girl is dreaming of at least a week in the mountains, and that's as practical as she gets on a cold, beautiful April morning. I'll see you at Blue's cabin."

"Hey, Reb, wait for me," Adam shouted. He kicked his horse Ricochet and pulled the pack mules forward, but their broken trot was no match for Brandy's distance-eating lope. Reb left him behind as she answered the beckoning call of the Rockies.

Chapter Two

KINCAID HAD REACHED THE LIMIT OF HIS PATIENCE WITH the garrulous woman who balanced her overdressed bulk on the narrow seat facing him and babbled incessantly about her daughter and the successful San Francisco merchant the fortunate young woman had met and married in New York. For the past fifty miles of the ride west, while the stagecoach had swayed on its heavy leather traces like a ship in a turbulent sea, he had heard how they begged her to join them and how much she would uplift the cultural and moral fiber of San Francisco when she arrived.

When he recognized a lull in the conversation he tipped his dark blue felt hat and agreed politely, "Yes ma'am, I'm sure you're right," although he had no earthly idea what she had just said. He let his gaze wander out the window to the receding view of the Laramie Mountains. Spring had barely touched the plains they now crossed, and the dull brown flattened grasses grudgingly gave way only here and there to the green of new growth.

Eula Thomas held a much higher opinion of the Yankee officer seated across from her, whose physical presence filled the cramped interior of the Overland Stage. She would have given a lot to be twenty-five years younger and a hundred, no, she admitted honestly with a cackle, a hundred and fifty pounds lighter. She perused the mobile mouth and square jaw. Eula guessed he was used to having his own way. A scar below his right eye lent his face a rakish look, but his eyes were what caught her imagination. Steely gray, rimmed in sooty black lashes and capped by finely arched brows as black as the errant curls that he brushed back occasionally from his forehead, they seemed to look right through her. Her knees went to jelly at the thought of those eyes turned on her in anger or in passion.

He was massaging his right thigh again. She had questioned him earlier and he had reluctantly admitted it was a war wound. He probably was a hero of some Civil War battle. He looked the type. He hadn't volunteered a tittle of information to satisfy her curiosity, however. All she'd been able to find out was that he was from New York and his name was Kincaid. Not "Major Kincaid," mind you, although she could see his rank perfectly well from his uniform, just "Kincaid." He seemed preoccupied, and she had to tap his knee with her fan to get his attention when she spoke to him.

"I noticed you're headed away from Ft. Laramie, Major—I mean Kincaid," Eula said with a girlish blush.

"Yes ma'am," he replied.

"Are you headed someplace in particular?"

"Yes ma'am."

"Can you tell me where you're going?"

"No ma'am."

One of the soldiers in the cavalry escort from the fort drew alongside the coach and addressed Kincaid.

"Sir, we've sighted a couple of renegades."

"I'm just a passenger, Corporal Jennings. I don't have authority to give you any orders."

"Yes sir, I understand, sir. I just thought I'd let you know we're planning to go after them."

"Do you think that's a good idea?" Kincaid could hear the painted braves baiting the recruits—"Come fight us, you sons of she-dogs!"

"We don't have to take that from those red devils, sir!"

The youth crimsoned when it became apparent Mrs. Thomas had heard the taunt as well.

"No need to be alarmed, ma'am. We're going to rid ourselves of those two vermin in the shake of a beaver's tail. Begging your pardon, ma'am," the lad added, tipping his hat to the rotund woman. He raced with the rest of the escort after the two Sioux rapidly disappearing over a rise to the west.

Kincaid shook his head at the misguided exuberance, and at the same time pulled his Colt from its holster to check the rounds. How many kids had he heard make the same brash promise about some Johnny Reb. He hoped the results were not the same for these inexperienced recruits. He scanned the countryside keenly for signs of danger, then laid the gun down on the worn leather seat next to him with his finger wrapped around the trigger. God, he was glad the war was over. It had been over for him for a while now, he thought ruefully, as he rubbed the ache

16

in his leg. He wished he had more space to stretch out and ease the stiffness.

His father had pressured him to take this assignment from General Dodge, outlining the details he and Dodge had worked out, but Kincaid hadn't resisted much. The task had the intrigue of being a secret mission and, although he had resigned his commission from the army, he'd been authorized to perform his investigation in uniform. He had harbored no desire to become one of the northern carpetbaggers that ravaged the South, nor could he seek solace by assisting those he had helped defeat, since that meant acknowledging his complicity in the events leading to the death of his wife during the war. To his mother's dismay, two days after the talk with his father he'd headed west. A wry smile widened on his face. His mother would consider it poetic justice to know his hurried timing had gotten him to the Overland Stage depot at the same time as Eula Thomas. They were nearly at his destination and she hadn't talked him to death yet—although it was a very near thing. All in all, Eula Thomas was certain to make him appreciate the opportunity this mission offered for solitude.

Standing Buffalo bared his teeth in a cruel smile as he watched the progress of the Overland Stage toward the gully where he waited in ambush with half his braves. The other half hid beyond a rise to rain arrows on the raw recruits being led to them by the two decoys. They had used the plan successfully many times over the winter. So far it was working perfectly in spite of High Forehead's whining complaints that they should quit raiding and join Spotted Tail at Ft. Laramie.

It had taken some convincing to overcome High Forehead's objections. Standing Buffalo had reminded the hawk-nosed brave (who should have been named for that prominent feature, rather than his moderately low forehead) about the thieving agent of the White Father, who stole their goods and left them to starve and freeze in the winter. He'd argued that they could not trust the white devils and must kill those who came to drive the buffalo away. Before they returned, he'd shouted, his knife must taste the white man's blood and leave his bones as bare of flesh as the hungry women and children of the tribe. The graphic picture of starvation, too vivid in their memories, had convinced the other braves to join him and, at their urging, High Forehead had capitulated and this attack had been launched.

The inexperienced soldiers, fresh from duty in the East, did not get far before a hail of arrows decimated their ranks. Then a cluster of Indians charged from behind a slight rise in the flat terrain. The Sioux suffered casualties when some of the soldiers had the presence of mind to fight back, but, of the eight troopers, only three remained alive to rue their underestimation of the enemy. They turned back to the stagecoach in panic. The two decoys, Spotted Elk and Strangling Wolf, gave chase, exhibiting superb horsemanship as they closed the gap. Guiding their ponies with their knees, they used bows and arrows to summarily end the lives of two of the fleeing men.

Corporal Jennings raced his lathered horse onward. When he located the stagecoach, the full folly of their escapade became apparent. The four stage horses were down in their traces, peppered with arrows, and the driver had already been scalped. The Indians were mutilating the body in a way they believed made it difficult, if not impossible, for the white man's spirit to find its way to the land of Wakan-Tanka. Not waiting to see more, and convinced he was the lone survivor of the raid, the soldier thundered away toward the nearest Overland Stage station.

Had he paused a moment longer, he would have seen a very tall man emerge from the interior of the coach to take a stand before the open door, his handgun blazing. Several warriors screamed and fell before the rest sought refuge out of range.

Kincaid was unaware that Standing Buffalo crouched above him, hidden amidst the baggage on the coach. He threw the emptied Colt aside in the sagebrush and stood boldly facing the Indians, empty-handed, in obvious contempt of their prowess.

The Sioux yelped in glee. Here was an adversary worthy of their attention.

"I will be first to count coup," Black Horse shouted exultantly.

"First after me!" Rolling Thunder bellowed back in the voice that gave him his name.

The two painted braves raced away on their ponies, competing for the honor of counting coup first on the large man. It soon became apparent that this was a rash action on their part.

Soundlessly, Kincaid reached out with his bare hands to unseat Black Horse, who was then brained with his own tomahawk. Seconds later he swiftly and accurately threw the bloody tomahawk at Rolling Thunder, who tumbled backward off his horse, dead.

It was a sign of their admiration for his courage that the Indians did not then attack the white man with bow and arrows. The deaths were unfortunate, but within the rules of this deadly game that allowed the opponent on whom the Indians attempted to count coup to do his level best to kill them. More wary, however, they raced back and forth in front of their tall adversary, waving their lances and screaming insults. Unarmed, the man faced them calmly, seemingly undaunted. He brushed a black curl back from his chiseled face and waited.

Standing Buffalo's younger brother, Smaller Bear, took up the silent challenge, seeking to count coup with the tip of his lance, a little safer distance than the coup stick allowed. Standing Buffalo watched in satisfaction. It is good for my brother to fight as a man, he thought.

Sadly, it was the end of Smaller Bear's life as a man for, as he raced past, Kincaid rolled over in front of the Indian pony with a grace and speed that denied his size and his lameness, causing the animal to rear in fright. In the moment before the pony could speed its rider to safety, he disarmed the boy, broke his neck with a sharp upward jab of the lance, and then backed up slowly in his halting gait to the stagecoach, lance in hand, to await the next foe.

Stunned by this turn of events, each Indian searched his heart to determine whether he stood in as good stead with the Great Spirit as this white man obviously did.

Wakan-Tanka smiles upon him, Standing Buffalo thought, noting that the white man was not even breathing hard from his exertion.

The tension mounted as several warriors in turn danced their ponies toward the white man, only to wheel them back into the crowd. Standing Buffalo realized that if he did not take matters into his own hands soon, it was possible all his warriors would be sent to the Happy Hunting Ground one at a time.

Moving stealthily, he reached the edge of the coach

above the powerful white warrior. Swinging with all his might, he brought his stone and rawhide war club crashing into the man's right temple. The giant dropped to his knees, still clutching the lance, then fell forward like a mighty tree cleaved from its trunk.

The Sioux thanked the Great Spirit for this good fortune with whoops of delight. Such a great warrior was strong war medicine, and they rushed up to obtain talismans from his person.

Rides-Two-Ways, one of the younger braves, had already stripped the shirt from Kincaid's body before the groan sounded that evidenced life. Startled, and a little fearful at this complication, the young brave raised his tomahawk to solve the problem. Standing Buffalo descended from the stagecoach in time to grab the youth's arm on its downward arc.

"He is mine. Do not take the scalp that protects his soul. I want his strong spirit to find its way to the Happy Hunting Ground to serve my brother and the other braves who died today. I will test the limits of this man's strength. Then we will truly know the worth of this enemy that took my brother's life. But you may keep the shirt," he added to assuage Rides-Two-Ways' anger at being thwarted in his murderous intent.

"Another enemy, but already dead!" High Forehead yelled. He referred to the heavyset older woman discovered inside the coach, who had been killed by a stray arrow in the first attack.

"Let me help," Rides-Two-Ways offered, joining the braves dragging the woman's body out onto the ground and stripping it. Others tore through the baggage.

"Look at me!" one commanded, as he paraded cockily in a bright lavender opera cloak.

Standing Buffalo ignored the cacophony around him, concentrating instead on his prisoner. He perfunctorily checked the man's pockets looking for booty. A grin spread across his face when a heavy gold pocket watch, bearing the inscription, "To Kincaid with Love from Laurie," appeared in his hand. He searched the other pocket eagerly, but was disgusted to find only a folded piece of paper. He opened it up and perused it but, as with the inscription, the writing meant nothing to him.

April 15, 1865

Christopher Lyle Kincaid
Fifth Avenue and 28th Street
New York, New York

Dear Major Kincaid:

After our successful association in Atlanta during the war I am ready to set another task of equal, or perhaps even greater, importance for you now that General Lee has surrendered. I realize you have barely had time to recover from your wound, but your father and I have discussed the necessity of your participation in this effort on behalf of the Union Pacific railroad and are agreed you are the best man for the job. Your father can fill you in on the significance of making the right choice between the two alternate routes. I need you here as soon as possible. Meet me at the second Overland Stage station west of the Laramie Mountains no later than May 15. I'm counting on you.

Maj. Gen. Grenville M. Dodge, Commander
Dept. of the Missouri

Standing Buffalo started to let the wind carry the paper away, but on second thought folded it again and stuck it in the sacred medicine bag that hung around his neck. Perhaps some of the white warrior's power-ful aura might wear off on him.

Having completed their destruction, the remainder of the contingent of braves that had attacked the soldiers rode up to join the rest of the band. They were greeted by the excited shout of Rides-Two-Ways, who gloated, "I have the shirt of a great white warrior. It will ensure my conquest of the white man."

Each group of Indians boasted of their bravery, but the exploits of the unconscious man, when recounted by the Sioux who had seen them, acquired a little of the supernatural in the telling.

Standing Buffalo ordered several braves to take their dead comrades back to their families along with the soldiers' horses, with instructions they would follow soon. "Strangling Wolf, you and Spotted Elk put our captive on my brother's pony," he com-manded.

It was a struggle for the two short, stocky Indians to move the large man. "Rides-Two-Ways," Spotted Elk shouted to his friend, "stop bragging and help us get this big man up here." He panted with the effort of getting the captive up onto Smaller Bear's pony, which had been chosen to bear this last burden before its life ended. As the dead Indian's favorite mount, the little mare's head and tail would be cut off and tied to the scaffolding supporting Smaller Bear's body, enabling the pony to serve her former master in his travels in the afterworld.

With extra-human effort, the three Indians com-pleted the task. When they stood back to survey their work, Rides-Two-Ways could not suppress a snigger. He was joined by Strangling Wolf's raspy chuckle and Spotted Elk's outright guffaw. Seeking the source of this mirth, the other Indians took one look at the prisoner and convulsed with laughter. The white man's fingertips touched the ground on one side of the pony, and the toes of his boots dragged the ground on the other. Even Standing Buffalo, weighed down by the sorrow of his brother's death, could not keep his lips from quirking at the edges.

"The Council will long sing the praise of our capture of this white man who is too big for horses," Standing Buffalo said solemnly.

"Yes, Too-Big-For-Horses was a brave warrior in battle," High Forehead agreed, sealing the label on the man.

"Let us go now to tell Spotted Tail we will return to the Powder River and hunt the buffalo. We will test the strength of Too-Big-For-Horses along the way, and tell his tale to our children around the campfire." Standing Buffalo grasped the rawhide lead on Smaller Bear's pony and headed north.

The Indians rode far into the night, then camped high in the mountains, where they believed themselves safe from pursuit. Always cautious, however, Rides-Two-Ways was selected to stand guard while the others slept. With sunrise only moments away, the boastful brave was tired, but still exuberant over his prize. It was a good thing that the sun was rising, since it meant his vigil as lookout was nearing an end.

He noticed the white man they had named Too-Big-For-Horses was awakening. The prisoner stood where they had tied him spread-eagled between two ancient spruces. He had not died from the blow to the head from Standing Buffalo's war club that would have killed an ordinary man. Soon the other braves would be stirring, and the testing of the white man promised by their leader could begin.

We will find much pleasure today helping Too-Big-

A LOVING DEFIANCE

For-Horses seek the Great Spirit, Rides-Two-Ways thought, fingering with pride the white man's dark blue shirt that dwarfed his figure. He hoped Too-Big-For-Horses manfully withstood the exquisite torture planned for him, since that would make his token all the more valuable.

"Today your trip to the afterworld begins. Be strong, Too-Big-For-Horses," he chanted. "This conquering brave wills it so."

Chapter Three

KINCAID WOKE TO THE THROBBING PAIN IN HIS MASSIVE shoulders and arms, which were stretched out taut away from either side of his body. The effort to flex his benumbed hands resulted in agony as tightening thongs bit into raw wrists. His head hung forward, so that when he blinked open his eyes to the early morning light he saw only the muddy ground, strewn with pine needles, below him. A slight turn of his pounding head in either direction revealed his black-booted feet, spread far apart and secured by rawhide at the ankles. His eyes followed the rawhide on one side to where it wrapped around a thick spruce. Kincaid closed his eyes and struggled mentally to orient himself.

A pulsing ache in the muscles of his right thigh took him back to a scene from the past. The scream of shrapnel that had left him with a slight but permanent limp, resounded in his ears, and he jerked unconsciously at the memory of that first awful impact of metal on muscle. It was a nightmare he relived time and again, but always with the same painful ending. He remembered anxiously watching the slender woman, her long blond hair windblown around a terrified, heart-shaped face, racing toward where he had been pitched from the saddle by the blast. He had warned her to get down, but was unheard amidst the chaos of defeated soldiers fleeing on horseback and on foot.

Suddenly, a blossom of red unfolded on the front of her high-necked gray wool dress. A tentative hand reached up to admire the deadly corsage, and she sought Kincaid's steel gray eyes with her own silvery blue ones, a poignant sadness replacing the fear for him on her face. Stumbling unsteadily, she took one more step. Then, he watched helplessly as his wife crumpled, like a flower trodden to the ground.

He dragged himself to her side, forced to pause occasionally by the bursting shells around him. Finally, he cradled her head in his arms as he lay full-length beside her on the red clay. He searched her face for signs of life but, when he saw none, gathered her close to him, their long bodies molding perfectly, and pressed gentle kisses on each closed eyelid, and finally on the still-warm mouth. The taste of his loss was bitter on his lips. Tenderly, he laid her head down and rested his own cheek beside hers on the cool clay.

His throat constricted so that he could not breathe without turning his gaze away from the precious young face to the sky above, dotted with ugly clouds of black smoke. If only she hadn't insisted on being where she didn't belong in the first place! If only he had demanded she obey him and leave! But, oh, how he had secretly admired her for staying.

"Damn you, Laurie!" he raged. He hugged the

lifeless body to his own in frustration, while tears of anguish squeezed from eyelids drifting closed in unconsciousness.

But the war of brother against brother was over now and had been for more than a month. Kincaid realized he'd remembered too far back in the past, and wished he hadn't. He'd awakened an ache in his heart as persistent as the one in his wounded thigh. He forced his mind to focus on solving the puzzle of how he had come to be tied, spread-eagled between two trees in the middle of a forbidding pine forest.

Two other minds worried over the same problem from another perspective.

"I count nine Sioux, including the lookout," Adam whispered to his lanky, buckskin-clad younger sister. "Too many for us to kill before one of them kills him."

"Why do you suppose they kept him alive?" Reb asked, as they observed the unknown man from their hiding place behind a mammoth boulder.

"Don't expect we'll ever know. Could be his size. That is one *big* man. Maybe they just want to see if the extra inches give him extra courage." Millions of pine needles and spruce branchlets rustling in the wind muffled their voices, and the strong breeze carried the softened sound away from the Indian camp.

Reb appraised the body that was stripped to the waist and suspended between two trees. She found no fault in the impressive shoulders and chest, the defined muscles across the abdomen or the strong, sinewy thighs molded into a pair of Union Army pants. She was curious to see the face that went with such a body, but the head hung forward, hidden in the shade of the forest.

They were several hours' ride south of Blue's cabin, on their way home with the beaver skins they'd picked up from the loner in exchange for the coffee, flour and beans they'd delivered to him. Located where the Laramie River crossed the plateau-like summit of the mountains, the cabin was more than fifty miles, as the crow flies, from Ft. Laramie on the plains directly to the east, and equally distant from their home at the base of the mountains to the southwest. Reb wondered whether the presence of this captive meant another massacre of soldiers on patrol like the many throughout the winter.

"Aside from the blood on his forehead, he doesn't appear to be hurt," she offered finally.

"Not yet," Adam replied quietly. "Those eagle feathers identify that lookout as one of Standing Buffalo's renegades, the ones Dad warned us about. I've seen samples of their handiwork. The kindest thing we can do for that stranger is shoot him."

Reb's senses rebelled against the mutilation planned for the magnificent specimen of mankind she saw before her. Surely the fates that had caused them to stumble onto this warrior camp could not have intended they pass without changing the now dismal outlook of this stranger's life.

"There must be a way we can save him. Think, Adam."

He squatted down with her to go over the alternatives. "Whatever we do should be done soon, before those sleeping Indians wake up. Or, we could take a chance that they're planning to postpone their entertainment until they get to wherever they're headed. We might be able to steal their prisoner away at some point during the journey."

Adam figured the band was headed for the Powder River far to the north near the Black Hills, where Red Cloud's Oglala and other Sioux less inclined to peace than Spotted Tail, were congregating. If so, he did not like the idea of trekking across mountains and plains after the Indians. They were too likely to be discovered and share the stranger's fate. He said as much to Reb.

"You're right," she agreed. "What about a trade?"

"We don't have a snowball's chance in the sun of bargaining with Standing Buffalo for that man's life, even if I were willing to give up Blue's beaver skins, which I'm not. Those Brulés won't trust us as far as they can throw us. They'll kill him sure if we charge in there. No, I'm afraid he's a goner, Reb. There's nothing we can do." As he finished speaking a far-fetched idea came to Adam of how to save the doomed man.

He rose, a smile tugging at the corners of his mouth. "Yep. The kindest thing we can do is shoot him."

Adam clamped a hand over Reb's open mouth as she jumped up to protest.

"Listen," he whispered excitedly. "I've got a crazy idea, but it just might work. What's the first thing those Sioux will do if we start shooting?"

Reb mumbled against Adam's hand, but he ignored her in his exuberance.

"Kill that stranger, that's what! So we're going to 'kill' him first. That is, we're going to make them *think* we've killed him, so they're more concerned about escaping our ambush than hanging around here to carve up a dead body."

The large, liquid brown eyes rimmed with long

black lashes, together with the light dusting of freckles across Reb's nose visible above his calloused hand, reminded Adam of a startled fawn. When she mumbled again in frustration, he took his hand away from her full, still-parted lips.

"How?" she hissed.

"You're going to shoot him. I think if you hit him just above the heart, that ought to convince them he's dead."

Reb sucked in a breath of air between clenched teeth, but said nothing.

"I'll sneak around to the far side of the clearing. When I'm set I'll shoot the lookout. That'll leave eight Indians. We've got two seven-shot Spencer rifles, four Colt repeaters, our knives and the element of surprise on our side. We can't lose," he said with a lopsided grin. "When the lookout falls, you shoot the stranger. I'll unhobble the Indian ponies so that they stampede when the noise starts. Don't stop firing till they're all dead or all gone. I'll be doing my part from the other side. Any questions?"

"What if I miss?"

"You miss those Indians and we'll be dead ducks," Adam joked.

"You know that's not what I mean. What if I accidentally kill that stranger?" She gnawed her lower lip with her straight white teeth, her forehead wrinkled in concern. She was a crack shot, but had never aimed her gun at a man before, only at animals and standing targets.

"Like I said, the kindest thing we can do is shoot him. Reb, in the first place, you're too good a shot to miss. In the second place, if it bothers you so much, we can just leave the way we came. In the third place, he's no worse off if we leave him dead than if we leave him alive."

Adam might be a pragmatist, but Reb was an eternal optimist. Besides, she very much wanted to see the stranger's face, and she was more likely to get her wish if they tried to save him.

She had no such mental qualms about killing the nine Sioux when she remembered the Morgans. Those horrible deaths, among others over the winter, were evidence that there currently existed a state of undeclared war with the Indians. At least it was undeclared on the white man's side.

The previous November, Col. John Chivington had ordered the murder of Cheyenne men, women and children waiting at Sand Creek to begin peace talks. In retaliation, the Sioux, Arapaho and Cheyenne had indulged in what many mountain men considered a quite justifiable rampage. The unprovoked attack of the army on the peaceful Cheyenne was the last straw. The Indians began paying the white man back for the degradation of drunkenness caused by his whiskey, for diseases brought back to Indian husbands by wives who prostituted themselves with the soldiers for scraps of food, for the theft of government annuities by dishonest Indian agents and, above all, for the lies of the White Father who broke treaty after treaty.

The Sioux were incensed by the story of how the Cheyenne Chief White Antelope, who stood alone and refused to fight the white man at Sand Creek, was shot down, then scalped and castrated by the soldiers. When his story was told, the Sioux smoked the war pipe gladly. They became the scourge of the Overland Trail, killing soldiers and settlers indiscriminately, and pillaging or burning everything in their path. The atrocities committed over the winter had included the riddling of one body with no fewer than 97 arrows. Both sides had given sufficient warning that when one met the other, the rules were "kill or be killed."

"All right, I'll shoot him," Reb agreed.

Adam disappeared silently into the forest. She lifted her Spencer to her shoulder and sighted down the barrel to a spot several inches above the stranger's heart.

Reb's hands shook at the enormous responsibility she had undertaken. Knowing that she held the stranger's life on the tip of her trigger finger, she wanted to know very badly who he was and where he had come from. She wanted to know the color of his eyes, to hear the sound of his voice. She wanted to know if he had a sweetheart, or worse, a wife and children.

"Look at me."

She willed the stranger to respond. As though reading her thoughts, his head rose slowly on his shoulders until he stared proudly forward, directly at Reb. His whole face wasn't visible, only his eyes, lit by a narrow shaft of sunlight that blazed through the towering spruce and two-hundred-foot lodgepole pines, so named for the use to which the Indians put them. She was unable to discern the color of the unwavering orbs that bored into her own, compelling a response, demanding her soul. Lost in his piercing gaze, Reb momentarily surrendered to the stranger's power, willingly giving to him a part of herself never before offered to anyone. In that fleeting instant Reb experienced a feeling of belonging so intense that it took her by surprise. This feeling was not the same sense of well-being that had always been provided by the support and love of her family. It was much more. Unused to domination of any kind, Reb's spirit shook off the pleasant, but still unwanted, yoke of attachment.

"I will never belong to any man, including you," she whispered in response to the stranger's unspoken demand for her soul, "who does not also belong to me." As the daughter of a one-time trapper and mountain man, Reb had learned not to give without taking a fair trade.

She took careful aim once more and waited for Adam's signal. Her eyes drifted to the lookout, who had begun strutting boldly before the stranger.

At that moment, Adam fired.

Pandemonium hit the camp. Rides-Two-Ways clutched the gaping hole in his chest, his dying thought one of furious anger for the ruin of his wonderful shirt. The Sioux threw off their blankets and buffalo robes, grabbed weapons and looked through sleep-crusted eyes for an enemy to fight.

"We are attacked!" Standing Buffalo cried.

"But I see no enemy!" High Forehead whined, uselessly holding his tomahawk.

Reb took a deep breath, her smooth white cheek pressed to the equally smooth brown rifle stock, and squeezed the trigger. Surprise registered on the stranger's face before it sagged forward.

"Too-Big-For-Horses has been shot!" Strangling Wolf exclaimed.

The Indians howled in outrage, certain now where at least one enemy lay. Reb chose another target immediately, knowing she must make each shot count. Her repeating rifle roared in her ear and an Indian unceremoniously died.

The gunfire stampeded the unhobbled ponies through the camp, increasing the confusion. Adam aimed and fired again. He caught High Forehead, who had paused in hopes of taking the "dead" stranger's scalp, with a bullet in the middle of his namesake. Adam struggled to avoid a charging brave who ripped open his right arm when he raised it to deflect a slashing knife blow. He hit the Indian in the throat with his left fist, crushing the windpipe.

Reb killed two more Sioux who were barely awake enough to realize they were meeting their eternal rest. Then Strangling Wolf and Spotted Elk attacked Reb. She dropped her rifle, thinking her two revolvers would be more useful in this situation. Moving desperately, she barely had time to free one gun and fire before Strangling Wolf fell dead on top of her with a final garbled cry. Adam's revolver spoke from a spot near the stranger and Spotted Elk screamed his death song before reaching Reb. Adam rushed to his sister, who was shoving her way out from under Strangling Wolf's unpleasant corpse.

"Are you all right?"

In shock, although she was not aware of it, Reb answered calmly, "I'm fine, Adam. Did we get them all?"

Adam counted quickly, confounded to discover they were one Indian short. Colt in hand, he searched the forest surrounding the camp, but found no sign of his prey. He checked each dead Indian, but none was Standing Buffalo.

"Damn! That renegade will probably high-tail it back to Spotted Tail for reinforcements. He isn't going to find any help there, thanks to Dodge. All the same, I'm not sure enough of what any Indian will do to stake my life on it. Under the circumstances, I suggest we pack up and get moving."

Noticing several Indian ponies still lingering nearby he added, "We can probably make sure he stays on foot for a while if we scatter the rest of these ponies. I presume your stranger is still alive?"

"He's alive, but he's unconscious."

"It makes the most sense for us to go back to Blue's cabin. It's closer than going all the way home and you can tend your stranger there."

Reb looked around at the slain men, then said so softly he barely heard her, "Let's get out of here, Adam."

Standing Buffalo watched the white man, who was nearly as tall as his former captive, cut down Too-Big-For-Horses, wrapping him securely in the blanket offered by his partner. When they lifted Too-Big-For-Horses across High Forehead's pinto and tied him down, Standing Buffalo smiled grimly and thought again how well the name fit the man, whose arms and legs nearly touched the ground on either side of the larger pony.

He waited patiently as the rest of the Indian ponies were scattered in the forest by several shots. He noted the direction of his favorite mount and set out at a brisk trot after him. He was not a superstitious man, but his former captive seemed to be having more than his share of good luck. He would leave it in the hands of the Great Spirit to bring the white man back to him, for he did not doubt that Too-Big-For-Horses still lived. Now he must meet Spotted Tail at Ft. Laramie and tell of the daring theft of Too-Big-For-Horses, and of the white man's evident favor with the Great Spirit. He did not wait to see Reb and Adam mount their horses, collect their pack mules and head back in the direction from which they had come.

It was not until they had traveled some distance that Reb came out of shock sufficiently to notice the blood covering the front of Adam's shirt.

"You're bleeding!"

"You call that bleeding? Why I've seen a stuck pig do better than this!" Adam rejoined.

"Adam, be serious." She was more annoyed with herself for failing to notice his injury, than with him for being so characteristically facetious. Upon a check of the sun to determine how long they had been traveling, she was startled to find it was well past noon. She had no recollection of the trip from the Indian camp and was surprised to see she was leading the pony that carried the stranger.

Although he had pressed his injured arm against his body in an attempt to stop the bleeding, Adam so far had been unsuccessful. The result of this tactic, however, had been to soak the front of his shirt with blood, so it looked like he had a belly wound. Adam might have been more concerned if the danger of pursuit was greater, but they soon would be able to stop and he was confident that Reb would be able to take care of him.

"It's just my arm, really, see?" He held out his arm to Reb, who raised an eyebrow appraisingly. "We should be back at Blue's cabin soon. You can play doctor for both me and your stranger there," Adam teased.

"Yes, and you can play nurse," Reb retorted irritably. She accepted the fact that she would take the more active role in ministering to the two men, dreading it all the same. All of her experience had been gained as an assistant at the Old One's side. More softhearted than she cared to admit, what Reb hated most about doctoring was inflicting the necessary pain that so often accompanied the panacea.

The fact that Adam could never be serious about anything was a little irritation she had learned to live with. In fact, the more dangerous the situation, the more he tended to treat it humorously. However, those who knew Adam well never underestimated him because of the smile on his face or the laughter in his voice.

She tried to look objectively at her brother. His green eyes glittered in a tanned face topped by sun-streaked, sandy gold hair. Clean-shaven, unlike most frontier men, his face revealed a firm jaw. He had joked that he wanted the ladies to be able to find his lips. He did have a good mouth, she admitted, with pleasant, full lips prone to smile, and to quirk when he was teasing, which was often. His nose had once been aquiline, but it had been broadened at the bridge by a break when he was ten, adding character to an otherwise too-perfect visage.

Adam yanked on the pack mule line with his good hand. "Blue's skins will just have to get delivered a little later. Come on, cheer up," he cajoled. "Not only did we rescue your stranger, but we're still alive and well enough to greet him when he comes to."

"He's not *my* stranger!" Reb protested hotly, out of patience with his constant ribbing because he was a little too close to feelings she was not yet willing to admit existed.

Adam's knowing grin was too wide to be measured.

She turned away to hide the embarrassing blush that rose in her cheeks. His reference to the motionless man made her consider for the first time what she would say to the stranger when the opportunity finally arose to have a civil conversation. What should she ask? What would his first question be? It's rather like stumbling onto a sleeping mountain lion, she thought. The action doesn't begin until the lion wakes up.

Chapter Four

"HOME AGAIN, HOME AGAIN, JIGGETY JOG," ADAM recited as he straightened up after helping Reb place the stranger on the long, extra-wide bed that was centered along one pine wall so that it took up most of the space in Blue's one-room cabin.

"Take your shirt off, Adam, so I can check the damage," Reb commanded from her place beside the unidentified man.

"And all the king's horses and all the king's men couldn't put . . ."

Reb's flat-brimmed hat interrupted him as it sailed into his face.

"Yes sir, yes sir, three bags full," he said, bowing comically.

Reb surveyed the room, where she had lived as a child, as a potential infirmary. The furniture consisted of a wooden chest Matt and Blue had fashioned from cottonwood planks, a roughhewn table and two chairs of the same material shoved against the wall opposite the bed, and an iron stove in the corner that they had salvaged from that great dumping ground to the north, the Oregon Trail, and carted here for Rachel at great effort. A high window sealed with a thin layer of animal skin let in the light, if not the heat, of the late afternoon sun. It blazed a bright spot on the dirt floor she had so recently swept in anticipation of their departure for home. A cupboard was built in along the mud-daubed wall near the table, with numerous cracked dishes, also salvaged property, arrayed on the open shelves. Several barrels for flour and beans were stacked next to it.

"I kind of expected Blue to be here," Reb said.

"I know what you mean," Adam concurred. "I guess he must have gone out somewhere. He'll be back soon, I'm sure." His fingers fumbled at the strings that tied his shirt.

It never occurred to Reb that anything could have happened to the mountain man. That was as unthinkable as that pigs could fly. There were things about Blue that Reb questioned, but none of them was his ability to take care of himself. Still, his absence was puzzling. When they had said good-bye to him that morning he had not talked of any plans for the day, in fact he had indicated quite to the contrary that he planned to sit back and relax, maybe even whittle some. Once Reb started thinking about Blue, the question she'd asked herself more than once rose automatically to her lips.

"Have you ever wondered why Blue didn't join Dad to start the ranch?" she asked Adam.

"Why don't you ask Dad?"

"I did. He told me that if Blue wanted me to know he'd tell me."

"Sounds like Dad. So?"

"Blue's never said and I've never asked."

Reb focused for a moment on the dark bruise and scrape marring the rugged beauty of the stranger's face. "How old do you think he is?" she asked Adam.

"Oh, about forty-five or so."

"No, he can't be! He doesn't seem much older than you."

One look at Reb, whose eyes were riveted on the stranger, told Adam why the conversation had gotten so confusing. He was still talking about Blue. She was talking about the stranger. "I'd guess *he's* twenty-five or twenty-six," he said, an amused grin on his face.

Realizing she'd been caught staring, Reb turned her back on Adam to check the injured man. She tentatively lifted the wool blanket from around him enough to determine that it was stuck to the wound with dried blood. At least that meant the bleeding had stopped. She checked the pulse at his throat and found it steady, the breathing regular, if a little shallow.

"He's not likely to get any worse in the time it'll take me to fix you up."

"I just have a scratch," Adam protested.

She knew that the seemingly innocent slash could be dangerous. Therefore she decided, as rationally as a sister could, that Adam needed attention now. The stranger could wait. "You first," she insisted, "or I don't take care of either one of you."

Adam shrugged in submission. She watched him finish unlacing his buckskin shirt nearly to the waist and make a one-handed attempt to pull the blood-soaked leather up over his head. He grunted as he painfully raised his cut arm to ease the torn shirt off. As the grunt became a groan, Reb came around the bed to push him into a chair.

"Sit down and let me help." Reb carefully skinned the shirt over Adam's head and down his arms until he was free, revealing the jagged slash that ran along the length of his forearm from wrist to elbow.

"That needs stitching," Reb said when she could see the cut clearly. "I'll get some water from the creek. You'll find Blue's whiskey stashed behind the stove, and there should be a needle and some thread in that chest beside the bed. Also, see if you can find something in there to use for bandages." Noting the steady drip of blood running off his fingers, she added, "Try not to dribble blood all over everything!" She grabbed a chipped blue Dresden china pitcher from the cupboard and hurried out.

She avoided patches of melting snow as her moccasined feet literally raced to the narrow creek that burbled downhill at the left end of the cabin. She sat on her haunches, chasing away a feeding trout as she dipped the pitcher into the icy water. Then she paused momentarily, finally locating the beautiful violet-green sparrow perched singing on a budding willow above her, its feathers varying from bronzy-green at the head to purplish-bronze at the tail. Once raised, her eyes were drawn to the pine-covered ridges laced with snow, visible through the naked cottonwood trees along the creek.

She wondered what had brought the stranger to these mountains. It occurred to her she might never know if he didn't recover. She dismissed the chance he might die as slight. It would not take long to stitch Adam, and then she would tend the stranger's wound. He had survived the flight from the Indian camp and it was a good sign that the blood had clotted around the bullet hole. He was strong. She knew the shot had hit him in the exact spot where she had aimed. The wound was serious, but not deadly, she tried to convince herself.

But who was he? Probably another Yankee seeking his fortune in the West now that the war was over, she thought. Most of the skinny, white-skinned Easterners she'd seen passing through with the wagon trains had trouble staying on their horses at more than a trot. Their aim was so poor she didn't mind their shooting at the buffalo, because they seemed to enjoy it and it didn't hurt the buffalo. She believed most didn't have the strength of both body and spirit demanded out here. That was why they didn't stop here in the Southern Rocky Mountains, but kept on going to Oregon and California, the lands of milk and honey. At least this stranger had a powerful body, as evidenced by the knotted shoulder muscles and bulging biceps that had supported his Herculean form between the trees . . .

"Reb! What are you doing down there? Taking a bath?"

Reb started at Adam's shout from the doorway, flushed at the reason for her delay, and retorted, "I'm coming. Hold your horses, if you can do it one-armed!"

Besides the needle and thread, Adam's rummaging had turned up an old sheet, which he deemed a fitting sacrifice for bandages. He observed that the stranger was still unconscious and more than a little pale, although his own face, if he could have seen it, didn't have much more color.

As Reb reentered the cabin Adam said, "Don't you think you ought to take care of him first? With this arm I don't know how much help I'll be, but he looks awful!" He gestured limply toward the unmoving man, leaving red bubbles across the floor that were gradually absorbed by the hard-packed dirt.

"He'll be fine," she responded, then realized she believed that firmly. "Let's get your bleeding stopped. Then we'll see about him."

Adam sat down while Reb rinsed his arm as free of blood and dirt as possible. He couldn't control the trembling that resulted from the combination of the icy water and the pain.

"It's a deep cut," Reb murmured, carefully prying the flesh apart. "Give me the whiskey, Adam." She accepted the bottle from Adam, uncorked it with her teeth and poured whiskey liberally over the slash in preparation for the next step in his treatment.

"Damn, Reb, that stings like the devil," Adam yelled in response to her ministrations.

"Sit still and stop acting like a baby," she scolded. She set the bottle aside, then wrinkled her nose as Adam handed her a whiskey-dipped threaded needle. Before recorking the bottle, he helped himself to a healthy slug of the golden liquid to counter the pain.

"You certainly have chosen the hard way to find out whether I can sew a neat stitch," Reb said.

Adam's laugh was stifled by his gasp as Reb inserted the needle through a flap of skin on his wrist and pulled it through to meet the skin on the other side. By the time she finished her work, the needle had been rethreaded several times, and two sets of lips had tightened into grim lines.

Reb used a strip of the sheet to make a sling in which to rest and protect the wounded limb. As he stood to escape her attentions, she reached her arms up around Adam's neck to tie the sling in a knot. She was tall enough to manage easily without the need to rise on tiptoe.

"It's getting dark. Light a lantern, please, Adam," she sighed quietly in his ear. Then, turning back to look at the stranger, she shivered noticeably. Adam rubbed his good hand up and down quickly along the golden fringe of her buckskin shirt to create some warmth.

"You're cold. I'll light a fire, too," he said. Reb agreed, although the shiver was more a reaction to the silent stranger than to the frigid early evening air.

Blue still had not returned and, knowing she could avoid him no longer, Reb moved to the wounded man. She watched his face as she unwrapped once again the blanket that had been so hastily slung around him at Standing Buffalo's camp. There was no reaction as the material was dampened and cautiously pried away from the dried blood that crusted the gunshot wound. Reb reached carefully behind the stranger's shoulder, probing with her fingertips, expecting to find that the bullet had passed all the way through. She groaned inwardly when the search revealed only hard, taut muscle.

"The bullet's still inside. I'll have to dig it out."

Adam gave Reb a sympathetic look, but did not offer to relieve her of the job.

She pulled her knife from the brightly beaded sheath at her belt. The feel of the beadwork gave her courage as she remembered the occasion on which the beautifully ornamented object had been bestowed.

On the eve of her first trip to Blue's cabin alone with Adam her father had advised her to use her head, to think carefully before she acted and to heed Adam since he had five more years of living under his belt. It was then he'd pulled out an intricately worked beaded sheath made to fit her knife. She would never forget his words as he had bestowed the gift.

"As your knife will always be with you, protected by this sheath, the love in my heart will always be with you, safe in your heart wherever you go." Almost to himself, but loud enough for her to hear, he had added, "Someday you'll understand that the love in a Hunter's heart is a great and powerful thing. It can withstand disappointment and pain, and be stronger for the testing. Remember that."

He'd offered her the beaded sheath as a symbol of infinite love. She'd promised to keep the precious token with her always. And she always had. Reb ran her fingertips comfortingly over the familiar pattern of knobby beads, then once more uncorked the whiskey bottle and poured some of its contents over the knife. She walked over to the lantern on the table, removed the globe and ran the blade back and forth through the flame, in preparation for the overwhelming task before her.

I can do it, Daddy, she thought, as she watched the whiskey burn in muted orange and blue glory. You taught me well.

Adam glanced up from the fire beginning to smolder in the stove and offered, "If I can hold my horses one-armed, I can hold him still for you."

Reb rewarded his effort to lighten the situation with a weak smile and, rather than say out loud how much she appreciated his support, merely nodded. She set the sharp knife down on the chest, taking care that the blade did not touch the surface. Tossing the bowl of bloody water out the door, she refilled it from the now tepid water in the pitcher, tore several more strips of cloth from the sheet and laid them on the chest. Then she sat down on the edge of the bed at the stranger's side to wash the area around the wound. Once she had disinfected it with whiskey, she alerted Adam and then waited for him to take his place near the head of the bed.

Both men were naked from the waist up, and Reb could not help making a physical comparison. She had seen Adam shirtless innumerable times. Indeed, her father had encouraged his five children away from modesty and, much to her mother's chagrin, when they were younger, she and her sister had gone swimming in the nude several times with their brothers. The sight of a male body was not a new, or even unusual sight, so she had no explanation for her sudden avid curiosity. It did not occur to her that this stranger was neither a relation nor a youth, or that she herself had matured since her last playful splash with her brothers in the swimming hole.

Both men were deeply tanned and broad of shoulder, although she reckoned the stranger must be broader by at least the width of her outspread fingers. Reb's glance paused at the stranger's collarbone and followed it to the small hollow of his throat. She avoided looking at the destruction wrought by her bullet in the area of the left shoulder, concentrating instead on the distance between the dark nipples, turgid from the cold, that indicated the breadth of the stranger's chest. Missing was the small triangle of sandy-colored curls that accented the center of Adam's chest. She found the bared muscle oddly enticing, and nearly reached to caress the stranger's smooth skin.

Instead, she counted the several ribs that could be seen before the stranger's form narrowed to a waist as slim as Adam's. The black line of curls leading from his navel boldly downward into a pair of dark blue britches was an exciting contrast to the light down found in the same place on Adam. Reb again fought the desire to touch.

The uncharacteristic direction of her thoughts unsettled Reb. Her gaze leaped guiltily to the stranger's face, offering penance for so intimate an examination. But the closed, wide-set eyes, framed by thick, sooty black lashes, denied her absolution.

Adam patiently watched Reb's visual assessment of the stranger, attributing a more clinical purpose to her darting glances than was the truth. When she finally lifted her solemn face to him, he questioned with his emerald eyes whether she was ready.

Reb directed with the knife for Adam to grip the man's right shoulder. When she began probing for the bullet, the stranger cried out hoarsely and writhed upward under her hand. "Hold him!" she barked.

Adam's strong left hand pressed the stranger downward. Reb turned with determination to the task before her, inserting the knife into the torn flesh as though it were not a totally new experience. The stranger wrenched once more under Adam's firm, one-handed grip, but made no sound as he slipped further into unconsciousness.

The work was not clean or as neat as Reb would have liked, although she tried to minimize what she knew would be a sizeable scar.

"The bullet got caught by the shoulder blade. That's why it didn't go all the way through. There are bone splinters that have to come out. This may take awhile."

Before long, perspiration glistened on her high cheekbones and dotted her forehead and determined chin. Unable to use her bloodied hands for relief when a drop of sweat rolled down to tickle the end of her nose, Reb stuck out her lower lip and sent puffs of air upward in an attempt to dislodge the offender. Adam grinned at her unsuccessful efforts.

"Don't just stand there, help me!" She sent him a ferocious look, meanwhile twitching helplessly.

"All you had to do was ask, Miss Independence." He gently brushed back the short, straight black hair covering her forehead. In the same motion he swiped his thumb across her damp brow, then down her small, straight nose, scratching the rounded tip lightly until Reb's relaxing features indicated relief from the itch.

"Ahhh," she purred. The uncontrollable locks settled back down on her arched eyebrows even as Adam finished his favor.

Reb had cut her waist-length raven black hair as short as a man's for the first time when she was fourteen. The deed had angered her mother, amused her grandmother and left her father in the middle, reluctant to side with either of them. The incident was typical of the constant dichotomy in her upbringing, caused by the differing outlooks on life held by her mother and grandmother.

It had always been a challenge for her to please equally the two demanding and headstrong women. That she could shoot the stranger in exactly the spot she chose, ride half the day escaping from the Sioux, and then calmly treat both Adam and the stranger, who at this very moment was under her knife, with capable medical skills gleaned from her apprenticeship with the Old One and her recent study of *Gray's Anatomy,* was a tribute to the success of both women's campaigns. Sometimes Reb wished that they had not both been so thorough—times like now, when she found herself digging splinters of bone out of a man's shoulder.

She finally located the bullet and retrieved it from the bone where it had lodged. She gratefully rinsed her hands and the knife in the bowl of water, then cleansed and disinfected the wound one last time before binding the shoulder with strips of sheet. "All we can do now is wait for him to regain consciousness and hope he doesn't develop an infection," Reb said at last. The sun was all but gone by the time she finished.

"I can take care of the bruise and scratches on his temple. Get a blanket from your bedroll to wrap around you before I have to treat you for pneumonia," she instructed Adam.

"Yes, mother," Adam hooted dutifully as he headed into the dusk, throwing back at her, "If you're sure you'll be safe all alone with your stranger, I'll make sure the horses and mules are bedded down and fetch some more water and firewood, too."

Reb gave Adam a disgusted look as he disappeared. She moved the lantern so that she could better examine the unknown face she found so inexplicably tantalizing. The bruise and knot at the temple had darkened somewhat, but the break in the skin was superficial. Already annoyed and confused by the depth of emotion the stranger aroused in her, Reb tried to detach herself from the hand that lifted aside the soft, midnight black hair from the scratch at the temple. Yes, her fingertips told her, as they threaded through the wavy mass, his hair was very soft.

She dabbed a damp cloth on the scratch and then set it aside. She hesitated only slightly before her fingers obeyed the impulse to trace an old scar highlighted on the man's cheekbone. She brushed away a small amount of dust and dirt accumulated there, and the tips of two fingers drifted down his cheek of their own volition to touch the stranger's full lips. She waited for the sleeping man to wake or react in some way to her touch, but he did not. As she watched her fingertips glide from edge to edge of the full mouth, unbearably pleasant sensations registered in a region far removed from their source. Reb fought, but could not control, the desire to smooth first one thick dark brow, and then the other, the gesture ending each time in the creases of tiny smile lines at the corners of his eyes. Her forefinger tested the bridge of a Grecian nose and then gravitated once more to the smooth scar across the prominent cheekbone.

Reb closed her eyes in the hope that by shutting the face away from view she could end its temptation. But, inexorably, her hands reached up until she cupped the stranger's face, gently feeling with her fingertips the heavy black stubble along square jaws. Her thumbs drew the strong chin for her mind, then retreated to the soft lips.

Reb had never been kissed by any man except her father and brothers. Nor had it ever entered her mind to encourage such a thing. Now, she imagined the taste of the stranger's lips on her own, imagined his breath smelling of the good brandy from the East her father treasured. Unconsciously, Reb's parted lips moved downward toward a destiny of their own.

The emotional turmoil of such unaccustomed behavior finally forced Reb's eyes open in alarm. Her hands still framed his face and her mouth was poised an inch above the stranger's lips. She jerked herself upward, hands flying outward in knotted fists, as though escaping the strike of a rattlesnake. She expected his eyes to flash open accusingly at any moment. His peaceful visage, totally unaware of the conflict stirring within her breast, forced a savage, inarticulate cry from deep within her throat.

At the sound of her own voice, Reb lurched away from the bed, appalled at what had transpired. What's happening to me? What are you doing to me, her mind shouted at the figure on the bed. Dillon might welcome such emotional entanglements, seek such sensual attraction, but not Reb. "Besides, you're probably married and have three kids," she threw at him.

At that moment it occurred to her that she had never checked for a wedding band. She rushed back over to the bed and grabbed the lantern in one hand and the stranger's left hand in the other. No ring! Unaccountably, however, there were numerous abrasions, cuts and scratches from the tips of his fingers to his knuckles that she had not noticed before.

She dropped the hand and leaned across the stranger to check his other hand, her firm breasts brushing lightly across his naked chest. She tried to ignore the exciting sensation that resulted. Both hands were in the same condition. Raw places on his wrists also should be treated. Reb set down the lantern and once again prepared a bowl of clean water and tore more rags from the decimated sheet.

Forced once more into contact that she considered too personal, Reb held the stranger's long slender fingers tenderly in her own. She could not have guessed in her wildest dreams the result of this tactile stimulation. The man's abraded fingertips burned into her own, and the tingling that began in her palm traveled up her arm until she was shivering, whether from delight or fear she could not have said. She concentrated on removing all traces of dirt and pebbles from hands that were covered in the same black curls found on his belly. When the job was complete, she brushed the unmarred portion of one ravaged hand across her cheek. It was happening again. She was not in control. She was no longer sure who was possessor and who was possessed.

"No!" she whispered through gritted teeth, firmly setting the stranger's hand down upon the bed next to his body. With the dearth of women in the West, she had faced such male temptation before, and she had conquered it. True, the magnetism had not been this strong, but if she had not relented to flowery words or tentative, and not-so-tentative touches, she'd be damned if an unconscious man would melt her resolve!

She knew she enjoyed the company of men, but she chose to focus on the opportunities for competition they provided. Deep down was the fear that if she submitted to their caresses she would lose the freedom to be one of them—to dress in buckskins, to hunt and ride, and to enjoy their laughter around the campfire after a long day. She told herself frequently she would never make a choice between the two different lifestyles offered by her mother and grandmother—one as a member of civilized society, and the other as a roaming free spirit.

So, she tried to find a compromise between the two worlds. She observed her manners at home, learned to dance and read and write, but continued to cut her hair, downplayed her femininity, and met the mountain men on equal terms. She avoided physical or emotional relationships with them and worked at being reasonable and practical and not allowing her emotions to govern her life. Consequently, the independent souls who often sat by the Hunters' campfire accepted her on the terms she specified. Because she earned it, they bestowed on her the respect and admiration usually reserved for their male peers.

Reb had no plans to give up her hard-won status at the tender age of seventeen. It was absolutely infuriating to find that she had become the aggressor. Her traitorous body simply would not resist touching this stranger for the pure pleasure of the feeling.

"It must be the mystery of discovering an unknown man in the middle of nowhere," she muttered to herself. Well, if mystery was the problem, she could solve that.

"Just wake up, stranger, and tell me who you are," she growled softly, "and then we'll see who controls whom!"

She turned away confidently to begin preparations for the evening meal.

Chapter Five

"I'VE BEEN THINKING," ADAM BEGAN, A SPOONFUL OF beans poised in midair before his mouth, "about what we should do now."

"And?" Reb helped herself to another cup of coffee from the black pot on the stove.

"Ummmmm," Adam modulated, indicating with the now empty spoon that, in obedience to his mother's training, politeness forbade talking with his mouth full.

"I've been thinking, too," Reb said. "If we hadn't run into this stranger, we'd be home by now. Dad expects us to show up to help with the spring roundup. One of us ought to ride down to the ranch and let him know what's going on. The other could stay here with the stranger until Blue shows up to take over."

"I agree," Adam surprised Reb by saying, then left her aghast when he added, "You stay here with your stranger and I'll go down and round up cattle with Dad and the boys." As Reb started to object, Adam hurried to explain his logic. "Blue should be back any time now, but until he shows up, you're the one with the medical skills. Besides, even one-armed I'm a better roper than you." As Reb grimaced he said, "You're not afraid to come down the mountain alone, are you?"

"Of course not!" she replied indignantly. "It's just that I thought you should be the one to stay since . . . I mean, since the stranger is a man and . . ." She was unaccountably embarrassed to admit to Adam, the same Adam to whom in the past she had always confided the antics of the forward swains she rebuffed, the effect the stranger had on her.

"Yes?" Adam waited while Reb stammered helplessly, then said matter-of-factly, "He doesn't have anything you haven't seen before." Ignoring her rolling eyes he continued, "He'll be incapacitated, so you shouldn't be in any danger of physical harm from him. What's the problem?"

Reb didn't know whether Adam was being purposely blind to her dilemma or not. If she could have seen the private smile behind the fist with a spoon sticking out of it pressed against his mouth, she would have struggled less for a valid reason, besides her inexplicable attraction to the man, not to stay alone with the stranger.

"The Indians?" she ventured.

"No." Adam watched Reb's shoulders visibly sag in defeat. "You ought to keep an eye out, but I'm not expecting any trouble. We've put Standing Buffalo out of commission for a while and all the other Indians have gone to the Powder River except Spotted Tail's Brulés. They're now considered 'prisoners of war' and on their way to a reservation, thanks to that idiot Dodge. Just because he was a good general during the

War Between the States doesn't mean he knows how to deal with the Indians. How Washington could have assigned him to command the army out here is beyond me. If he thinks Spotted Tail's tribe will sit still for being moved to Pawnee country . . . doesn't he realize the Pawnee and the Sioux are mortal enemies?"

The question was rhetorical, of course. Adam mounted a soapbox when he wanted to change the subject painlessly. Reb listened, knowing that, if past experience held true, the oration would be short-lived, and the subject would be changed by the time he finished speaking.

"And do you know why he's made this unbelievably stupid move of holding Sioux who have come to make peace as 'prisoners of war'?"

"Why?" Reb obediently asked.

"Because it's an embarrassment to have Indians making friendly overtures while he's planning a grand revenge campaign against the Sioux. No matter that these are 'friendly Brulés' and he's after the 'unfriendly Oglala's. If that bastard Grenville Dodge keeps it up, he'll eliminate any difference between the 'friendlies' and the 'unfriendlies.' They'll all be out for scalps! Dodge has got to be stopped!" he exploded, slamming his fist on the table.

"Shhh," Reb soothed. She placed her hand on Adam's fist to calm him. "You're making enough noise to wake the dead. We'll figure out a way to control Dodge so that we can get the result we want," she coaxed, all concern for the problem of staying alone with the stranger forgotten for the moment, as Adam had intended.

The "dead" had indeed been awakened by Adam's outburst, which intruded on Kincaid's senses, nudging him to consciousness in time to hear Reb's last remark about "controlling Dodge."

"If only we knew who this stranger is," Reb said, "we could contact his people and have them come to get him. That would solve a big part of our problem."

Where was he, Kincaid wondered. The last thing he remembered was waking up in the Indian camp, and just when he had begun to worry about how he was going to get out of the fix he was in, being shot. Who were these two? Had they learned of his mission and captured him to thwart Dodge's plans? No, that couldn't be the case, since they didn't know who he was. If they wanted to be rid of him, why not just let the Sioux kill him? What was the problem they needed to solve? He was confused and knew he was missing some pieces. They planned to control Dodge, he thought foggily. He must find out their plan, if possible, yet keep his own identity and mission a secret. Kincaid surreptitiously glanced at the pair seated at the table in the shifting lantern light.

The larger and apparently older of the two had leaned his chair back against the wall, one hand stiffly holding a buckskin shirt while his other hand sewed the sleeve. His left boot was up on his right knee, the right toe holding the chair in place.

The smaller had shoved the chair back far enough to stretch long legs out fully, heels resting on the table top, hands cupping a mug.

Both had short, shaggy hair, one sandy colored, the other pitch black. The older one had a day's stubble on his chin, while the younger had a face as smooth as . . . he struggled for something to compare it with, but the more he examined the complexion turned peach by the flickering reddish light, the more he

59

thought "baby's bottom" appropriate. The lad probably hadn't reached puberty yet, and his husky voice spoke from a mouth and jaw that seemed too soft for a man. He gave the youth the benefit of the doubt, guessing that the face would strengthen as the boy matured.

One of these two probably had shot him. Time enough later to figure out the reason for that if they didn't know who he was. He tested his shoulder by lifting slightly. Pain raced briefly across his upper body, and it was with great effort that he suppressed the need to express his discomfort aloud. Clearly he would be in the custody of these two for some time. Certainly until he healed enough to think moving was preferable to dying, he told himself wryly. His tongue felt thick and fuzzy, and his head ached.

"Why is it so important for you to know who he is?" Adam asked.

"I'm just curious," Reb fibbed, admitting to herself that that was only half the truth. She believed the stranger's identity was the key to unlocking the tenacious hold he seemed to have on her heart. "Don't you want to know what happened to his companions? Surely he wasn't out here all by himself."

Kincaid absorbed this additional information. Although they didn't know who he was, their discussion suggested they would ask questions he couldn't answer. If only his head would stop hurting so he could think. Of course! He'd been hit on the head. The ache in his head eased as he put into action a plan he thought might solve some problems, even if it created others. At least it would give him some time.

"Water," he rasped.

Reb froze in her chair. Adam poured a cup of water

and offered it to the man, who took it weakly in his right hand. While Adam supported his head, the thirsty man greedily drank the entire cup. Reb rose slowly and moved as in a trance to a spot beside Adam. He has gray eyes, she thought, such sad gray eyes.

The stranger held out the cup when he was finished. Reb was forced to reach for it, since Adam had no free hand. Trying to avoid contact with him, she inadvertently dropped the cup, which landed with a thud on the floor. She quickly retrieved the vessel. Mumbling an apology for her unusual clumsiness, she set it on the table, then returned to stand slightly behind Adam's shoulder.

Adam eased the stranger's head back down onto the pillow. He stood with one hand on his hip, waiting for the silent man to speak. Reb was dying of the curiosity she had so recently professed to her brother. The revelation of the stranger's identity would free her from his spell. She was sure of it. When the unknown man had a name he would lose his indefinable lure. She leaned in slightly to catch his faint words.

"Who am I?"

"What?!" she blurted incredulously.

"Of course!" Adam interjected. "The blow to his head! We should have suspected this might happen."

Reb forced Adam to spell out in words what she feared to be true from the stranger's remark. "What are you saying?"

"He seems to have lost his memory." He asked the stranger, "Can you remember anything at all about yourself, or how you got here?"

Reb held her breath.

The stranger stared intently first at Adam, noting

his genuine concern, then at Reb, noting her nervous anxiety, and answered positively, "I'm sorry. I can't seem to remember anything."

"Well, I'll be damned!" Adam crowed.

Reb groaned out loud in misery. She turned to Adam, pleading in desperation, "You can't leave me here now. Not with this . . . this . . ." She turned to look at the virile young man, who had cocked one eyebrow speculatively in anticipation of her description. ". . . mindless Yankee tenderfoot!" she finished.

A fleeting smile crossed the stranger's face.

"Watch me," Adam replied. "Come morning I'm heading down the mountain. I'll check at Ft. Laramie to see if anyone knows who you are," he addressed the stranger.

Kincaid relaxed, unaware he had been tensed. They believed him. It was going to work. And he couldn't believe his good fortune. The older one was actually going to leave the younger one here alone with him. "Thank you. By the way, where am I?" he asked so quietly Adam had to bend down to hear him. "How did I get here?" The last question came out as a kind of sigh.

Adam realized the stranger was struggling to keep his eyes open. "Tomorrow's soon enough for all that. You just rest now. Reb'll tell you anything you want to know tomorrow."

Reb gave Adam an angry glare and crossed her arms defiantly across her breasts.

"Reb?" the stranger whispered, eyes closing. A chasm opened and Kincaid plunged into an exhausted sleep.

"Yeah, my baby sister Reb . . ." Adam stopped when he realized the stranger had not heard him. "He's asleep."

"I can see that," Reb snapped, letting the full measure of her anger at the stranger fall on Adam. "Adam," she began in a loud voice.

"Shhh," he said. He placed a finger before his lips. "You don't want to wake your stranger."

"You're not seriously going to leave me here with him in this condition, are you?" she hissed back at him.

He folded his sister in his good arm to comfort her. "Reb, Reb, think what an opportunity this will be. He's like a clean slate—a man with no bad habits to contend with. With total ignorance like his, you can turn him into a right fair human being by the time Blue shows up," he teased.

Reb didn't see the twinkle in Adam's eyes as he smoothed her shorn locks. His suggestion, although humorously intended, put a bee in Reb's bonnet. She jerked out of Adam's grasp in her excitement.

"You're right!" she said. A grin broke across her face for the first time since they had encountered the stranger. "I wouldn't miss an opportunity like this for all the mountain oysters in the world. By the time I get through, he may still be a Yankee, but he won't be a mindless tenderfoot," Reb said smugly. "I'll teach him a thing or two! Why he'll be *so* polite! I can't wait to get started!"

Adam looked askance at Reb. "Don't overdo it."

"Don't worry." Reb smiled with the knowledge that she was once more absolutely in control of the situation. "You just go brand and castrate calves with Dad and the boys and don't worry one little bit about me and *my* stranger. I'll be fine. Now, are we going to let this man sleep in his boots?"

"Uh, no." Adam was too concerned that Reb had a little castrating of her own in mind to focus on her question. "No, I guess I'll take his boots off. You want his pants off, too?" he asked suggestively.

"Yes," Reb said, ignoring his leer. "Take everything off and give it all to me."

Adam did as he was bid, both of them registering in silence the extensive scar on the stranger's right thigh. Finally, Adam covered the naked man with the sheet and wool blanket on the bed.

"Now we'd better think about getting some sleep ourselves," Reb instructed Adam. "Dawn comes early and the sooner you get started the better."

Adam followed her lead, but wondered whether he had made a mistake in his evaluation of Reb's feelings toward the nameless man. He had thought she was attracted to the stranger, but her plans to "remake" the poor man made him stop to reconsider. He didn't want to leave Reb in an untenable situation if he had misjudged her feelings. He decided to give her one last chance to trade places with him. "Maybe I ought to stay here, after all," he suggested tentatively.

"Oh, no you don't," Reb responded immediately. "I'm planning this party, and you aren't invited. Pillow?" She offered Adam a folded-up blanket, a serene smile adorning her flushed face.

Adam thought at that moment she was beautiful. He wondered what the stranger would think. Only time will answer that, he thought. He lay down, wrapped up in his buffalo robe and, not aware how much the efforts of the day had drained him, fell asleep immediately.

"Adam?" Reb queried from her place beside him on the floor several minutes later. A small snore indicated Adam was no longer of this world. "I only wanted to ask," she whispered anyway, "whether you think my stranger isn't a handsome man?"

Chapter Six

ADAM UTTERED A LAST GOOD-BYE, VISIBLE IN THE FROSTY air, and moved down the mountain, pack mules in tow. Reb watched and waved until he disappeared into the dim forest, prolonging until the last possible moment her reentry into the quiet cabin. At last the chilly wind and cloudy skies forced her back into the somewhat warmer refuge.

Like a homing pigeon she headed for the stranger, approaching hesitantly, then more surely as she noticed he seemed feverish. Immediately concerned for him as a doctor for her patient, Reb placed her palm on his forehead. It was hot to the touch. She pressed the back of her hand to his whiskered cheek, also hot.

Suddenly, a powerful hand grabbed her wrist in a paralyzing, but not painful, grip, and she found herself gazing into the flinty gray eyes of the fully wakened man.

"You have a fever," she said softly, attempting to free herself. "I need to check your wound."

"Who are you?" He tightened his grasp.

"My name is Reb."

"As in Johnny Reb?" he asked menacingly.

"No, no," she reassured him, "it's . . ." She hesitated, unwilling to let him know it was a masculine shortening of Rebecca. "It's just a nickname," she offered placatingly.

Kincaid suspected the young man was hiding something, but continued his interrogation. "That other fellow . . ."

"Adam," she supplied.

"Are you his brother?"

"He's my brother," Reb answered evasively. Apparently the stranger did not recognize her as a woman. So much the better, she thought.

"Where is he?"

"He's gone. Don't you remember? He went to Ft. Laramie to see if he can find out who you are. Do you remember anything about yourself this morning?" she questioned hopefully.

"No." He sighed, already regretting the necessity to pretend amnesia.

"I need to check your wound," she reminded softly.

He released her hand reluctantly, then waited stoically for the changing of bandages with which he had such recent familiarity.

"Go ahead." His face closed to all emotion.

Reb watched the hardening features age the young man before her eyes. She proceeded to quickly unwrap the bandages with a deft, yet gentle touch.

Reb gasped when she saw the wound.

Kincaid braced himself for bad news. "Infection?" He refused to look at himself, having seen enough of his own torn flesh.

Reb's gasp had been the result of surprise at what

she did *not* find. There was no bright red skin, no oozing pus to indicate the anticipated infection that would explain the stranger's fever. The wound looked —ordinary. A scab was forming and the skin surrounding it had the expected colorful black and blue bruising.

Reb met the stranger's gaze and answered in amazement, "No infection at all."

Kincaid frowned at her contrary diagnosis.

Reb rebound the wound snugly with clean strips of sheet. Forced to look for another cause for his fever, Reb started asking questions, fearing the answers she would get.

"How do you feel?" she asked, flustered by the turn of events.

"How should I feel?" he retorted.

"How do you feel!" she shot back impatiently. "Are you hungry?"

"No!" That answer surprised him even as he admitted it. He should be hungry, since he hadn't eaten in over twenty-four hours.

"Are you thirsty?"

"Yes!" His tongue felt furred, in fact.

"How about your head?"

"I have a headache! Is that any surprise?"

Reb reached out to lay her fingertips on the pulse at his throat and the stranger once again stayed her hand. Kincaid wondered at the slenderness of the wrist he held, which reminded him once more of the youth of his physician. The commanding tone of the boy's next words belied his apparent youth.

"I need to feel your pulse," Reb ordered.

"Are you a doctor?" he demanded, curious about the competent self-confidence of the lad.

"Do you have someone else in mind for the job?"

she asked sarcastically, gesturing around the deserted cabin.

Kincaid allowed the boy to place his fingertips on his throat. The increased rate alarmed Reb. "I want to listen to your breathing," she warned. She lowered her ear to his chest. The labored breathing, rapid and shallow, revealed the answer she sought.

"Are you always so irascible?" she asked, to postpone thinking about what her examination had revealed.

"I don't know. Are you always so kind to your patients?"

Reb laughed out loud, surprising Kincaid with the warmth of the sound.

No infection for this huge, irritable and irritating man, she thought, amused at the ludicrous conclusion she had been forced to draw by her examination. This stranger, unfazed by a bullet wound that had narrowly missed his heart, had caught a cold from exposure. Of course, the head and shoulder wounds probably hadn't helped, she thought cynically, and God only knew if he would develop pneumonia.

"You have a fever, and I think it's the result of your exposure to the cold. You should drink lots of water, and it would help get the fever down if I apply wet cloths. Are you willing to cooperate?" Reb wasn't sure what she would do if he refused.

Kincaid studied the serious young man. It disturbed him to hand over his well-being to the youth, but he had seen younger men handle even greater responsibility during the war, so he was hesitant to deny himself the boy's services. He avoided answering by asking another question.

"How did I get hurt?"

"The head wound you had when my brother and I

found you strung up by the Sioux. I . . . I shot you. It was the only way we could think of to rescue you," she rushed to explain. "You see, there were too many Indians for us to kill before one of them would have finished you off, so we decided to 'kill' you first. The bullet broke your shoulder blade. I guess I miscalculated a little," Reb finished lamely, unwilling to continue in the face of the stranger's obvious skepticism, and angry that she should feel the need to apologize.

Kincaid heard in the story the excuses of a child caught doing something he should not, and seeking parental expunging of guilt for the wayward action.

"Are you that good a shot, that you had no qualms about shooting someone to 'save' him?" He was not yet ready to oblige in the matter of forgiveness.

"Yes," Reb answered, then added defiantly in response to the eyebrows rising in disbelief, "You're alive, aren't you?"

"Just barely," he muttered under his breath. Reb heard him and an unwanted blush began to rise at her throat.

Returning her earlier sarcasm, he asked, "And I'm to believe you and your brother risked your necks to save a total stranger?"

"You can bet I'll think twice before I do it again," she spat, as she headed for the door.

"Hold it, kid," he said to the retreating form.

Reb whirled and lashed out, "I'm not a kid, I'm . . ." She hesitated, not willing to reveal her true age lest he judge her by her years. "I'm not a kid," she repeated. "I know more about how to survive out here than a tenderfoot like you, so if you expect to live through this ordeal I suggest you think twice before drawing similar unfounded conclusions."

Kincaid admired the boy's spunk. "Whoa!" he laughed. "You're a Rebel, all right!"

Reb watched the years fall away from the man and was tempted by the change to try once more to help him. "Are you going to cooperate?" she repeated testily.

"Sure," the stranger answered easily. "By the way, where are we?"

"A cabin in the mountains, about fifty miles from Ft. Laramie," she replied. "It belongs to a friend of my father's, a trapper named Blue. He should be showing up here any time now."

Damn, Kincaid thought to himself. Another complication. He was very tired. Aloud he said, "I could use some sleep," and closed his eyes.

Before she would let him rest, Reb forced the exhausted man to drink some water and provided a pot from under the bed so he could relieve himself. She refused to be embarrassed by the necessity for this assistance, and his lack of knowledge that she was a woman made the duty easier.

The murmur of Reb's voice as she applied the cooling cloths over his upper body and face lulled Kincaid to sleep. When he was resting comfortably, Reb busied herself making a nutritious broth. When she sought some wood for the stove, she noted the supply was low and decided to take advantage of the respite from her duties with the stranger to split some more logs. The fresh tang of the pine chips assailed her nostrils, replacing the distinctive masculine scent of the stranger that she only now realized she had been savoring.

When it was nearly noon, she felt the first cold snowflake land on her eyelash. She blinked it away, only to have it replaced by two more on her cheek and upper lip. Licking the snowflake away from her mouth, Reb suddenly became aware of the brisk, icy wind that whirled around her.

She hurried to ensure that her horse, Brandy, and the Indian pony that had carried the injured man had plenty of water and feed, pausing to caress her mount. "What do you think, Brandy?" She slid her fingers across the smooth nose of the mare. "Who is my stranger? A famous hero, or a dastardly villain? He is pleasing to the eye, don't you agree?" The horse nickered softly. Reb laughed aloud at the fanciful conversation. She gave the horse a final pat on the withers. "Don't worry, Brandy, I won't let him ride you. He is a little large for a dainty lady like yourself."

Reb shivered at the picture of being mounted by the stranger that drifted through her mind. "Although I'm sure he'd be very gentle," she murmured. As she left, she closed the door of the shed to protect the horses from the blowing snow.

Reb gathered a last load of wood to carry to the cabin and was grateful to be going in out of the cold, which she could feel now that she was no longer warmed by the physical exertion of chopping wood.

The stranger was awake again.

"It's snowing," she said, to make conversation.

"Oh," Kincaid replied, unsure what to say. "Is that normal for this time of year?"

"A May blizzard isn't normal, but it's not uncommon either, up here. I hope Adam doesn't get caught in the storm," she worried out loud, catching her lower lip in her teeth.

Kincaid observed the fear in the wide eyes and spoke to calm the urchin. "He's probably halfway down the mountain by now, don't you think?"

Reb regarded him with a tremulous smile. "Yes,

you're probably right. I'm worrying for nothing, I know. It's just that Adam and I are very close."

Kincaid envied Adam the apparent devotion of his brother. The love of his parents had alleviated the loneliness of being an only child, but he had discovered during the war the deep feelings of brothers for each other and the shared camaraderie that was so different from the parent-child relationship.

"He's lucky to have a brother like you," he found himself complimenting the youth, who blushed with pleasure, making him look slightly cherubic.

"I'll get you some broth." Reb moved away to escape the stranger's scrutiny.

Kincaid allowed himself to be spoon-fed to keep the boy's mind off his brother. Somehow the lad appeared younger and younger the more he observed and listened to him. Pretty soon I'll have him in knee britches, he mused to himself disgustedly.

The protective instinct that rose sparred with the logical side of Kincaid's mind that told him however young the boy looked, however kindly he acted at the moment, the brat had shot him. Even now, the kid must be thinking up ways to interfere with Dodge's plan.

"Is Adam your only kin?" he asked gruffly, determined to find a subject to dispel the aura of pervasive goodwill in the room.

"No," Reb answered good-naturedly. "I have another older brother, Garth, and a younger sister and brother, Dillon and Jesse."

"What about your parents?"

"My father, Matthew Hunter, is alive and my grandmother, the Old One. My mother was killed in the war," she finished bitterly.

Kincaid could not imagine how the war had reached out here in the wilderness to snatch this boy's mother.

"The war?"

"You don't remember the war?" Reb wondered what it would be like to have such an earth-shattering event wiped from one's memory. "You were in the war, I think. I've seen your right leg." She paused to watch the stranger massage his thigh for a moment.

Kincaid had not realized he was rubbing the pitted scar on his upper leg. It was a habit born of necessity, since without massage or some activity the muscle stiffened and ached. He met the boy's wide eyes and the two shared a moment of common pathos.

"The war seemed so far from us. It was a fight between Northerners and Southerners. We were no part of it. The only difference out here was that fewer soldiers were stationed at the forts. I had no objection to that. The fewer Easterners out here, the better."

Kincaid recognized Reb's attitude toward Easterners from her tone of voice. It reminded him of the disdainful attitude of Johnny Rebs toward Yankees.

She continued, "My grandfather, my mother's father, who lived in Philadelphia, somehow talked the Yankees into making him an advisor. He wasn't supposed to go near the fighting, but he did, and was hit by cannon fire. We got word that he was dying. My mother hadn't seen him since she married my father, but she insisted on being with him.

"My father couldn't stop her from going, and for some reason he wouldn't go with her. She took a stage until she could catch a train." Reb could barely speak with the strain of holding back unmanly tears.

"You don't have to continue," Kincaid said, empathizing with the boy's loss. It was difficult to imagine people ignoring the war, pretending it wasn't happening. He thought of his own parents, back in their Fifth Avenue brownstone mansion in New York, who had done a pretty good job of it. Apparently, these people had not been entirely successful.

He was not prepared for the string of invectives that spewed forth from the youth suddenly, and he was so surprised he only caught the words "filthy Yankees" and "killed by a damned train."

"What?"

"A Yankee train! A Yankee train!" she repeated, breathing heavily, barely under control.

"Is it Yankees you have no stomach for, or trains?" Kincaid probed gently, certain now, with the mention of distaste for trains, of his original suspicion that the two brothers had not come upon him accidentally.

"Both!" Reb knew she should not be revealing the overwhelming distaste she had developed for Yankees and the irrational fear she had of trains since her mother's accident. This was one area where knowing she should stay calm and actually accomplishing that goal were two different things. Both her hate and her fear had condensed into dread of the dragon her mother had warned her was coming: civilization.

"Would you care to talk about it?" Kincaid inquired carefully. He didn't wish to upset the now agitated youth any further, but he did want to find out as much as he could to protect his mission and perhaps save his own life.

"My mother is dead because some Yankee was too greedy to spend any money maintaining his train and the track it ran on," Reb accused.

"Men out here aren't guilty of greed?"

"No mountain man could be as greedy as you Yankees."

Kincaid noted his inclusion among the offensive group.

Reb ranted at her captive, "The South only wanted to maintain its way of life. The North wouldn't let go. It destroyed the South rather than give it up. A mountain man would never hang on if doing so would destroy the worth of that which he sought to hold. There are rumors that the Northerners want to build a railroad out here. That's a perfect example of Yankee thoughtlessness. Did they ask us if we needed it, or even wanted it? No! But they'd put it here, to ruin our way of life without ever considering the consequences. I'll never let that happen if I can help it!"

Reb's statements destroyed any doubt Kincaid had had about the reason for his capture. It was difficult to argue that the North had not wreaked havoc with the South. Kincaid had seen enough carnage to convince him that if not ruined, the South was very close to it. For his own reasons, he didn't agree with her comparison between the results of the war and the results of building the railroad.

"Don't you think that's being a little unfair? What about the positive things a railroad could provide?" Kincaid argued back.

Reb shuddered. "Trains will bring people. We don't need them out here." It was the Old One speaking, through Reb. "It's one thing my father and I agree about."

Kincaid glanced at the fierceness of the kid's countenance as he defended his way of life. Then he amended his impression. That is no child, he told himself.

"What does your father do?"

"Mostly, he raises cattle. We all help. Adam went to join him for the roundup." Reb gladly left the topic of railroads. It was easy to discuss with the attentive stranger the monotony of herding cattle balanced by the pleasure of hearing new-born calves bawl for their mothers. Before either of them was aware of it, darkness was falling.

"Time to feed you again," Reb interjected when she noticed the failing light.

At the thought of more broth, Kincaid uttered an "Ugh!" that made Reb laughingly reply, "I never said I could cook!"

He watched the boy efficiently stoke the fire and warm the broth left over from lunch. Soon he found himself once more full, sponged down, relieved and tucked in to sleep.

From the sound of the wind drifting the powdery flakes around the outside of the cabin, Reb guessed the storm was abating. She thought how apt was the local saying, "We don't get much snow, but a lot blows through." In acknowledgment of the cold, she quietly stripped off her buckskins and underclothes in the dark to don the full-length nightshirt she kept at Blue's cabin for just such occasions. She gloried in the feel of the soft, warm flannel against her bare skin.

It was a relief to have the stranger asleep, even though his fever remained high and he restlessly tossed in the bed. She thought ruefully how wrong Adam had been about the stranger having no bad habits. He was extremely argumentative for someone with no memory. And good at getting me to talk, she thought. Adam probably was wrong about the danger of physical harm, too, she added silently, rubbing her wrist where the stranger had enveloped it in his grasp. Even injured, his strength exceeded that of most men she knew.

She spread a buffalo robe on the floor beside the

stove and dropped down to curl up inside it. She wished she hadn't been so glib with the man. Why had she gushed out the story of her mother's death and her aim to fight against the takeover of her wilderness by the Yankees? After all, he was a Yankee, too.

Enough of regrets, she admonished herself. Instead, she should be congratulating herself on how well she had suppressed even a moment of desire for the stranger throughout the day. "I do not need him, I do not want him and he will not have me," she pledged as she drifted off to sleep.

The frantic shouts of the stranger woke Reb in the middle of the night. She did not take time to light the lamp, but bounded over to the thrashing man. Fearing he would further injure himself, she sat on the bucking Yankee to keep·him in bed. She pulled her nightshirt up to straddle his waist, quickly placing a knee on each arm to hold them down. She put one palm on the center of his chest and one on his right shoulder, leaning down to his face to talk soothingly to the struggling man, who seemed to be having a nightmare.

"Don't leave me," he pleaded desperately.

"I won't leave you," she reassured him. She laid her cheek next to his to check his temperature. His skin was on fire. When he began to talk again, she decided he must be suffering from delirium caused by the high fever.

"I'm not that rich, arrogant Yankee spy Christopher anymore," he entreated. "I'm just plain Kincaid. I've changed, Laurie. I've changed."

So he was a Yankee spy named Christopher. Or Kincaid. Who was Laurie?

"It's all right, Kincaid," she comforted, hoping to keep him still. "I'm here."

"Let me love you," he urged, his head, the only unpinned portion of his body, coming up from the pillow seeking contact with the feminine voice in the dark.

"No!" Reb jerked away from the stranger when his mouth found hers, freeing his arms. They came up around her instantly, pulling her down to him, binding them breast to breast, her right hand caught between them.

She could feel the heat from his fevered body through the flannel nightshirt. Amazed and startled at how fast the situation had gotten out of hand, Reb forced herself to remain calm while Kincaid murmured love words in her ear and kissed her tenderly along her jaw and down her neck behind her ear. She waited, expecting the period of delirium to pass momentarily. She was unprepared for the strange feelings elicited by her close contact with the man's hot skin. Intensely aware of her bare thighs touching his waist, the constriction of inner muscles warned that Kincaid's affectionate attentions were not without their effect.

She listened to the endearments, anxious for a way to ease the unfamiliar erotic tension mounting moment by moment. She did not struggle, mistakenly thinking she could ignore the physical sensations generated by the hallucinating man.

"So beautiful," he whispered in her ear. "So soft, so lovely."

Reb closed her eyes and envied Laurie, whoever she was, while she fantasized that Kincaid spoke to her.

"Let me touch you," he implored. One hand forced her upward enough to enable him to cup her breast in his hand. She reached up to stop him, but ended by resting her own hand upon his instead, while he gently caressed her nipple until it stood out in an excited peak. Without warning, the nightshirt was pulled up and Kincaid's warm, wet mouth replaced his hand and gently tugged on the sensitive point. The whiskers that scratched her delicate skin roused her to action.

Her hands flew to Kincaid's hair, her fingers threading through it. Grasping the silky stuff with both hands, she tried pulling his head away. But it was too late. He increased his hold, swirling his tongue around the responsive tip while his calloused fingertips caressed her velvety skin, until at last she abandoned all resistance, pressing him to her and arching backward, offering him freer access to her body.

His tongue titillated first one breast and then the other, while his hands continued their quest over her sleek form. Wrapped in delight, Reb lost track of time until Kincaid slid her down his belly into a prone position so that her most private place made contact with his swollen shaft. She instinctively pressed her body closer to his. He grabbed her naked buttocks to help her in the pleasurable endeavor.

His tongue dipped slowly into her honeyed mouth, then delved deeply, seeking sweeter nectar. Unaccustomed to the intoxicating feelings he generated, Reb relented further to Kincaid's explorations. She could no longer act, she could only react. In a haze of sensation, she felt herself pushed upright to a sitting position once again, as Kincaid's hands set out on a delicious assault of her breasts and belly.

"Perfect," Kincaid praised. "Breasts like ripe fruits, belly so firm, one day to grow large with my seed . . . we'll make beautiful babies."

Bombarded with the satisfaction of itches she had not known needed scratching, she did not resist when he grabbed her waist with both hands, intending to join himself with her. Reb was ready, anxious even, for the consummation of an act she only hours earlier had denied she needed or wanted.

At the last moment, Kincaid hesitated and placed her back upon his belly, away from the source of satisfaction. Reb moaned in rebellion, pressing her rosy crests enticingly back down upon his chest and pushing her body back down against him, seeking gratification.

"No, no, love," he said gently in her ear, scraping her sensitive breasts along his chest in sweet pain as he put his hands under her arms and raised her up and away from temptation. "You're right. Must wait, must wait," he chanted, resisting her entreaty with great effort. "Marry me. Be my wife, Laurie," he said, stroking the hair tenderly from her damp forehead.

The shock of being denied brought Reb back to bitter reality. Kincaid was delirious. He was making love to another woman, not her, one he had wanted to marry and have his children. Appalled and ashamed at her behavior, and enraged at Kincaid's unknowing callousness to her, she hit out at the source of her humiliation.

"Let go!" she screamed, slapping Kincaid across the face and struggling to escape his embrace.

"No, I won't let her go!" Kincaid shouted, lost again in his nightmare. "She's my wife. She's not dead! She's not dead, I tell you! Don't die, Laurie, don't die," he cried in agony. "Don't leave me," he whispered desperately. Reliving his loss, Kincaid relaxed his hold long enough for Reb to scramble off the bed.

"Don't take her away!" Kincaid shouted angrily, arms flailing. One powerful clubbed fist caught Reb in the eye and knocked her across the room, where she stumbled against a chair and fell backward. She hit the door hard enough to knock her unconscious. Kincaid swung his feet over the side of the bed, but when he tried to rise, he fainted from the effort.

When Reb came to, she found herself slumped in front of the door, one eye swollen shut. Sunlight streamed through the skin window, reflecting off the frigid, white snow. Kincaid sprawled sideways across the bed, naked and shivering. The fire in the stove had gone out and she could see her breath in the room.

She rose painfully, stiff from the cold and the fall, and crossed to look down at the man who had rejected the offer of her virginity.

"How sad," she mused, recognizing in the shivering man symptoms of the deadly pneumonia, "for both of us. He's in love with a dead woman, and I'm in love with a dying man."

It's all my fault, she thought guiltily. If I hadn't wanted him to make love to me, I would have been able to control him, to keep him from hurting both of us. She'd broken her own cardinal rule. She'd gotten involved and the results had been disastrous. Well, I won't make that mistake again, she vowed silently.

She rearranged Kincaid correctly on the bed, covered him with the sheet and blanket and then added the buffalo robe from the floor as well.

"You're not going to die," she addressed the unconscious man firmly. "You're going to get well, Kincaid, and then you're going to get out of my life!"

Chapter Seven

"HEY, BLUE, WAIT UP," ADAM SHOUTED LOUD ENOUGH
to be heard across the barren parade ground. He tied
his horse and the mules at a nearby hitching rail in
front of the officers' quarters and marched diagonally
across the length of the austere compound separating
him from the mountain man. "Hi there, Trapper," he
greeted Blue's wolfish dog. He dropped on his knees
to grab the thick, gray fur at the animal's neck,
roughhousing playfully with him. "What are you
doing here at Ft. Laramie, Blue? I thought you never
came down here," he said when he stood again.

Blue squinted at Adam, who had his back to the
sunset. "Usually I don't," the wiry, long-limbed man
replied. "But I was tracking somebody, and this is
where he came." Blue had spent so much time in the
sun his face deserved the "beaten" in the word
"weather-beaten." The unevenly cut black hair that
fell into his arched black brows and the several days'
growth of black and gray stubble on his face gave him

a grizzled look, but the flame in the warm, mahogany eyes testified to the fiery spirit that dwelled within. "I could ask the same about you." He gestured toward the arm Adam still carried in a sling. "You look a little the worse for wear. What happened?"

"It's a long story. Let's go sit where we can talk without being ogled." Adam glanced around at the beardless new recruits lining the barracks wall who gawked rudely at the two men.

They headed for the sutler's store, which supplied the soldiers with combs, writing paper, thread, sweets and other sundries not issued by the quartermaster. It was deserted except for the proprietor, a long-toothed man named Sam. The store was off-limits to the soldiers unless they had money to spend. Fortunately for Adam and Blue, the recruits had long since gambled away the pittance they'd earned, and payday was weeks away. While the Indians usually traded there as well, none were present now.

"Hi, Sam," Adam called to the sutler.

"Jes' make yerselves ta' home," the white-bearded coot said from behind the long, waist-high wooden counter cluttered with bolts of cloth, canned goods, tobacco, ribbons and jars of candy. The old man disappeared through a doorway hung with a tattered, red wool blanket muttering, "Got some unpackin' ta' do in the back."

"He's not much for company," Adam excused the old-timer.

When they settled in rickety wooden chairs before the huge, black iron stove, Trapper lolling on the uneven dirt floor between Blue's outstretched feet, Adam reached for a peppermint stick from one of the jars on the counter and, while he sucked on it, recounted the events of the previous day.

"That Reb, she's something," he said, finishing his story and the candy at the same time. "Nothing would do but we save that stranger, and we did."

"You left her alone with that man?"

Adam could hear Blue's concern, but remained confident as to his initial assessment of the possible danger. "We expected you to show up at any minute. I didn't think she'd be alone with him long." He licked his sticky fingers clean, then shared his observations with the older man. "It's a funny thing. I've never known Reb to show any female interest in a man, but she sure is all-fired attracted to this stranger."

"Mooning over him?"

"Not exactly," Adam replied with a grin. "As a matter of fact, when I left, she was all set to teach him some manners." Adam filled Blue in on the man's amnesia and Reb's pledge to instruct the "mindless Yankee tenderfoot." "I came here to see if I can find out who he is. I don't have any doubt Reb can handle the situation so long as Standing Buffalo doesn't show up unexpectedly."

"You don't have to worry about Standing Buffalo," Blue said, his eyes narrowing.

"What makes you say that?"

"I followed him. He's here at Spotted Tail's camp outside the fort."

"You followed him? From where?"

"From where you ambushed him," Blue said quietly.

"But if you were there . . . ?" Adam could not fathom that Blue should be there but not make his presence known.

"I guess you're old enough to know the truth and not get huffy," Blue said resignedly. Then, looking into Adam's eyes, man to man, he said, "I've followed you down the mountain from my cabin every year since the first year you came."

"You what?!" Adam sprang up in disbelief of this secret intrusion into his life.

"Sit down," Blue said, brooking no disagreement and staring Adam back into his seat. "Hear what I have to say."

Adam sat down, but the tension in his powerful young body belied the blankness of his features.

"I made an agreement with Matt that first year that I'd be sure you and Reb got back down the mountain safely."

Adam's mouth tightened perceptibly at the corners at the thought his father hadn't trusted him. As if reading his mind, Blue added, "Your father knew a sixteen-year-old boy doesn't want a wet nurse. Anyway, it wasn't you he didn't trust."

"Reb."

"Yes," Blue confirmed. "She had the skills of an adult and the curiosity of a child. She was just as likely to listen to you as to wave your opinion away and do what she wanted. It was only meant to be a precaution, and only the first year," Blue soothed patiently.

"But you said . . ."

"I know," he interrupted. "It was so pleasing for me to watch the two of you on your own, growing up, I couldn't help myself. I followed you down all the other years without your father's knowledge. Once or twice I was glad I was there," he confessed grimly, reflecting back over the years.

"The bear!" Adam recalled the year when Reb had disappeared, making him frantic until she suddenly came up behind him with a black bear cub over her horse's neck, saying it must be an orphan. "Then you must have provided the distraction that kept that hornet-mad mother from catching up to us!"

Blue nodded. Adam could remember as though it were yesterday the cub scampering away after its mother when Reb released it, and their fear.

"And the wolves," Blue reminded gently of the time the pair had been trapped by a blizzard and besieged by a large, hungry pack.

"I'd forgotten that," Adam murmured, a sardonic smile erupting on his face. "I thank you now for the help, although you're right. I would have been highly offended at the time to think I couldn't do it all myself."

"You've come a little further than Reb," Blue said, returning the grin. "She still thinks she can."

"Oh, I don't know about that. She's expecting you to show up at your cabin any moment to help her out with the stranger," Adam informed Blue.

"I think we should let her stew in her own juices for a little while," Blue replied with a conspiratorial smile. "How about you?"

"So long as it's you she vents her wrath on and not me, that's fine," Adam answered. "Since you plan to go back up, will you ask around about the stranger's identity for me?"

Blue had seen the captive hung, spread-eagled in the forest and wondered himself where the man had come from. "Be glad to check up on him for you."

"I'm heading for home tomorrow, then." Adam stretched one-armed as he rose. "Think I'll go find a place to bed down and get some sleep."

"I prefer to sleep under the open sky, but if you can stand the stares, there's some room in the barracks," Blue offered.

"It beats the ground." Adam took a good look at

the awkward youngsters drilling outside. "Pretty green," he finally said.

"Yeah. They got a new bunch in, fresh from *not* fighting the Civil War, that's supposed to head out tomorrow. They'll escort Spotted Tail and his Sioux to a reservation near the Pawnee. You got a picture of that?"

"You're expecting trouble." A frown furrowed Adam's brow.

"Let's just say I plan to stick around to make sure nobody starts an Indian war," Blue replied calmly.

"Good luck. If I don't see you tomorrow morning before I leave, send Reb home as soon as you can. We can use her help. She's a pretty good roper—for a girl."

"Don't let her hear you say that," Blue said, chuckling.

"I may be crazy, but I'm not *that* crazy," Adam threw back over his shoulder.

Blue watched Adam unhitch his animals and head for the stables. "Rachel, Rachel, my love, your children are growing up . . ." he sighed to himself, then ran his hands over his moist eyes and up through his hair. "Come on, Trapper, let's go," he called to his old friend, and they headed for a spot to sleep out under the stars near Spotted Tail's camp.

The strong smell of bear grease awakened Blue. He slowly opened his eyes to find Spotted Tail squatting next to his head, knife in hand, muscular forearms resting on his knees, his black eyes glittering intently, watching for Blue to become alert.

Without moving, Blue greeted the chief of the Brulé Sioux. "Welcome, my friend."

"You're getting careless in your old age. Were I not

a friend, you would be a dead man," Spotted Tail said with a chuckle, setting the point of his knife in the hollow of Blue's throat.

Blue looked around furtively for Trapper.

"Your dog has gone to chase a rabbit. You should not depend on him to be your ears. Someday your ears may not be there when you need to hear."

"I will take your words to my heart," Blue said, gracefully accepting the lesson as Spotted Tail sheathed his knife. "What makes Spotted Tail seek out an old friend in the dark?" Blue rose slowly to a sitting position and crossed his legs, Indian fashion.

"Tomorrow the soldiers take us to the land of our enemy, the Pawnee."

"I know."

"My people will not accept the will of the White Father that we live so near our enemy."

"I know," Blue repeated. "My heart is heavy for the people of Spotted Tail."

"Is your grief great enough to help us escape?" Spotted Tail was not shy about putting to the test his friendship with the white man he had always found honest.

"What can I do for my brother, Spotted Tail?" Blue asked earnestly. "I will not kill the soldiers myself, nor help you kill them," he admitted.

"That is not needed. We have a way to be free of the Blue Coats without killing. You can help us by keeping them from overtaking us before we reach the Powder River. With the women and children, we cannot travel as fast."

"How can I do that?"

"You will find a way," Spotted Tail said confidently, placing the burden squarely in Blue's lap. "Then you can go back to Too-Big-For-Horses."

Blue's eyes hooded.

"Standing Buffalo says his prisoner was stolen by two young trappers. His picture of them is like that of the two who visit you each new season of growth."

"And if this is true?"

"In return for your help I will keep Standing Buffalo close by my side, and we will not find Too-Big-For-Horses on our journey north."

Blue sat quietly thinking for a moment. "I will do what I can to delay the soldiers because we are old friends. But I make no guarantee."

"That is all I can ask."

"Look well to your path. I would not like it if the young trappers should come to harm. Then I might think you no longer value the friendship you gave in return for the saving of your life."

"I have not forgotten I owe my life to you, my friend," Spotted Tail replied soberly, his black eyes bright. "But for you, my scalp would be the prize of a Pawnee warrior."

The men measured each other by the light of the evening stars, pleased with what they found.

"I will keep my part of the bargain," Spotted Tail finally said, rising and breaking the silence.

Blue slowly unfolded from his sitting position and held out his hand. Spotted Tail clasped Blue's arm to his own, so that the men were joined elbow to wrist. Blue, a head taller, looked down into the grave eyes of the Brulé chief.

"And I mine." Blue increased the pressure of his grip to seal the agreement. With an understanding reached, they released each other and Spotted Tail disappeared into the night.

Trapper picked that moment to reappear. "Thanks a lot, pal," Blue said, dropping to his haunches to scratch the animal lovingly under his chin. "That could've turned into more than an embarrassing moment if it hadn't been Spotted Tail. Try to stick around a little closer, will you? You know my hearing's not what it used to be. All right?"

Trapper whined and gave Blue a look of understanding.

"All right," Blue repeated quietly. He pulled the old dog close and gave him a hug. "All right."

Chapter Eight

KINCAID ROLLED FROM HIS BACK TO HIS RIGHT SIDE ON the soft, overstuffed mattress, drawing his bare left leg up and out from under the oppressively warm covers until his knee sank into the ticking at a right angle with his sweat-soaked body. His powerful right arm curled childlike around the matted black curls on his head, protectively cupping the crown. Somewhere, deep in his consciousness, it registered that the pain that resulted from the change in position was located in his left shoulder, not his right thigh.

He opened his eyes and quickly shut them again, then blinked slowly several times to adjust to the daylight streaming in through the opaque window. He waited for the film that blurred his vision to clear.

The first thing he saw was the boy, Reb, sprawled sleeping, legs akimbo, in a chair next to the bed. His head was cradled in his arms on the edge of the mattress. Kincaid reached tentatively with three fingers of his left hand to touch the youth's frail arm and wake him. He got no reaction.

"Rebel," he managed to whisper, weakly applying more pressure to the boy's arm.

With a languor that bespoke the eight sleepless days and nights Reb had fought death, she gradually raised her tired head to peer half-asleep at the source of the rational baritone voice.

"Kincaid?" She feared she was dreaming because she wanted so badly to find the fever broken and death defeated.

Kincaid noted vaguely that she called him by his name. "You look a little under the weather," he said, attempting a grin that caused his dry lips to crack from the effort. He licked them with his equally dry tongue, then added, "Where'd you get the shiner?"

Reb heaved a private sigh of relief that Kincaid did not remember the events leading to her blackened eye. She caressed with her fingertips the still tender yellow and purple skin.

"I have you to thank for this," she said with a rueful grin that softened only slightly the drawn look she wore from too little rest.

Kincaid's eyes widened in surprise as he prepared to protest.

"Delirium," she explained and excused all at once, anticipating his plea for pardon.

Understanding washed across Kincaid's features. "Sorry," he apologized sincerely.

"It's much better now." It embarrassed her to hear him take responsibility for actions she considered her fault. "Are you hungry?" Although she'd force-fed Kincaid regularly, she didn't know when she had eaten last. She was aware of a gnawing in her stomach that suggested it had not been filled recently. She stretched each arm upward as far as possible from her aching body, palms outward and long fingers outstretched, while a huge yawn forced her mouth to open wide and her eyes to squeeze shut.

"I could eat a horse." Kincaid drew the last word out as his mouth fell open, echoing her yawn.

Reb braced her palms on the sagging mattress and pushed herself up out of the hard, uncomfortable chair, pausing to arch her stiff back and massage her tingling buttocks with her hands. She checked Kincaid's brow with the palm of her hand and found it cool and moist.

"Fever's broken. Gone," she said with a sigh, continuing the laconic conversation. "I'll get your . . . lunch," she finished after checking the angle of the sunlight.

Tears welled up in Reb's eyes and she turned quickly to the potbellied stove lest Kincaid discover her extreme emotional relief that he was not going to die. When she had regained control, Reb returned to Kincaid and helped him sit upright in the bed. As she propped the poor excuse for a pillow behind him, the sheet dropped to his hips, barely covering his manhood. Reb hardly noticed the bare flesh, having been on intimate terms with every part of the sick man's body as his physician.

When she spoon-fed him with a variation of the steamy, bouillon-like broth he remembered so well, Kincaid questioned Reb on the details of his bout with pneumonia.

"So I talked while I was delirious," he said with some trepidation. "What did I say?" He had visions of his entire secret mission exposed. With Reb's dislike of Yankees and railroads, there was no telling what the youth would do with such information.

"A lot. And nothing," she replied cryptically. "I know you were a Union spy."

Kincaid's face remained blank.

"I know your name is Kincaid, or Christopher. You seemed to prefer Kincaid," she said mysteriously, paused, then screwed up her courage to add solemnly, "and you had a wife, Laurie, whom you loved very much, who died."

"You know enough," Kincaid said bitterly, reacting to the grief still evoked by even the mention of Laurie's name.

"You remember?!" Reb was so excited that Kincaid's memory might have returned she spilled a spoonful of breath-cooled soup. It dribbled down the front of his brawny chest, pooled in his navel and then ran over down into the line of black curls on his belly. Reb anxiously sopped up the warm mess with the sweaty sheet. Her efforts took her where the curls thickened to a bush, and she suddenly felt the pangs of a different hunger. She looked up quickly to find Kincaid staring coldly at her. It was as though he knew what she was experiencing in that moment and condemned her for it. She was so distracted by the unexpected return of her desire that she overreacted to Kincaid's next despair-induced remark.

"I remember I had a wife who was killed. How I felt about her is none of your damn business," he snapped.

His consideration for the dead woman renewed her pique over the events during his delirium, and she abruptly thrust the whole bowl of hot soup upside-down in his lap.

"Thanks for saving my life, Reb," she mocked furiously. "I owe you so much, Reb. I don't know how I'll ever repay you, Reb," she snarled at Kincaid.

"You ungrateful bastard." Anger, frustration, fear and exhaustion had all taken their toll, and the need to remain in control had been dispelled by his recovery. "It's none of my business how you get well! You can take care of yourself!"

She was out the door and it had slammed behind her before Kincaid realized she'd dumped the scalding contents of the bowl on his lap. With a nimbleness that left him prostrate afterward, he hopped out of bed and wiped the remains of the disgusting meal off his heat-pinkened skin with the ends of the stained sheet, which he ripped off the bed in his haste.

Reb still saw red even after she reached the creek. She followed it quickly to the deep, calm pool hidden in a thick stand of fresh-smelling lodgepole pines that formed an oval at the center so the sun shone through on the sparkling water. She stripped off her filthy, rankly odorous buckskins and stepped across the muddy bank, where the drifted snow of the previous week had only recently melted.

She immersed her long, naked body slowly in the frigid wetness—toes, ankles, calves, knees, thighs. Shivering, unable to withstand any longer the apprehension of the cold, she plunged herself forward headfirst, diving with fingers delicately forming a V, piercing the small, circular pond without a sound or a splash. Suddenly she simply was no longer there.

Reb held her breath as long as she could, swimming strongly with smooth strokes underwater. Finally, she burst upward, breaking the surface with a gush of white spray, enjoying a freedom of spirit she'd missed while nursing Kincaid. Then, she dog-paddled in place while her rage cooled.

Whether I like it or not, she concluded after several fatiguing minutes of this exercise, I'm responsible for this aggravating man. I *will* mold him into someone capable of surviving in this wilderness, and I won't lose my temper again no matter what the provocation, she promised herself faithfully as she stepped from the water.

She dreaded the thought of pulling the crusty, sweat-salty buckskins on over her dewy skin, but having no other clothes available that hid her female form so well, she reluctantly donned the offensive garments.

She took advantage of the opportunity to walk in the woods after being cooped up for so long and when she returned to the cabin several hours later, a contrite Kincaid, naked and seated cross-legged on the thoroughly rumpled bed, chin in hands, elbows perched on knees, greeted her warily, "Welcome back."

"Are you ready to behave yourself?" Reb responded frostily, immediately taking the upper hand and putting him on the defensive. She moved purposefully to pick up the bowl and spoon from the floor where they had landed.

"Are you?" he shot back, determined not to kowtow to a stripling youth.

Reb ignored the question and gritted her teeth, equally determined not to allow him to goad her into uncharacteristically losing her temper again.

"Get off the bed," she ordered.

"What for?" Kincaid asked suspiciously.

"I have to wash the sheets, unless you want to sleep in this mess," she answered caustically.

"Oh." Sheepishly, he moved off the bed and stood wavering barefooted on the cool dirt next to Reb.

She suddenly became aware of him again as a man—a vulnerable, naked man.

"Put this blanket around yourself before you get sick again." She stuffed the red-striped gray wool blanket against his barrel chest and suppressed her disturbingly persistent passion by concentrating on her work.

"Well?" she said when she had the sheets in hand.

"Well?" he repeated expectantly.

"Even for a Yankee tenderfoot, you don't have much common sense. Get back in bed. I'll change the dressing on your wound when I get back."

Kincaid ignored the jibe and gratefully climbed back into the soft haven. He was asleep almost before Reb left the room.

She rinsed the sheets and beat them on flat stones near the creek to clean them, then hung them over the forked branches of a cottonwood to dry in the fresh, cool, ever-present breeze.

Reb decided that, having been deprived of lunch, Kincaid should have something more substantial for dinner. By the end of the afternoon she had snared two rabbits and harvested some wild onions and mushrooms she had located earlier in the day. She collected the dried sheets and returned to the cabin. Soon, a savory rabbit stew permeated the cabin with delicious smells. It was Kincaid's nose that woke him.

"Aaaah, ambrosia," he sighed, breathing in deeply to absorb as much of the luscious odor as possible and smacking his lips loudly.

Reb wafted a large bowl of the chunky, mouth-watering concoction under his nose. Kincaid obediently opened wide and waited for Reb to feed him. He ate ravenously, gulping the stew so quickly that he choked at least twice on hunks of meat before Reb insisted that she would not give him any more unless he chewed more thoroughly.

"If you don't slow down, it will all come back up again," she warned.

"Where'd you get the meat—rabbit, isn't it? I didn't hear a shot," he said, chewing and talking at the same time.

"I used a snare." Reb should have left it at that, but she could not resist the urge to begin remaking the man. "You shouldn't talk with your mouth full. Obviously nobody ever taught you any manners. You're as bad as Adam, and even he knows better."

"What did you expect from someone you've labeled a 'mindless Yankee tenderfoot'?"

"If the shoe fits, wear it."

"Spare me," Kincaid groaned as he looked skyward.

"I guess if your mouth is empty enough to talk it means you're all done eating." Reb mocked as she started to move away.

"Wait!" He grabbed the fringe on Reb's grimy buckskins. "I could be persuaded to eat a little more." However, he was not true to his word. "Guess my eyes are bigger than my stomach," he commented wearily in chagrin when he had eaten only two more bites.

Reb placed the bowl on the table, then came back to change Kincaid's bandage. She carefully unwrapped the sheet and was relieved to see the wound scabbed over and healing nicely. "Sore?"

"You could say that. Although it doesn't hurt as much as . . . I expected it to." Kincaid had been about to say "as my leg did," but remembered at the last second he was supposed to have amnesia. Still, his eyes were awash with remembered pain that Reb immediately attributed to his memory of the war and the loss of his wife.

"Just take it easy and rest, and you'll be well before you know it," she reassured him, but she avoided the hurt in his eyes by moving back to the stove.

Reb slowly poured heated water from the black pot on the stove grate into a large, silvery-colored tin bowl, as she had every evening since Kincaid first evidenced signs of pneumonia. She used a towel as a mitt to carry the bowl over to the chest next to the bed.

As if he were a limp rag doll, Reb began methodically washing Kincaid from head to foot with a soapy rag, starting at the bottom. He struggled like a child as she washed between each toe and then scrubbed the sole of his foot, pushing his grief aside with her ticklish onslaught.

Kincaid's fingernails clutched the mattress and one leg writhed to escape Reb's unmerciful attention while she stubbornly held on to the other ankle and continued the ritual cleansing. He endured it as long as he could without saying anything, holding in the laughter until it hurt his chest, then finally burst out with, "This is torture! What are you doing?"

"Giving you a bath."

Reb dutifully soaped upward from his long foot to the knee, to the deeply-scarred right thigh.

The moment Reb touched the scar Kincaid's grief returned in full force, and his pain and guilt.

"Leave that alone," he said in a gravelly voice, all traces of humor suddenly gone from his eyes. He grabbed Reb's hand in a steely grip that was meant to hurt.

"Ouch!" she yelled, yanking her wrist away as Kincaid simultaneously released it. "What's the matter with you?"

"Don't touch that scar."

"I've been washing that scar for eight days, and I see no reason to stop now," she said, nostrils flaring dangerously.

"Eight days?!" Kincaid bunched his brows in consternation. He calculated the days and realized he'd missed the meeting with Dodge. He felt a pang of sympathy for his parents, who would surely worry when they got a telegram from Dodge saying that he hadn't shown up.

"Why do you think the leg's not stiff? Just who do you think has been massaging it all this time? Little green elves?" Reb hissed sarcastically. "Now sit back, get your hands out of the way, and let me finish so I can eat. I'm hungry and tired and I've had just about all I'm going to take from you today!"

She recommenced her task. She soaped the pitted scar, and then set the warm, soppy rag on the opposite thigh while she used all her strength to firmly and thoroughly work the muscles of the right thigh from knee to groin until they were supple. She found the area near the groin less pliant than usual and worked until the muscle yielded.

When he had been unconscious, Reb had deemed the job a labor of love. Now that Kincaid was awake, she was embarrassed to be manhandling him so familiarly. Actually, she would have been perfectly comfortable performing the service if only she weren't so conscious of the deception she practiced on him regarding her sex. She shuddered to think what the arrogant Yankee would do if he knew she was a girl. Her recent experiences with him had convinced her that the last thing she should do was reveal her female nature.

"Thanks, Rebel." Kincaid smiled pleasantly as Reb finished.

She stared into his fathomless gray eyes. "That's the second time you've called me that. My name is Reb."

It irked him to have the brat return his thank-you with a complaint, but it made his explanation all the more fitting. "You remind me of a Rebel." He gazed away, lost in memories, then turned granite-gray eyes back on Reb. "By the end of the war most of them weren't much older than you."

Reb snorted.

"But they had lots of the same kind of misguided fighting spirit. Which are you denying—that you're young or that you've got spirit?" he taunted.

"I ain't—I'm not denying nothing—anything," Reb gritted out between clenched teeth. She felt like a heifer backed up by a mountain lion. She could feel herself flushing red from the roots of her hair. She hadn't made a slip in grammar like that since she'd been six! How could he rattle her so successfully?

Kincaid noticed the embarrassed blush and thought it couldn't do the boy any harm to learn a little more politeness to his company, whether that company was welcome or not. "And you ask why I call you Rebel? If the shoe fits, wear it," he mocked, throwing back her own aphorism.

Reb finished rewrapping the wound in furious silence as quickly as she could. She got the pot out from under the bed, practically threw it at him, and then left to eat her own meal alone outside. There she contemplated just what it was about Kincaid's comments that upset her so much. She realized that it was his attitude more than the words themselves that galled her. The man assumed from his lofty male perch an "I know best" tone that he probably used for all women and children, and although he didn't know she was a woman he had apparently categorized her as a child. She hadn't thought of herself as a child since she was eleven and first came up here to Blue's cabin with Adam. She reminded herself that she had vowed to create a "new man" out of this Yankee. Well, he could certainly use a new outlook about women and children, and he would soon learn this was one young female who could teach him a few things! Her self-confidence restored, she returned to take the pot out to empty it, then came back with the sheets.

"Up, so I can make the bed," she ordered.

Kincaid willingly vacated the soft, warm comfort of the mattress while Reb quickly and efficiently made up the bed.

"Now get in." It made her feel immensely better to add under her breath, "You mindless Yankee tenderfoot."

When she had Kincaid tucked in, Reb moved over to the stove, banked it for the night and lay down on the buffalo robe before it.

"Wait just a minute," Kincaid said, disturbing her. "Are you planning to sleep on the floor?" He tried unsuccessfully to mask his concern.

"I have for the past week," Reb answered antagonistically, "when I wasn't unlucky enough to be sitting in that chair next to the bed."

"Well, that ends now. You can sleep here with me. There's more than enough space for the two of us," he insisted and punctuated his words by shifting over to make more room.

"You're hurt. I might roll over on you in my sleep," Reb countered frantically. She didn't want any part of Kincaid being gracious. He'd only offered out of his noble sense of duty to women and children! God forbid he should discover she was not the boy he thought she was!

"Either you sleep here with me or I join you on the floor," he threatened and threw his feet out to the side of the bed.

"Wait!" Reb rushed to keep him under the warm blanket. "All right, if it'll keep you from making yourself sick again, I'll share the bed. Anything to get you well and out of here!" she said, glaring at him.

She walked around the foot of the bed and sat cautiously on the edge opposite from Kincaid, peering over her shoulder at him, but he had already lain down again to sleep.

She pulled off her moccasins and removed her belt and sheath, but left on the stinking buckskins, thinking to herself smugly that the smell would wake him if he got too close. She lay stiffly on her side, as far as possible from the man who had aroused in her an unaccountable curiosity along with a totally accountable ire.

"Rebel?" Kincaid said into the silent, dusky dark a few minutes later. "You need a bath."

"Go to sleep, Kincaid," Reb sighed with a secret smile.

Chapter Nine

THEY CALLED AN UNEASY TRUCE THAT LASTED THREE days, while Kincaid mended apace. Just after supper on the evening of the fourth day, while he lay naked on the bed after his daily sponge bath, Reb began the questioning that would be the basis of her education of the tenderfoot.

"You can begin by telling me everything you can remember. That will give me some idea of how much I need to teach you," she said imperiously. She pushed the chair far enough back from the disheveled bed to plop into it and extended her moccasined heels up onto the dirty sheets, rationalizing that she would wash them again tomorrow. Slouching down a little more comfortably, she crossed her arms and waited patiently for him to begin to speak.

Kincaid cocked a skeptical eyebrow. Inwardly, he passed through a number of reactions to her command, from incredulity, to chagrin, to stubborn refusal. Finally, not unmindful that Reb had saved his life, he grudgingly offered, "I remember several events surrounding the things you've reminded me about, nothing more."

"That's a good beginning," Reb said confidently, as though speaking to a recalcitrant child. "Perhaps if we talk about those things, you will recall other facts about your life."

"Don't be so sure," Kincaid muttered under his breath.

"What was that?" She leaned forward at the waist to hear better.

"I said 'sure,'" he replied, recovering quickly. "Where would you like to start?"

Reb thought seriously for a moment. Then she said deliberately, "With spying for the Union."

Kincaid could imagine how that sort of intrigue would appeal to the boy. He'd never spoken to anyone about the events during the war, but hesitated only a moment before he started talking.

"It all began one warm, moonlit summer night. It was that night I first met my wife."

Reb could see his tension in the tic in his cheek and the white knuckles of the clenched fists lying on the sheets beside him. She immediately pictured a long white front porch with two lovers reclining on a squeaky wooden swing, baby-pink roses on a nearby trellis cloying the still air with their perfume.

"On my ship," he continued, breaking her reverie and forcing her to refocus her thoughts.

"Your ship?" she asked dumbly, jaw dropping.

"My cover as a spy was a ship's captain smuggling goods past the Yankee blockade." He reached over casually to push Reb's mouth closed with his forefinger.

"Laurie Simmons was, believe it or not, my Confederate contact to move the smuggled goods inland to Atlanta. I knew I was to meet a woman, but I had no idea she'd be so beautiful." His face lit with a special glow at the cherished memory.

Reb had to bite her lower lip hard to avoid a jealousy-provoked comment about the dead woman. She spied the whiskey bottle on the cupboard shelf and moved without thinking first to pour herself a stiff drink to anesthetize her raw, sensitive feelings against the coming revelations.

"That's hardly medicine I would have thought you'd prescribe, but if it's what the doctor orders . . ." Kincaid held his hand out for the full glass.

Reb hesitated only a second before extending the drink. Then she moved to pour another for herself. Kincaid watched her without saying anything until she raised the glass to her lips.

"Are you sure you're old enough for that?" he inquired with a raised brow.

"Plenty old," Reb retorted, taking a big gulp. She immediately gasped and put her hand to her throat, trying desperately to breathe. She managed to wheeze a breath of air, then bent over in a fit of coughing. When the coughing subsided, she looked up at Kincaid through watery eyes.

"Salute," he said, toasting her and taking a delicate sip of whiskey.

Reb watched with satisfaction as Kincaid's eyes widened ever so slightly when the whiskey hit his stomach.

He sipped in silence, apparently waiting for some indication from the sprite that he should continue.

Reb was warmed and more lightheaded than she had expected to be from the whiskey. She could only guess the effect the spirits would have on the ill man.

At least he would keep talking about himself, she thought. When she could speak again, Reb rasped, "You were saying?"

"She was only eighteen," he picked up as though there had been no interruption. "My job was to get close to her, make love to her, whatever was necessary to gain her confidence, and obtain the list of men working with her. The Union wanted to shut down Atlanta's supply channels."

"Didn't it bother you to use her like that?" Reb asked, her distaste for the assignment plain on her face.

"War is Hell," Kincaid defended. "Anyway, you're not giving the lady enough credit if you think the job was easy," he remonstrated with a cynical smile. "She had me pegged as a rich, arrogant Yankee profiteer within minutes of our first meeting and I had my work cut out for me."

"Is that when you changed your name from Christopher to Kincaid?"

"I didn't change my name. I merely resorted to using my last name for my first."

Reb's face mirrored her confusion. "Your full name is Christopher . . . Kincaid?" She tried out the name, rolled it around on her tongue with a sip of whiskey, and decided she liked it.

"Christopher Lyle Kincaid, to be precise." He felt an unaccountable sense of relief at having at least that part of his charade over.

It occurred to Reb in her alcoholic euphoria, looking at Kincaid sitting stark naked on the bed, black stubble on his face, hair askew, eyes bleary, that learning his name was not the momentous occasion she had imagined it would be. Her feelings for the stranger did not miraculously disappear when she learned his name. Nor had she suspected the jealousy she suffered on account of a dead woman—one who could get a man to change his name. A touch of her incredulity, mixed with a dab of envy, came through as she voiced her thought aloud. "No, I didn't give Miss Simmons enough credit if she managed to get you to change your name."

"Oh, it was my idea," he assured, "but it came after I'd completed my mission."

"After?"

"She took me into her proper Southern home in Atlanta; I got the names of her supply network and I gave them to the army," he said without pride in his accomplishment, eyes focused into the empty whiskey glass. "Another," he demanded, and passed the glass to Reb for a refill.

If her own senses had not been so dulled by the strong spirits, Reb would not have allowed it. Instead, she rose unsteadily and poured him a second cup—to the brim.

Kincaid took the cup from her carefully and drained an inch of it quickly. They both sat in moody silence for several minutes until Kincaid added softly, "And I fell in love with her."

"But she didn't love you." The words came slowly and were somewhat slurred.

"Not at first. Especially when she found out what I'd done. No, it would be more accurate to say she hated me," he admitted sadly.

Neither of them realized the effect alcohol had at this high altitude. That, together with the fatigue both felt, meant that by this time the two were feeling rather numb and decidedly more relaxed. Kincaid talked of things he'd kept hidden even from himself.

"I changed my name because I wanted Laurie to know I was different. I wasn't the Union spy Christopher anymore. I was just plain Kincaid . . . and I loved her."

Reb's eyes sought the ground guiltily as she recalled Kincaid's prayer to Laurie in his delirium.

"She didn't believe it would work," she whispered, not meeting Kincaid's glance.

"How did you know?" he asked, his eyes drooping in spirituous melancholia.

"Lucky guess." Between sips of whiskey Reb murmured, "She knew you loved her . . . but that you hadn't really changed what you are . . . what you think and feel deep down."

"Maybe you're right." Kincaid scratched the whiskers on his chin thoughtfully in slow motion. "Anyway, I persisted in my pursuit until I caught her," he said wryly. "She married me, but she was such an unbroken filly, even then there was no tying her down. That's what I loved most about her . . . and what killed her," he concluded morosely.

"Killed her?"

"We both knew it was the end for Atlanta. Everyone was fleeing. I begged her to leave with her family. I even ordered her to go, but she wouldn't. She insisted on being there to help the Confederacy to the last. There was an ambush. She was where she didn't belong," he said in drunken bitterness, "and a stray cannon fragment killed her."

"Where she didn't belong?" Reb asked, somewhat confused, the whiskey having dulled her senses. "Working for what she believed in was where she didn't belong? I don't understand. It wasn't wrong for you. Why was it wrong for her?"

"She was a woman," Kincaid argued, "trying to do a man's job."

"What?" Reb found herself ominously close to anger. "And I suppose I'm a *boy* trying to do a man's job," she challenged.

"You did childishly lose your temper earlier," Kincaid chided, tenderly touching his scalded skin where Reb had dumped the hot soup in his lap several days before.

"Oh, yeah?" Reb yelled. She jumped up to pose feet apart, hands defiantly on hips, and swayed slightly from lack of equilibrium. "Where is it written that women can't think or feel or be dedicated to a cause?" she flung at him. "Your wife was fighting for the South the same way you were fighting for the North—only a whole sight more honorably from the sound of things. If you'd really loved her, you would have understood that!"

"I *did* love her," he insisted heatedly. "And I still do!"

Reb flinched openly at Kincaid's ardent declaration and staggered back a step.

"I loved her enough to let her have her own way even though I thought she was wrong. She died because I allowed her to do what she wasn't capable of doing," Kincaid threw back at the lad in guilt-ridden anger.

"Wasn't capable of doing!" Reb sputtered furiously. "A woman can do anything a man can do, and she can do a whole passel of things better!" Perilously near to revealing herself, Reb amended, "And so can a boy like me!"

"I'll believe that when I see it," he retorted, smiling cynically.

"You will. Tomorrow morning, bright and early, we

begin your lessons. We'll see just how capable a Yankee tenderfoot like yourself is in areas that matter out here."

"Such as?"

"Shooting, riding, roping and tracking," she spat.

"Fine," he said confidently and handed her his empty glass. "Now, if you'll excuse me, I need to rest up."

Reb stood aghast at his audacity while he turned over to sleep.

"Tomorrow," she grumbled to herself. "Tomorrow the tables will be turned."

Because of his recurring mild fever, however, almost a week passed before Reb allowed Kincaid to venture beyond the cabin door, although keeping him in bed, resting, challenged the patience of both of them to the utmost. Reb had long since given up hope of relief from Blue.

"I think this is the day," Reb said when she placed a hand on Kincaid's forehead and found his temperature normal. His gunshot wound had not been giving him much trouble, but he remained worn down from the effects of the pneumonia. Finally, the fever seemed to have released its relentless grip on the large man.

"Hallelujah!" Kincaid snapped a sharp salute. "General, suh," he drawled. "Private Kincaid reporting for duty, suh!" An enormous grin of pure pleasure spread across his face.

Reb couldn't help laughing at the contrast between Kincaid's precise, square shouldered salute and his lazy imitation of southern speech. She spunkily returned his salute, falling in with his silliness, unable to repress her delight at his steady, almost miraculous recovery. "At ease, soldier. We have some unfinished

111

business to attend to. There's the matter of your frontier education, Private."

"Aw General, ya know us sturdy, pink-cheeked plowboys is too dumb to l'arn new regulations, suh," he mocked, eyes twinkling.

"Well, we'll start with something as simple as your mind, then," Reb said teasingly. "First you need to get dressed."

Kincaid exuberantly jumped out of bed to stand magnificently naked before her. "Ya mean I get a real uniform, General?"

"What you're wearing now is hardly sufficient, Private." Reb covered her rising blush with a smirk as she casually pitched him his Union pants and one of Blue's dark blue wool shirts she had found in the chest. Inside she felt anything but casual. Her heart pounded as she stood and watched, fascinated at the magical transformation from "patient" to "person."

Kincaid shimmied into the tight, yellow-striped navy britches, tugged on his tall black boots and donned the worn shirt, which fit snugly across his broad shoulders. He brushed his hand back and forth across his thick beard. "Now all I need is a shave to feel human."

"That can be arranged." Giving in to the desire to attract his attention she flipped her razor-sharp bowie knife across the room so it stuck in the bedstead an inch from Kincaid's right hand.

He slowly and carefully worked the large knife free. "I've only got ten fingers and I'd like to keep them all," he said a trifle sharply, eyebrow cocking in surprise and reluctant admiration.

"No problem," Reb replied coolly to his implied censure. "I never miss. Want some soap and water?"

"Not if they're delivered the same way," Kincaid replied dryly and waited for the brat's next move.

Reb chuckled. "They're not." She poured some warm water from the pot on the stove and gave the chary man water, a towel and a precious cake of soap. Then she returned to the table and sat, prepared to ogle Kincaid's toilette.

He took two strokes, then frowned. "You wouldn't have a mirror handy by any chance?"

Reb rose lazily from her chair. "No, but if you like I can play barber for you." She had observed his grimace of pain as he lifted his left hand to hold the skin on his neck firm for the knife and had surmised, correctly, that his left arm pained him when he lifted it.

"Just remember you're *shaving,* not *skinning,*" he bantered. He wiped the knife clean, balanced it momentarily in his palm and then threw it with a dexterity equal to Reb's, imbedding it in the log wall an inch above her head.

"Not bad," Reb replied somewhat shakily, eyes wide in alarm as she felt the shaft of the knife caress her hair when she turned to pry it free. She noted the depth to which the blade had penetrated and thanked whatever lucky stars had made his throw accurate. Anger replaced her fear as she sat Kincaid in the chair by the bed and tilted his chin up to make his neck accessible.

"Careful with that thing," he said distrustfully.

"Look who's talking," she muttered sarcastically. She grabbed her lower lip in her teeth and resisted the temptation to nick him on purpose. Reb regretted her impetuous offer when she realized just how close she needed to be to this infuriating man in order to remove the soap-lathered beard. She'd shaved her father and brothers on several occasions and she knew very well what she was doing. She was amazed, however, at what a different pleasure she derived from performing the service for Kincaid. It gave her a possessive feeling that wasn't at all appropriate under the circumstances.

"What other hidden talents do you have?" Reb asked as she worked.

When he could talk without endangering his chin, Kincaid replied, "Well, I don't know. What did you have in mind?"

"Marksmanship."

"You mean like with bow and arrows?" he asked innocently.

"No. I mean like with swords and battle axes!" Reb glared in irritated exasperation at Kincaid as she wiped the last of the soap and whiskers from the knife to the towel and replaced her knife in its sheath. When Kincaid did not respond to her taunt Reb forced herself to explain in a civil tongue. "I mean like marksmanship with a rifle."

"Oh, that." Kincaid smiled serenely as he felt his face with his hands. "I have absolutely no idea." Kincaid had to marvel at the boy's skill with the knife. Considering the kid's smooth face, he couldn't have had much practice doing this job for himself. "Close shave," he commended. "Thanks."

Reb rolled her eyes to the ceiling helplessly, then forgot her question, forgot everything as Kincaid stood. Reb looked up at her stranger and gaped in awe. Her heart hammered in her throat and she felt a tightening in her belly. She found that she wanted more than anything to touch the firm jaw that had been shielded first by stubble, then by beard.

Kincaid was puzzled at Reb's glazed stare and looked for something amiss in his appearance. "Something wrong?"

"Absolutely nothing," Reb whispered, jaws now clenched tightly together, although she still stared hard at his face. She abruptly turned, picked up her Spencer from where it stood next to the door, her hat from its peg and escaped outside into the glaring sunlight. It had been difficult before to withstand her eager appetite for "the stranger." She now discovered it was even more difficult to repress her ravenous craving to touch "Kincaid." She needed a little more time alone to think.

And Kincaid gave it to her. He followed on her heels, but not too close, since as a form of self-protection Reb had refused to clean her buckskins. The pungent garments did their job, keeping Kincaid at least three feet away at all times. He'd held his breath through most of the shave in the interest of self-preservation.

"You know, you could use a bath," he said when he caught another good whiff of Reb during their march into the forest.

"I haven't had time," Reb hedged, then changed the subject quickly, repressing her feelings in the role of teacher. "Knowing how to use a rifle can mean the difference between life and death." She stopped and turned to him as they reached a grassy clearing. "It's important not only for self-defense, but also for putting food on the table. Are you familiar with the Spencer rifle?" She held it before her for his examination.

"No," Kincaid replied honestly. The Spencer was an out-of-date weapon, usually carried only by the enlisted man. The more modern Henry rifle was purchased by the officers who could afford them, including Kincaid. So while he might claim expertise with the Henry, he could plead comparative ignorance of the Spencer.

"I thought not," Reb said smugly, misunderstanding his answer to mean he had no experience with rifles at all. "This is a .52 caliber weapon with seven shots, loaded here in the tubular magazine in the butt."

Kincaid listened with rapt attention and watched closely while Reb demonstrated how to load the weapon and sight down the barrel.

"We've had a lot of trouble with the Sioux the past few months."

"Really?"

Reb shuddered. "I've seen some sights I'd rather not have seen. It gave me a little more incentive to see you rescued. Now Red Cloud has retreated with his braves to the Powder River up in the Black Hills to spend the summer hunting, and General Dodge is moving the Brulés to a reservation. Adam and I are hoping Dad can talk some sense into Dodge and change his mind about sending the Brulés away. At least he should reconsider sending them to Pawnee territory."

"So Dodge has got to be controlled . . ." Kincaid mused quietly.

"Exactly," Reb replied, unaware of the connection Kincaid was making between this discussion and his foggy memory of the exchanges between Adam and Reb immediately after his rescue. Kincaid shook his head in disgust at his mistaken conclusions. Apparently, the boy only coincidentally disliked Yankees and railroads. He and his family would obviously be concerned with Dodge's handling of the Indian situation. Well, that certainly wouldn't interfere with his assignment. To reassure himself of this new view of things he asked, "What would you like to have Dodge do?"

"I haven't really thought too much about it. I guess I've had too much happening in my own life to think about trying to run somebody else's."

"Except mine."

"I haven't . . ."

"Yes, you have. But I forgive you under the circumstances," he interrupted with a laugh that cleared the tension he could see building in Reb's body. "Now, what did you want to teach me?" He relaxed fully for the first time since his rescue. He suspected his memory was going to return with amazing rapidity from this point forward.

"Let's start with standing targets," she began, eyeing his boldly grinning face warily. "See those four pines over there, the ones evenly spaced about two feet apart? You'll notice they each have the bark scraped off in a small circle about five feet up. The center of that circle is your target."

Reb shouldered the rifle, took a quarter turn from the targets, aimed and fired four quick rounds. Kincaid could see from where he stood that each bullet had found the bull's-eye.

"Your turn," she said as she handed him the rifle and some bullets. "You'll need to reload."

"You're a pretty good shot."

"I never miss."

"Only 'miscalculate'?" Kincaid taunted. He put the stock to his right shoulder and aimed, having some difficulty balancing the gun with his left arm, which was uncomfortably stiff from the recent injury. His first shot went far to the left, missing the tree entirely.

Reb smirked at Kincaid's obvious lack of skill, so typical of a tenderfoot, but inside felt a stab of disappointment. For some reason she had hoped he would be different.

The recoil on the gun surprised Kincaid, jarring his wound enough to make him tighten his jaws to avoid responding aloud to the pain. He braced the gun more effectively to absorb the shock, gritting his teeth at the stress this put on the knitting skin and bone of his left shoulder. The second shot hit the next tree, but at least a foot high of the mark.

Reb said patronizingly, "Take your time. There's no rush. This usually takes a little practice."

Kincaid examined the rifle sight, noticing that it was bent slightly. He grunted to himself, then aimed the gun again. He hit dead center of the circles on the next two trees.

It was Reb's turn to cock an eyebrow and speculatively observe the stranger. "I thought you said you never shot a rifle before?" she asked sharply.

"I said I wasn't familiar with the Spencer," he answered calmly. "I did most of my shooting with a Henry."

"Your memory is making remarkable strides," she said suspiciously.

"Your sight is crooked," he answered, ignoring her suspicion. "It marks the target wide and to the left."

Reb had the good grace to look abashed. The sight had gotten bent years ago and she hadn't thought to advise Kincaid of the problem since she automatically compensated for it herself.

"How are you with a moving target?" she asked to cover her dismay at her oversight.

"Fair."

He was more than fair. Kincaid never missed the

wood chips she threw as high and as far and as fast as she could.

"I guess I'm not going to teach you anything you don't already know," she said, not sure whether that pleased or infuriated her.

He reloaded, then handed the boy the rifle and picked up a handful of wood chips. "You haven't had your turn."

Mesmerized by his steady gaze, Reb waited too late to take aim after he threw the first chip, and to her intense embarrassment, she missed.

"Never miss?" Kincaid badgered mercilessly. He suddenly threw three chips at once.

She hit all three before they reached the ground. He immediately threw three more and she hit those as well.

"Bravo!" he congratulated, patting Reb heartily on the back, impressed by the youth's obvious capability.

"The lesson's over," Reb said irritably as she moved away from Kincaid's touch. "I hesitate to ask. How are you at tracking game?"

"Passable."

"We'll see. Follow me."

Kincaid turned out to be as skilled in the forest as he was with a gun. For every sign that Reb showed him, Kincaid responded with one for her throughout the afternoon.

"Because of the cottonwood and willow, this is a good habitat for beaver," she instructed.

"Yes, here are signs that one has passed," Kincaid said, pointing to the spot where a beaver had dragged by a felled tree. That must mean there's a creek around here somewhere, right?"

"Yes."

"A deep creek?" Kincaid inquired with a grin.

"Not very."

"Deep enough to rinse off the dust of the day?"

Reb realized now where the conversation was headed. As a matter of fact, they were not very far from her hidden pond. However, she had no intention of letting Kincaid know where she had been taking secret baths, for, although her buckskins might be filthy, the skin underneath was not. She had daily stolen away to bathe in her reclusive spot.

"How about a swim?" Kincaid urged.

"The creek's too shallow. Besides, we're out here so you can learn to survive in the wilderness, not so I can take a bath," Reb said acidly. "Shall we continue, or would you rather return to the cabin?"

"By all means, continue. I do want to learn how to survive in your wilderness, although with the Yankee railroad coming through, I don't expect it to be around much longer," he jibed.

Reb flushed, but led Kincaid away from the pond without saying anything. She pointed out a rabbit burrow. He found some day-old deer spoor. She discovered the feeding place of a black bear. He located a tree where they could count on finding honey later in the summer. She led him to the wild onions and mushrooms she had used in the stew. He instructed on herbs that were useful for medicinal purposes.

As the afternoon drew to a close, Reb circled back so they were very near the pond again when she noticed Kincaid's limp was more pronounced, his hand massaging the leg as they walked, his shoulders not as square as they had been earlier in the afternoon.

"How about a rest?" she suggested.

"I could use a break," Kincaid admitted. He lowered himself wearily to sit against a majestic spruce, his long legs stretched out in front of him. He closed his eyes and laid his head back against the rough bark. Reb squatted down beside him. She was in no hurry to return to the confines of the cabin.

Kincaid spoke with his eyes closed while he massaged his thigh. "The rustle of these pines is as rhythmic as the sound of hooves on cobblestones, a noise that lulled me to sleep more than once when I was flat on my back in New York with this leg wound."

Reb did not answer, merely watched as his face relaxed into sleep. She realized guiltily that she had pushed him too hard and too soon after his illness. She sat, her chin on her knees, and prepared to wait for him to awake. However, her nose wrinkled with disgust when she smelled the trousers she wore. She was as offensive to herself as she was to Kincaid. The pond was so close she probably could bathe and be back before he ever knew she was gone, she decided. So she deserted Kincaid for the icy water.

Reb had been gone only a few minutes when Kincaid knew something was wrong. Without opening his eyes, he bunched his muscles and quickly rolled away from the tree, coming up in a huddle behind a nearby outcropping of rock. Senses alert, he looked and listened for the danger he thought was near.

At the same time he conceded there was no threat, he discovered Reb was nowhere to be seen. Unable to believe the boy intended him harm, but nevertheless cautious, he set out to track the youth down. He was indeed as practiced in wood lore as Reb had suspected, but the task turned out to be surprisingly easy. Apparently the urchin had not expected to be followed, since he left a clear path.

When Kincaid approached a stand of scented pines and heard the sound of splashing water, he slowed his approach. He moved stealthily among the trees, approaching an open glade with a pool of glistening water in the center. Standing at the edge of the pool, back to him, was the curvaceous, peach-skinned form of a long-legged female.

The small waist would almost have fit the span of his large hands, but the hips were developed for childbearing, the buttocks enticing in their firm roundness. The statuesque legs went on forever, disappearing at the calf into the depths of the pond.

Kincaid stood stunned at his discovery. All thoughts of Reb were gone, his eyes riveted on the beautiful sight of the softer sex before him. His passion rose unbidden in response to this totally unexpected delight. Abruptly, he turned his head to determine the source of a noise in the undergrowth nearby. Satisfied that it was only a small animal, he returned his attention to the pond.

The woman had disappeared. Kincaid searched the glen anxiously with his eyes. Just as he was ready to conclude that he had suffered a hallucination, the apparition reappeared before him. She emerged from the water like a sleek crystal goddess with light-refracting droplets of water clinging to her small, firm breasts, her flat stomach, and to her long stemlike legs which made her so tall. She shook her glossy hair as a dog shakes its pelt, whipping it back to expose the clean lines of her softly feminine profile.

Kincaid couldn't believe his eyes. It was Reb! The *boy* Reb was a *girl!* No, he said to himself, taking a closer, longer, lingering look. Not a girl, a woman.

Chapter Ten

KINCAID'S UNBRIDLED LUST WAGED WAR WITH HIS REA-
son. His gray eyes were dilated with avidity, his face
frozen rigid with desire. He licked his lips unconsciously and, like a hungry puma, took two long,
graceful strides toward his prey. Then he paused,
tantalized by the beads of water surrounding Reb's
mouth. He imagined the tip of his tongue flicking each
drop away, finally lodging itself between her full lips
in the deep recesses of that honeyed cavern.

In the months since Laurie's death he had endured
a self-enforced celibacy. To seek another woman for
his needs had seemed a betrayal of his wife, and he
had felt guilty whenever the persistent reminder of his
virility made itself known. He felt no guilt now, only
the pulsing insistence of his manhood that he slake its
thirst.

Innocent of Kincaid's private battle, Reb titillated
his senses by cavorting playfully in the shallow pond.

The cold hardened her nipples into coral buds and tinged her skin rosy pink. She crossed her arms under her breasts to hug herself in an attempt to get warm, inadvertently lifting the tips so that they jutted out in an invitation to be kissed. Kincaid swallowed the saliva that had accumulated in his mouth, and held his body rigidly in check.

Rubbing her hands up and down along her body to flick off the icy drops, Reb moved completely out of the water. Once on the muddy bank, she looked around warily and then yanked on her buckskins. Kincaid watched her slim waist and rounded hips disappear under the blousy leather shirt that made her the same width from chest to thigh. A row of bright beadwork camouflaged her pert breasts, while her shapely limbs vanished in the wide, fringed leggings. She added the loose-fitting belt that held her knife sheath, then hopped on opposite feet as she tugged on her moccasins. Kincaid had already slipped away by the time Reb grabbed her rifle, pulled her flat-brimmed hat down low on her brow, and moved quickly but carefully back through the forest to where she had left the sleeping man.

A peaceful scene greeted her. Kincaid's head lolled back against the rugged bark of the spruce, his eyes closed, the long, inky black lashes lying peacefully on his tanned face, his breathing even and slow. In a moment of tenderness at his seeming childlike helplessness, she brushed back an unruly curl from his forehead. She jumped back as Kincaid waked from his torpor. He stretched in a leisurely way and slowly blinked his eyes open.

Reb could not know the effort Kincaid exerted to give the lazy appearance of a waking sleeper. It had taken all his willpower not to confront her when she brushed the lock of hair from his forehead. How could I have been so blind, he wondered as he stared into Reb's smiling freckled face.

"Have a good rest?"

Kincaid analyzed the voice that had deceived him so well. It was husky, mellow like good brandy, and, now that he knew Reb was a female, seductive as hell!

"Kincaid?"

"What?"

"Are you all right?"

Kincaid's glazed, unblinking stare had prompted the inquiry from Reb, who tilted her head quizzically at his expression. Kincaid nonchalantly waved away her question to cover the frantic scurrying of his mind. He was glad he had not revealed himself to her at the pond, since fast on the heels of his lust was the nagging suspicion that he had somehow been made a fool. With that suspicion rose an equally strong desire to repay Reb in full measure for her deception.

"I'm fine, really. I just wasn't quite awake," he said, yawning broadly.

"We should be getting back. Are you sure you're all right?" Reb asked with a nervous laugh.

"Your hair is wet."

Kincaid's stare stripped away at her veils of deceit until Reb dropped her eyes to avoid his penetrating gaze.

"I . . . I took your advice and . . . and rinsed off," she stuttered. "But we were talking about you."

"I'm fine. Just a little tired," he said softly. "I guess it would be a good idea to get back to the cabin so I can rest."

He rose in one powerful, fluid movement. If Reb had been paying attention, she would have questioned the limberness of his scarred leg. Instead, she hurried away to avoid Kincaid's steely gray eyes and missed this clue to his newfound knowledge.

This time, when Kincaid followed, he held his breath and stayed close, looking for signs of femininity. And he found them. Her hips swayed ever so slightly from side to side. The steps he had thought so sure he now decided were delicately placed. The leanness of youth was the fragility of woman. With his eyes opened to the truth, her womanhood seemed blatantly apparent, and Kincaid's disgust with himself increased. He pushed down the admiration for Reb that kept rearing its ugly head. What was there to admire in a woman who hid her charms in filthy buckskins?

His chagrin grew into anger as he thought back on Reb providing a pot so he could relieve himself, washing him like a baby, and changing the bed while he stood by like a naked idiot. That inspired the memory of the scalding soup dumped in his lap. *That* was something a spiteful woman would do, all right! And the confessions about Laurie! That was none of her business! The foibles he was willing to overlook in the "boy" he found intolerable in the "girl." Without taking time to fully analyze why he felt the need for it, Kincaid began to plan his revenge.

His jaw tightened in determination as he mulled over the best way to show Reb the error of aspiring to a man's role. He wondered that she had not seemed affected by his nakedness. But then, she did have brothers. Kincaid was willing to believe anything of a hoyden who could outshoot anyone he'd seen and nurse a sick man back to health in the bargain. He winced as he thought of the black eye he'd given her in his delirium. For that he was truly sorry. He'd never hit a woman before—but he'd already apologized for that.

Surely she must realize how ridiculous this pretense was. If not, then he would just have to give her a little help. But how? Kincaid's lips quirked into a sly grin as he hit upon the perfect solution—physical contact. Surely she couldn't ignore that. He'd never met a woman who could. He wasn't unaware of his own ability to arouse a woman, and this one would probably take all his expertise and then some. He had the perfect excuse to force her to touch him—his leg—his shoulder, too, for that matter. They both needed massage; she had admitted that herself.

Yet Reb hadn't seemed affected by touching in the past. After all, she had given him a bath every day without so much as a rosy blush. Or had she? He had not been watching for her reactions in the past. Perhaps she had not been so unmoved as he imagined. The grin became more smug and his stride lengthened, so he caught up with Reb and walked beside her the rest of the short distance to the cabin.

When they arrived, Kincaid immediately collapsed on the bed as though exhausted.

"Reb, can you help me?" he asked politely as he extended a booted foot toward her.

"Sure." She straddled his leg with her back to him and grasped the heel of the boot to pull it off. Kincaid placed his other foot on her rear to provide assistance and shoved hard just as the boot came free. Reb sprawled forward awkwardly on the dirt floor.

Why didn't seeing her on the floor like that feel more satisfying? Kincaid's contrition was genuine and he cursed himself for his weakness as he admitted, "Sorry. Guess I gave it a little too much."

Unaware that Kincaid knew her to be female, it was easy for Reb to dust herself off without embarrassment and come back for more.

"No problem," she assured with a grin. "Just take it a little easier this time."

She assumed her position over the other boot while Kincaid placed his socked foot upon her fanny, thinking to himself how lusciously soft it was. Again, at the most vulnerable moment he couldn't keep himself from giving a hefty push that sent Reb flying with the boot in hand.

"That isn't funny!" she came up sputtering, red faced.

"I don't know how that happened. I didn't do it on purpose," he said between gritted teeth. Kincaid couldn't explain to himself why he'd done such a despicable thing to a young lady. How could he begin to explain it to her? Kincaid pulled his scarred leg up onto the bed with both hands. "I guess I must have had a muscle spasm." He groaned piteously and clutched his leg, looking up sideways from under hooded eyes to see the effect his performance was having on Reb. He thought he saw something like disgust, a moue of distaste around her mouth as she chewed her lip with sharp white teeth, but then sympathy replaced that expression and she shoved him down flat on the bed.

"Let me see."

Before he could protest, Reb placed her hands on his leg in the area of the scar and let her fingers do the looking. Coming so soon after his recent perusal of her unclothed loveliness, Reb's manual investigation was nearly Kincaid's undoing. Her fingertips massaged his inner thigh and moved upward toward the groin. Kincaid closed his eyes and breathed deeply to dampen the fire growing in his loins.

"There does seem to be a great deal of tension in the leg," Reb volunteered.

Kincaid almost choked trying to hold back the burble of laughter in his throat. There was tension, all right, but she needed to look just a little higher for the source.

"Lie still a moment and I'll try to work it out."

Totally oblivious to the reason for the tensed muscles, Reb continued her massage. She worked her thumb into the muscle on top of his leg while her fingers pressed, then released, the sinewy thigh. As she worked her way upward, Kincaid's breathing became ragged and his forehead and upper lip beaded with sweat. He could feel the evidence of his desire rising in his tight pants and thought surely Reb could not miss it either.

Reb noticed Kincaid's difficulty breathing, and paused in what she was doing to glance at his face. She took one look at the strained features covered with sweat, then placed her hands on her hips and glared at him.

"You lied to me!" she accused.

Kincaid opened his eyes in alarm, wondering how he had revealed he knew her secret.

"You aren't fine at all. In fact you look positively *ill!*"

Kincaid's face contorted again; he truly was suffering—from the inability to release the explosive guffaw that grew deep in his chest.

"Can't fool the doctor, can I?" he managed to gasp, freeing a silly grin.

"No, you can't," she responded, unable to resist

meeting his grin with a relieved grin of her own. Then she chided good-naturedly, "I expect you wouldn't have had this problem with your leg if you had just admitted when you were tired. At any rate, now you should rest. I'll get us some dinner. We'll take it a little easier tomorrow."

Kincaid laid his head back on the pillow and stared moodily at the pine rafters in the ceiling. His revenge wasn't working out exactly as he'd planned. She was unaware that he knew she was a female, so of course she wouldn't act any differently around him than she always had. He'd had no idea his body would behave so traitorously, either. After all, there was absolutely *nothing* appealing about Reb in buckskins. She smelled! He decided to wait until bedtime to renew his attack. Surely in that confined environment she could not dismiss his attentions so easily.

Kincaid was wrong about Reb's lack of reaction to him. She had noticed his rising passion but had attributed it to the thoughts of Laurie that she assumed her massage of his war wound must be provoking. What else could it be? She tried to ignore the ache that invaded her chest when she admitted to herself that he still loved his wife enough to become physically aroused just by her memory. For the first time in days Reb wondered what had happened to Blue. She needed rescue from this man who was no longer a stranger. Immersed in her thoughts, she ladled up some leftover stew and absently handed the bowl and a spoon to Kincaid.

"Something troubling you?" he asked when he saw she was not paying attention to what she was doing.

"Huh? What?"

"What are you thinking about?" Kincaid prodded.

"I was just thinking how little I taught you today,"

Reb admitted irritably. She served herself a bowl of stew and shoved his legs over to sit down next to him on the bed.

She had sat next to him to eat at this same spot for many days, but this was the first time Kincaid was aware she encroached on his space. He edged his thigh further away so it didn't rest against her buttocks. After all, he was the one who was going to make the advances. He peered over his bowl of stew into the wide, innocent brown eyes, then focused again on the chunk of rabbit he pushed around with his spoon.

Neither said anything for several minutes and finally Reb broke the silence.

"I wish I knew what brought you out here."

Kincaid wanted to say, "I'm here on a mission for the Union Pacific railroad. It's my job to survey two alternate routes and report to General Dodge which is better. One goes through Denver. The other goes across the base of these beloved mountains of yours." Instead, he sighed and said, "I do, too."

Silence enveloped the room.

"Well, you're certainly no tenderfoot. You probably ride and rope as well as you track and shoot," Reb said disgustedly.

Kincaid couldn't keep his lips from quirking, but brought his hand up to cover his amusement at the disconsolate woman.

"I never said I was a tenderfoot. You did." He continued in spite of her wince. "I merely acceded to your desire to provide me with a frontier education. You're a very good teacher."

"I'm tired." She lowered her eyes dejectedly, crossed to the chair and sat with her clenched hands pressed into her face.

Kincaid felt a tenderness well inside him, a desire to alleviate her misery. He opened his mouth, then abruptly clamped it shut. The best thing he could do for her was make her see how wrong she was to pretend to this unnatural role. As a woman, she deserved to be coddled, and when she admitted she was a woman he would do so. Posing as a ragamuffin lad, she was not entitled to the same deference. He must make her acknowledge the advantages of her femininity for her own good. Armed with his good intentions, Kincaid boldly unbuttoned his shirt and pulled it off. He then unbuttoned his trousers and peeled out of them as well. Determined to arouse a response from her, he called to her when he was naked.

"Come to bed."

His gruff voice startled Reb out of her reverie. As she passed him on her way to her side of the bed, Reb shuddered slightly, but otherwise Kincaid noticed no outward reaction to his state of undress. Eliciting a response from her became not only a duty for her own good, but a challenge.

Reb perched on the bed to remove her moccasins as though she were on the edge of a high cliff, then raised the covers and scooted underneath. An unshaven and unconscious Kincaid Reb found enticing. A prepossessingly unclothed Kincaid provided a formidable temptation. Turning away from him, she pulled the blanket over her shoulder like a woolen shield.

So, she was not unaware of him, Kincaid mused, only purposefully ignoring him. Slowly and carefully he lifted the covers and moved himself underneath to join the brat. He crossed his arms behind his head, causing a twinge of discomfort in his wounded shoulder. He smiled grimly and launched the next phase of his attack.

"Reb, my shoulder aches. If you could rub a little of the stiffness out, maybe I could sleep better," he entreated.

"I'm not your servant," she replied sulkily. She couldn't touch him now, she thought. She couldn't handle much more of the kind of strain Kincaid was imposing on her self-control through his display of masculinity. She wanted to unashamedly look her fill and to touch what was forbidden. The possible results of succumbing to that desire, given her current pose as a young man, almost made her giggle in hysteria.

"I know. I know," he responded glibly. "But you are my doctor, and as a patient I'm asking for your services."

"I'm done for the day."

"And of course this particular ache is one that you inflicted," he added relentlessly.

"Oh, all right," Reb said petulantly, sitting upright in the moonlit dark that had fallen around them. Why not? she thought to herself. He believed she was a boy. What did she have to lose? "Turn over on your stomach."

Kincaid obeyed instantly. Reb crossed to him on her knees and adjusted the sheet and blanket over him so that he was exposed only from the waist up. She rose on her knees to gain leverage for the job, then leaned over to place her palms on the taut muscles of his left shoulder. Kincaid shivered under her fingertips.

"I'm sorry. My hands are cold," she apologized, removing the offending members and curling them against her chest.

"Please," Kincaid said tightly, more affected than he cared to admit, "go ahead."

A moment later Reb obeyed his command. She closed her eyes and devoted herself to easing his pain. She marveled at the corded muscles along the back of his neck, then smoothed the rippling flesh across his broad back to his shoulder and down the knotted left arm.

Kincaid knew Reb had been reluctant to come into physical contact with him. Her touch, however, was decidedly caressing. He closed his eyes and allowed her fingers to work their magic. The next thing he was aware of was Reb's voice in the dark.

"Turn over."

Incredibly, he had fallen asleep! Kincaid damned the illness that had left him so fatigued. Then, determined that he would not lose the effect of this lesson on Reb, he interrupted her by marching away from the bed to the table.

"Wait a minute."

He fumbled around in the dark. He scratched a match against wood, there was the smell of sulphur, and a brief red flare merged into a golden glow on his body as he lit the lamp. He carried the light with him over to the chest next to the bed and treated Reb to a view of the stalking lion. When he held the lamp up to her face, her eyes were huge mahogany pools in a visage blanched white. She stared at him like a rabbit trapped by a puma. He kept his eyes locked with hers as he placed the lamp on the chest and sat on the bed. He lifted the covers and slid under, laying his head down on the pillow, his arms relaxed at his sides.

"I'm ready."

He waited patiently for Reb to begin. As if in a

trance she raised her hands to his bared chest. Gently, lovingly, she fondled the warm, smooth skin beneath her fingertips, living the fantasy she had imagined the first day she saw him. All the while Kincaid watched for her reaction. His eyes hooded slightly and his lips pressed into a grim line. Reb worked away from the healing bullet wound toward the enticing bare skin in the center of his chest, then spread her hands outward toward each turgid nipple, skimming the hardened tips. Her fingertips slid down along the muscled ribs she could see delineated as well as she could feel them, coming to rest in the line of curls at his navel.

Kincaid knew desire in a woman's face when he saw it, and the bright shine in Reb's eyes, the soft, full, partly-opened lips that she wet occasionally with her tongue convinced him that she was not immune to his masculinity. He decided to move on to the next step in his plan.

Slowly, so as not to frighten her, he reached up to stop her hands in their motion on his abdomen. Searching her face, he was well pleased with the avid look he found there. "Thank you, Reb. That feels much better. Good night now."

Reb stared at him as though he had told her she could leave for the moon now, and removed her hands as though they belonged to someone else. A blush rose on her cheeks when he had to nudge her back to her own side of the bed. She jerked the sheet and blanket up over her, then breathed deeply to avoid crying out loud with mortification.

Kincaid listened to the muffled sobbing with only a small pang of regret. He was doing this for her own good, he reminded himself. He raised himself enough to blow out the lamp. Well, he had proved he could—what—disturb her? Certainly arouse was not the proper description for the sounds he was hearing from the other side of the bed. No, arousal would come later. With a fleeting smile that belied his own uncomfortable state, he closed his eyes in satisfaction and slept.

Chapter Eleven

REB SNUGGLED AGAINST THE WARMTH THAT ENFOLDED her, relishing the feeling of comfort. Soft lips caressed her forehead, then moved down her temple to kiss each closed eyelid. The endearments continued along her cheek toward her mouth, which she raised slightly in anticipation of the coming touch. Gently as a butterfly, two lips brushed across her own, hesitated, then briefly lit again. She shivered when calloused fingertips lifted her short locks away from the nape of her neck. That touch was followed by warm, wet lips, causing another shiver. The tantalizing caress worked its way up her slender neck to her shell-shaped ear, leaving behind a trail of tingling flesh. If this is a dream, Reb thought, I don't want to wake up.

"Laurie," a husky voice breathed in her ear.

Reb groaned inwardly as her heart sank to her toes. Kincaid dreaming! She couldn't let this farce continue! She wouldn't let it continue. She began the delicate process of extricating herself from his grasp. How in the world had they gotten so tangled up, she wondered. When she tried to edge backward, his hands increased their splayed hold on her bare ribs, thumbs resting up under her breasts.

"Come, love," he coaxed, "give me a kiss."

Reb's first reaction was to press her lips tight in refusal and pull away from the strong hands that had slipped under her buckskin shirt. When he stirred restlessly, she began to have second thoughts. What if her refusal caused him to wake up? Aside from the loss of pride she would suffer from being caught in such a compromising situation, she was not altogether sure she was ready to deal with Kincaid woman to man. Perhaps if she assuaged his desire for a kiss she could escape from this predicament without discovery. Then she would make sure they headed down the mountain tomorrow whether Blue had returned or not.

Never having taken the initiative, she was unsure how to proceed. She moved her head closer to Kincaid and tilted it slightly so their noses would not collide. Her eyes were open, but the moonlit shadows were deceptive. She edged closer until her lips touched lightly stubbled skin. She'd kissed his chin! Now what?

A voice sighed, "Again," and she could tell from the sound and the exhaled breath where to move her mouth to make contact with his. She inched her lips upward until she met the warm lips waiting for her. At the same time that their lips met, his thumbs reached up to brush her nipples, which hardened into coral pebbles under his caress.

Reb almost gasped at the concurrent tightening in her belly, but the surge of desire that rose in her center only made her more anxious to get away. She took advantage of his concentration on one part of her body to try to extricate her legs from under the powerful thigh he had thrown over them, but without much success. She didn't panic, although the urge to do something desperate was great. With reluctance, she admitted that until Kincaid was satiated she was stuck. Well, there was more than one way to skin a cat. She would tame the beast by feeding its hunger. When she had taken the edge off its appetite, she would make her escape.

Kincaid was delighted with the success of his plan. The greatest danger had been at the time of Reb's awakening. Apparently her fear of confronting him had been sufficient to make her compliant to his wishes. As long as Reb thought he mistook her for Laurie, she would do nothing to resist his advances . . . and he would be satisfied with nothing less than total capitulation. The next step was to get her out of those smelly clothes.

Without more effort than it takes to tear an autumn leaf from a limb, he pulled Reb's shirt up over her head. She immediately rolled away from him at the waist. He flung the shirt away and reached for her shoulders, bringing her bare breasts, now protected by her hands, against his chest. He slid his arms around her. She trembled and breathed shallowly from her mouth. He ran the fingers of one hand through her hair, smoothing it away from her ear so that he could nibble on it. Light pressure applied to her elbows brought her arms up and around his neck. Then he set about calming her obvious fear by running his hands up and down along her spine and across her shoulders, pressing her breasts flat against his broad chest.

Frightened as she was of discovery, Reb never questioned the vigor of Kincaid's actions. How should she know what a man might be capable of in his sleep? All she had for comparison was the episode when he was delirious. This activity seemed in total keeping with that. She was determined that her responses would be so compliant as to put him off guard. Then she could withdraw without waking him.

They were pressed together now, nose to nose and toe to toe, and Reb knew once again the warmth and strength of his desire against her flushed skin. The demands he made with his mouth she responded to as gentle, unspoken requests. She was surprised at her body's languid acquiescence to Kincaid's possession. She felt safe in his arms. It was time to feed the beast.

She threaded her fingers through his hair and arched her head sideways, offering her willowy neck for his kisses. She pressed her loins against his belly and slipped her knee between his legs. Her breasts she slid teasingly back and forth across his own. She shivered in pleasure when he kissed a path down her neck and throat to her shoulders.

Then she put her own mouth to good use, tasting his salty brow with the tip of her tongue and then bringing his head up with her hands, her tongue gliding down his temple. She tenderly kissed each closed eyelid, and the tip of his Grecian nose. She felt his strong jaw with her hands, celebrating the memory of her first touch of his mobile lips with another visit from her fingertips. Her tongue found the scar under his eye and she nipped it with her teeth. She could do all these things without self-consciousness because Kincaid would never know. He was asleep and thought she was Laurie. Her soul cried with wanting it otherwise. When she realized Kincaid was releasing his hold, she tensed in preparation for the move away from him.

The wanton sensuality of the woman in his arms surprised and confused Kincaid. She was supposed to resist his advances so he could overcome her objections, then expose her for the female she was. Instead, he felt a fierce protectiveness for the innocent abandon of her response to his premeditated stimulation. For all that, his body raged with a need that only she could fulfill.

The next thing Kincaid knew he had landed on the floor, his head striking a flour barrel with enough force to momentarily stun him.

"What the hell is going on here?!" a voice bellowed.

"Blue!" Reb shrieked in joy. She threw herself into the mountain man's arms, oblivious to her state of undress. While she was hugging him, the realization dawned that she was naked from the waist up—not that she was embarrassed to be so unclothed before Blue—but rather that it exposed more fully the nature of the activity she had been involved in when he entered the room.

He put his hands on her bare shoulders and pushed her away. "Put your shirt on."

Reb skittered to obey, hearing the censure in his voice.

"Do you mind telling me what's going on?" he growled, glaring at the naked man he'd laid out flat on the dirt floor.

Reb had to light the lantern in order to find where Kincaid had thrown her shirt. The dark frown she saw on Blue's face when she picked up the garment from the floor in the corner made her hasten to explain.

"He thinks I'm a boy," she began hesitantly.

"Then he must be blind!" he thundered.

Reb blushed and crossed her arms to hide her breasts. She turned around and yanked her shirt down over her head. "He thought I was his wife," she blurted over her shoulder.

"Well, which is it? Does he think you're a boy or does he think you're his wife?"

Kincaid controlled his twitching lips that kept threatening to grin at Reb's discomfiture. However, not knowing the limits of Blue's anger, and, after all, discretion being the better part of valor, he bit the inside of his cheek and remained still.

"Both!" Reb snapped in reply to Blue's question, her temper now a match for his. After all, he wasn't her father, and besides she hadn't done anything wrong. "He mistook me for Adam's *brother* and I saw no reason to disenchant him," she spat. "As for tonight, he was dreaming and thought I was . . . another woman. If you hadn't interrupted us, I would have soothed him and managed to disengage myself before he woke up and he'd never have been the wiser!"

So that's what she was doing! Kincaid marveled at her ingenuity, even while he rued his own willingness to once again be duped.

Blue glanced at Kincaid, who still appeared to be out cold, then back at Reb. No matter what she said, there was a whole lot more going on between these two than she was telling.

"I'd appreciate it if you'd help me get him back on the bed," she said. "It took a lot to get him well, and I'd just as soon not go through that again."

Kincaid grunted when Blue easily picked him up and threw him over his shoulder. When the mountain man dropped him on the bed, he opened his eyes to stare into two startlingly similar faces—bright mahogany eyes framed by arched black brows, shaggy, midnight black hair, prominent cheekbones, full mouths and stubborn chins. One was an older man he'd never seen before. He shook his head groggily. No wonder the man had laid him out. He was lucky nothing worse had happened.

"Your father?" he questioned Reb.

Kincaid watched the man flush and a curious expression flicker across his face when Reb answered with a smile, "No, this is Blue."

"What happened?" Kincaid asked, pretending ignorance while rubbing the knot on his head.

Reb and Blue exchanged looks and she put a hand on Blue's arm before she answered, "You were dreaming and you fell out of bed. Go back to sleep. Blue and I have some things to discuss. You two can talk in the morning."

Why, the little liar! Kincaid thought. Well, he had a few lies of his own to set straight. "Reb, I remember everything," he improvised quickly. "Must have been that knock on the head. My memory is back."

She quickly hid the pain in her eyes, but could not suppress a sigh. "Good. Get some rest and tomorrow we can think about sending you on your way." It didn't matter any more who he was, or what he was doing out here. She already knew all she needed to know about him—she loved him.

"Reb." He called her back to his side and pulled her down to whisper in her ear so Blue couldn't hear. "I can ride, but I don't know a blame thing about roping." He grinned. She chuckled, then laughed aloud. He joined her and soon the two of them were laughing so hard Reb had to wipe the tears from her eyes. Blue just watched them like they were crazy.

"Private joke," she giggled, then gave an unmaidenly guffaw and slapped her knee.

Kincaid was glad to see the pain gone from her face. Tomorrow was soon enough for pain.

Chapter Twelve

SEATED ACROSS FROM EACH OTHER AT THE TIMEWORN table, Reb and Blue talked quietly to avoid disturbing Kincaid, who had finally relented to Reb's pleas and turned over to sleep.

"Why can't you tell him you're a woman?" Blue demanded.

"It would be very . . . awkward to admit it now," Reb replied. "Anyway, what purpose would it serve? You've just told me that I have to take him down the mountain alone and it would only complicate things if he knew the truth."

Blue didn't argue, just shook his head. "When do you plan to leave?" he asked.

"Tomorrow, I guess, if Kincaid hasn't suffered any lasting effects from your overenthusiastic greeting."

Blue scowled. "My greeting was damned appropriate."

Reb laid a hand on Blue's sleeve, and she concentrated on her fingers as she toyed with a snag in the navy colored wool. "Thank you for caring, but things were not as they probably seemed."

"I know what I saw," he said brusquely.

Her deep brown eyes peered up into the matching orbs that were sunk deep in Blue's rugged face. "It was dark, Blue. What did you see?"

Blue recalled the scene to mind and a frown wrinkled his brow. His reflex action on finding the two in bed together had been to save Reb from the unwanted attentions of that rutting rogue. It dawned on him now that it was Reb who had been caressing Kincaid when Blue had interrupted them. It was hard for him to imagine his Reb desiring any man, but if his recollection was accurate, he must be mistaken. When Blue looked at her, the question was plain in his eyes, but Reb waited for him to voice it aloud.

"You were the one kissing him?"

Reb flinched, even though she had known the query was coming. It was true, though. She had been the one kissing Kincaid, not the other way around. What was wrong with her? Her throat closed on the admission she was about to make. She tightened her jaws to stop the trembling in her chin and took a deep breath before plunging into her confession.

"He was dreaming and asked for a kiss from his wife—she was killed during the war—and I guess I just got carried away by my feelings." She swallowed painfully over the lump in her throat before finishing in a frightened and confused whisper, "I can't seem to keep myself from wanting to touch him."

Blue watched the tears of frustration gather in Reb's eyes and, as a giant teardrop slid down the side of her freckled nose, he asked bluntly, "Do you love him?"

"I think so," she choked out.

"You think so?" Blue snorted and muttered in exasperation, "All this moaning and groaning and you *think* so?!"

Reb laid her head down on her arms to muffle her gulping sobs as the vulnerable child in her wailed, "He thinks I'm just a smelly, bratty boy!"

Reb's tears tore at Blue's heartstrings because he could not remember anything in the past that had reduced her to such a womanish display of emotion, not even Rachel's death. His knuckles whitened in clenched fists as he controlled the furious desire to strangle Kincaid for being the cause of Reb's unhappiness. At the same time, he was not able to hide his exasperation with Reb for acting so out of character. His mind raced for a solution that would resolve Reb's dilemma, and quickly concluded that, whether she liked it or not, the first step out of this pile of buffalo flop was to make Kincaid aware Reb was female.

When he came to this conclusion, he was aware of a sinking feeling in the pit of his stomach. His face took on a pinched, grim look as he admitted to himself the source of his distress. The Reb that had giggled in pleasure and wide-eyed adoration when he had dandled her on his knee had grown up. What she wanted —what she needed now—were the attentions of another man. It startled and pained Blue to realize he was jealous of the love Reb had bestowed on the unknowing Kincaid. He would not see that precious blessing go to waste.

"Dammit, Reb!" Blue interrupted his own thoughts angrily, "tell the man you're a woman! Tell him how you feel!"

"NO!" She grabbed his arm and her magnificent fiery eyes, glistening with tears, locked with his. At a stirring from the bed, she checked over her shoulder anxiously to make sure she had not wakened Kincaid with her outburst. While she waited for the sleeping man to finish shifting his position, she wiped her eyes with her dirty sleeve, leaving childlike smudges across her cheeks. When Kincaid quieted, she confronted Blue once again. "You don't understand," she hissed. "His wife was killed, but he hasn't stopped loving her. There's no room in his life for anyone else."

Blue tugged his bottom lip in thought. Perhaps Reb was right. There had only been one woman for him. Even though they hadn't been destined to share their lives together, he had never desired another. But he well knew that not all men were so constant. "How do you know unless you ask?" he said calmly to the dirty-faced waif.

Reb was reluctant to disclose everything she'd learned about Kincaid over the past weeks, not to mention the episode during his feverish delirium. "I just know," she said miserably. She tipped her chin up in a way that made it clear this was not a subject she wished to discuss any further.

Blue knew better than to argue with her. When Reb's mind was made up, it was made up. As he'd taught Reb, however, there was more than one way to skin a cat. He would just have to talk with Kincaid himself.

"All right," he said, seeming to concede the issue, "we might as well get some rest if you're going to leave tomorrow." Blue excused himself from the table.

Reb sat forlornly watching the lantern flicker. It wouldn't make any difference, she kept repeating to herself. There's no way Kincaid could feel anything for me at all. He thinks I'm a boy, for heaven's sake!

She laid her head back down on one arm and her eyelids drooped further closed with each twist of the lantern flame. Her other hand dropped down to scratch Trapper's head as Blue's dog laid down across her feet.

"Reb."

Drowsily, she responded to the parental tone of Blue's voice and slid from the chair onto the buffalo robe he had spread on the floor next to the stove. She tossed and turned like a cat in a basket until she had achieved a comfortable fetal curl inside the robe, then mumbled, "Goodnight, Blue." Trapper waited for her to quiet, then chose a spot as close as possible to Reb and, after a canine version of Reb's nesting efforts, settled himself on top of the buffalo robe next to her.

Blue bent to one knee next to Reb. Parting the hair on her forehead, he brushed it back to each side with his forefinger to make a place for the soft kiss he pressed on the center of her brow.

"Goodnight, Rebecca," he whispered.

After breakfast the next morning, it was Kincaid who first brought up the subject of leaving the cabin.

"Now that you're here, perhaps you can help me get to my destination," he said to Blue.

"Just what is your destination?" Blue asked.

"The second Overland Stage station west of the Laramie Mountains."

Blue and Reb exchanged surprised glances. Seth Barker's stage station, where Kincaid would have met his party, was one stop beyond Matt's ranch. If Kincaid had completed his original journey, Reb observed with unaccustomed green-eyed jealousy, he would have eaten a meal in her home served by her sister, Dillon. Reb, being a part of the roundup crew, would have known about Kincaid only through her sister's glowing reports. Reb bit her lower lip to control the smug satisfaction that she experienced because she had met Kincaid first. Reb loved her sister, but Dillon tended to sweep most men off their feet with her beauty. She did not relish the idea of facing Dillon's competition where the tall Yankee was concerned. Blue interrupted her train of thought when he spoke to Kincaid.

"I'll be glad to get you started on your way," Blue began. "I should tell you first that I asked some questions about you at Ft. Laramie, and apparently there was quite a stir at your disappearance. A Corporal Jennings reported that everyone on the stage he was guarding had been killed. Of course, when they went to retrieve your body for your folks, it wasn't there. General Dodge left word with the commander of the fort, Colonel Moonlight, to send word to him immediately if you were found.

"When I informed the army that Adam and Reb had rescued you and that you were safe, but had lost your memory, they provided a horse for you and instructions where you were to be taken. Moonlight wired your parents to advise them you're alive."

"Thank God for that," Kincaid interjected quietly.

"I've brought the horse, but I'm not able to be your guide. I have some unfinished business with Chief Spotted Tail," Blue said.

"Wasn't he being sent to a reservation?" Kincaid asked, recalling his discussion with Reb.

"He was." Blue grinned. "He changed his mind."

Blue explained how the cavalry had considered itself more an escort than a guard and, unsuspecting that there was any resistance to moving to the reservation on the part of the Sioux, had marched in front of the Indians rather than following them. The troops hadn't even been issued ammunition. Three days away from the fort, the Sioux had slipped away from their camp before dawn to cross the Platte River, heading north for the Powder River region west of the Black Hills. It was a while before the soldiers even realized the Indians weren't asleep in their tepees. By that time, most of the Sioux women and children had crossed the Platte.

"Although the Indians' ponies were trained to ford rivers, the army horses weren't," Blue said, "and most of the soldiers couldn't swim. Besides, there were only a hundred and forty soldiers against nearly four hundred armed warriors. You see, they never thought to take the Indians' weapons from them, either." He scratched the stubble on his jaw, then shook his head in disbelief. "Sometimes the stupidity of the U.S. Army amazes me."

"You won't get any argument on that from me," Kincaid laughed ruefully, recalling his own disastrous encounter with the army's protection.

Blue continued, "The Sioux harassed the soldiers just long enough to allow their women and children to escape. When the braves quit chasing them, those army boys raced for home. That's where I came in.

"When Colonel Moonlight heard what had happened, he sounded boots and saddles and lit out from the fort with over two hundred men. I volunteered to act as scout. I suggested to Moonlight that we pace ourselves, but he was so anxious to catch Spotted Tail and his Sioux that we rode a hundred and twenty miles in two days. Of course that ruined a lot of horseflesh, and about half the men had to go back.

"We stopped for breakfast the third day along

Deadman Creek, and we unsaddled the horses to let them graze between the walls of the narrow canyon there. I warned Moonlight we should hobble the animals, but it seems every suggestion I made on that trip he did the exact opposite." A wry smile lit Blue's face when he remembered how easy it had been to manipulate the bullheaded Colonel.

"He insisted the horses were too tired to move very far on their own. Unfortunately (or fortunately, he thought to himself, depending on whose side you were on), there was a surprise attack by Spotted Tail. He and his braves came down into the canyon shooting and yelling and waving blankets. Scared a year's life out of those fledgling recruits and sent the horses flying.

"I tried to explain to the good Colonel that I was shooting my gun to try to head off a few of our mounts, but it seems he saw it otherwise. He accused me of being in cahoots with those Indians. We did manage to catch about twenty-five horses, but Spotted Tail's Sioux got clean away with the rest."

"You lost all but twenty-five horses?" Reb repeated in awe.

"Unbelievable," Kincaid murmured.

"Moonlight was furious. He burned the extra saddles and all the tack and supplies we couldn't carry, and we walked back. It was a long, thirsty four days for those young boys. When we arrived at the fort, the Colonel threw me in the stockade. Nobody thought about me again until Moonlight got relieved of his command. I remembered to inquire about you then," Blue said to Kincaid. "You know the rest."

"Oh, Blue, you've been in jail!" Reb exclaimed. "I've been thinking so much of myself, I never wondered what could have kept you away so long."

Kincaid ignored Reb's outburst, more intent on the other information Blue had revealed regarding his relationship with the Indians. If the mountain man did have some connections with the Sioux, it might be a good thing for the railroad to know about. "Were you working with the Indians?" Kincaid inquired innocently.

"Not exactly," Blue hedged. "You could say I helped make an opportunity that the Sioux took advantage of. I'd promised an old acquaintance of mine I'd do what I could to slow the army down."

"An old acquaintance?" Kincaid prodded.

"Spotted Tail."

Kincaid did not mask his incredulity. "The chief of the Brulé Sioux is a *friend* of yours?!"

"I saved his life once."

Reb also was startled at Blue's unexpected revelation. If Spotted Tail were his friend, might not Standing Buffalo be a friend as well? For a horrified moment, Reb feared she and Adam might have killed someone close to Blue in their slaughter at the renegade camp. "Standing Buffalo isn't . . ." she began.

Blue squelched Reb's concern immediately. "Standing Buffalo and his braves are murdering renegades and deserve whatever happens to them."

"I never knew, Blue. You never told me you were friends with any Indians," Reb accused, still shocked at the idea of Blue sitting down peacefully with the same Indians who scalped and murdered the white man with such violent ease.

"You never asked," he answered simply. "General Connor was the one who urged General Dodge to relieve Moonlight of his command. He convinced Dodge at the same time to let him lead his own

153

expedition to the Powder River to solve this Indian situation. Blast the army for its ignorant generals! I owe it to Spotted Tail to warn him things are bound to heat up for the Sioux."

"Owe it to him? I thought you said you saved his life, not the other way around," Kincaid said.

"He did save my life." Blue let the sentence hang alone in the ensuing silence without offering further explanation before he added firmly, "I only came by to bring you that big-devil black horse the army sent—Satan, I think the hostler called him—and to tell you where to meet your people. Reb'll have to lead you back down the mountain."

"Reb?" Kincaid asked skeptically.

Reb immediately flared up at this uncalled-for questioning of her capabilities, especially since the insult had occurred in Blue's presence.

"Yes. Any objections?" she snapped.

"Would it matter if I did have any?" he retorted.

Blue watched the tension sparking between the two pairs of flashing eyes, and wished he knew more about what had happened between them before his arrival.

"No," Blue said quietly, causing them both to turn and stare at him.

"Do I meet my party at the same place as before?" Kincaid asked.

"Yes, it's one stage station after Reb's place."

"Reb's place?"

"My father's ranch also serves as a rest stop for the Overland Stage," Reb supplied.

Kincaid went through practically the same speculation as Reb had, mistakenly concluding, because he was not aware she would have been gone on the roundup, that if things had gone as initially planned he would have met Reb when he stopped at her father's way station. He eyed her surreptitiously. Would she have been wearing a form-fitting print calico dress like the farmer's daughters he'd seen back east? Probably not. He corrected his image of her, mentally redressing her in a pair of *clean,* sturdy buckskins. He rubbed his thigh to still its aching, but did not repress the smile that flickered across his face. "When do we leave?" he asked Reb almost jovially.

"After lunch," she replied in a more subdued tone. "That'll give us plenty of time to get to the base of the mountain to camp by dark. We'll arrive at your point of rendezvous tomorrow."

Reb couldn't believe they were having this calm discussion planning Kincaid's departure from her life. Although once she had wished fervently for just such an eventuality, that was no longer true.

Kincaid was also reluctant to part from Reb. There was unfinished business between them. She still had not paid for her deceit. Perhaps an opportunity would present itself on the way down the mountain. He would have to make sure one did.

Blue sent Reb out to feed and curry the horses to give him an opportunity to speak with Kincaid alone, warning her to take care with the mount he had brought for the tall Yankee. Reb looked back and forth between the two of them seated at the table and grumbled something about child labor, but did as she was bid.

Blue leaned back in his chair and took a sip of coffee. "You know, the army never did say what you're doing out here."

Kincaid had expected Blue's interrogation, so the man's indirect question came as no surprise. He had no particular reason to trust Blue, and yet he did. If the mountain man had intended to do him deadly physical harm, he'd already passed up the perfect opportunity, and words alone would not deter Kincaid from his mission. He decided to take the grizzled character into his confidence.

"That's because the army, except for Grenville Dodge and a few generals in Washington, doesn't know what I'm doing out here," Kincaid admitted.

Blue raised a quizzical eyebrow that encouraged Kincaid to elaborate.

"The Union Pacific is trying to determine the best route for their half of the transcontinental railroad. The businessmen in Denver have been trying to convince railroad officials that south through Denver City is the way to go. Grenville Dodge is a qualified engineer himself and, when he got a look at the terrain out here, he suggested that my father privately check it out. I studied engineering at Harvard and that made me a logical choice to survey the mountainous grades in this area. So, here I am."

"What about the uniform?"

"That was to get me in and out of my meetings with Dodge without raising questions," Kincaid acknowledged.

"Your father's a railroad man, then."

"That and several other things—banker, financier, industrialist. You name it, he has a probing finger in the pie," Kincaid said wryly.

"You'll be going back east then when your job is done, I expect," Blue said, trying to determine where Reb might fit into this blueleg's plans.

"No," Kincaid replied pensively, "I don't think so. There's nothing for me back there now." He massaged his thigh, which seemed to ache more than normal this morning, perhaps as a result of his trip to the floor the previous night, and maybe because the past few hours had stirred up the distressing memories that had only begun to soften their grip on his heart.

"I'm sorry about your wife," Blue said softly.

The grizzled man's perceptive insight surprised Kincaid. He replied with a gruff curtness intended to cover his feelings, "I'll get over it."

Blue didn't miss the regret that crossed Kincaid's face. He knew the emotion well. He also knew from his own experience that regretting something didn't change the fact it had happened. It was time, if not more than time, that this young man got on with his life. Reb loved Kincaid. Blue set his mind to determining whether there was a way in his power to have this providential stranger recognize and return that love.

"Reb's quite a . . . boy," Blue began.

"Yes, he is," Kincaid readily agreed. That was an understatement.

"You don't have to worry about getting down the mountain safely. Reb's one of the best trackers I know."

"A crack shot, too," Kincaid muttered.

"Yes. How did you know?"

"She gave me some lessons," he said, smiling at the recollection of Reb's reaction to her one missed shot. It was not until he had the sentence out that Kincaid realized what he'd said. The smile faded and he looked quickly at Blue to see if he'd noticed the slip. He had.

"How long have you known?" Blue asked ominously. This was a twist in the trail he had not counted on, and he hoped that what he found around the corner would not be a polecat.

"I just found out yesterday," Kincaid admitted reluctantly. "She has played her role very well."

Blue gave an inaudible sigh of relief but remained tense, searching Kincaid's face for any indication of his feelings for Reb. What he encountered was a stony visage to outmatch anything he'd ever seen, even on the close-faced Matt Hunter. He had to find a way to crack that facade and make this Yankee reveal his intentions toward Reb.

"Are you going to tell her you know?" Blue demanded in an icy voice.

"Why should I?" Kincaid countered defiantly. "We've managed very well up to now. She seems perfectly happy with the current arrangement. There's certainly no modesty on my part," he sneered. "I'm perfectly happy to parade around naked while she plays doctor! She's even welcome to bathe me when I'm bare as a babe!" Kincaid snarled furiously.

A throaty growl drew his attention to the corner of the room. What he saw there would have terrified a lesser man. Trapper crouched with fangs bared, and silvery gray hackles raised on the scruff of his neck, in readiness to spring at the man whose tone of voice threatened Blue. Kincaid was certain that any movement from him would precipitate an attack by the wolf-like animal.

"He belong to you?" Kincaid asked without taking his eyes off the dog.

"Friend, Trapper," Blue commanded.

The dog immediately relaxed and came over to investigate Kincaid, who held his hand out tentatively for the canine to nuzzle. When Trapper had satisfied his curiosity, he dropped to the floor and rested his head on Blue's foot. Blue was somewhat surprised by his own tolerant patience with the younger man's challenging response, but, when he put himself in

Kincaid's place, the attitude was pretty understandable. Kincaid's belated awareness that it had been no ragged lad that had attended him, and the stinging knowledge of Reb's highly successful pretense, had injured this proud man's pride.

On the other hand, it had been Kincaid who had asked Reb for a kiss. Blue was not at all fooled by the nonsense about a "dream." He was sure Kincaid had known exactly what he was doing. Was the request for a kiss the gesture of a man who was not at least a little interested in the woman beneath the rags she wore? Apparently, taking advantage of Reb's naiveté was part of some plan of Kincaid's to get back at Reb for her breach of feminine conduct. It was necessary, then, to make it clear to the angry man that, if Reb were hurt, Kincaid would have to answer to Blue.

Blue sat forward and braced his palms on the table before him. "If you're offended by her lack of modesty, then I suggest you don't have any more 'dreams' that require Reb to administer immodest attentions," he said.

Blue spoke so softly Kincaid barely heard him, but he could not misinterpret Blue's aggressive posture, his narrowed eyes and the iron in his voice. It was obvious that Blue saw through the ploy he'd used with Reb. It was equally obvious that the older man was setting himself up as Reb's champion.

"I think that how this matter is resolved is between Reb and me," Kincaid said slowly, with a steel in his voice that parried the iron in Blue's.

"I don't want her hurt," Blue slashed back.

Kincaid bristled at Blue's commanding tone and answered angrily, "Reb started this game and she set the rules. I don't intend to throw in my hand just when the pot has gotten interesting."

"Reb isn't playing a game with you," Blue responded hotly.

"Then what do you call it when a beautiful woman pretends to be a dirty, stinking ragamuffin boy?" Kincaid raged. His anger forced him to his feet so violently that his chair fell with the crash of splintering wood behind him. He towered menacingly over Blue, letting his full height intimidate if it would.

At Trapper's warning rumble, Blue laid his hand calmly on the dog's head and ran it down his back to once again soothe the raised, black-tipped gray hackles. Blue was amazed at Kincaid's vehemence and the all too obvious resentment manifested at Reb's ruse, but he was more sure than ever that all was not lost. In fact, he had to tense his jaw to keep from smiling ear to ear. Perhaps he could help these two find each other before it was too late. Kincaid's fury at the tack Reb had taken would have to be soothed. Thanks to the Yankee's most recent outburst, however, Blue was confident that his job was not going to be as difficult as he had thought at first. What virile man, and Blue had no qualms about Kincaid on that count, wouldn't want to be persuaded that the "beautiful woman" who had masqueraded as a "dirty, stinking ragamuffin boy" had done so because she was afraid she would not be able to resist his masculine charms?

"Reb wasn't raised to play coy games," Blue said softly. "Her father . . ." he stumbled over the word, then continued, "her father saw fit to teach her things a girl wouldn't normally learn. Reb was a good pupil, and what seemed strange at first became pretty normal over the years. She's only doing what's natural for her. Reb is an innocent where men are concerned," he finished pointedly.

Kincaid snorted his disbelief. He walked in a limp-

ing circle in the small room, glad for the opportunity
to exercise the cramped muscle in his leg, and to
observe Blue from behind without being subject to
the same scrutiny. He found it hard to connect Reb's
wanton sensuality with inexperience. Yet, she had
been shy at first when responding to him. That kiss on
the chin was certainly not the work of a practiced
lover!

"At least she was innocent before she met you,"
Blue turned and added probingly.

Kincaid stopped and glared at Blue. He found the
insinuation that he regularly deflowered helpless vir-
gins strongly repugnant. He also could not help a
twinge of guilt when he acknowledged at the same
time that he had set Reb's virtue as the price she must
pay for her masquerade.

"I've never known Reb to treat any man as other
than a friendly competitor," Blue continued, undeterred.

"Friendly competition?! That's what you call the
way she's been leading me around by the nose?"

Blue had to struggle against a guffaw at Kincaid's
indignant question. He managed to control himself
and to reply with some measure of calm reasoning,
"I'm sure Reb used her best judgment under the
circumstances. You can hardly blame her for not
admitting she's female—alone with you, not knowing
what kind of man you are . . ." Blue let his voice trail
off significantly.

Kincaid's brow arched in thought. "I wouldn't have
hurt her," he said, although it was true that, had he
known sooner that she was a woman, events might
very well have led him to bed Reb. He couldn't deny
the heat in his loins when he remembered her striking
appearance in the pond.

Blue couldn't resist forcing the issue. "Do you find Reb attractive as a woman?" he asked.

Disconcerted by the question that followed so closely his own train of thought, Kincaid paced away from the older man. "What's attractive about a woman in filthy buckskins?" he spat sarcastically, echoing his earlier thoughts aloud. However, to be perfectly honest with himself, he had admired many facets of the woman beneath the clothes. Capable, competent, caring Reb. Beautiful, enticing, lusciously soft Reb.

Kincaid turned back to Blue with a troubled look that caused the mountain man to adopt his severest expression to hide his inward satisfaction. Clearly this was a subject Kincaid had never examined closely. Good. Let him think.

"I do admire her . . . capabilities," Kincaid grudgingly admitted. "Are you going to tell her I know?"

Blue made a tepee of his hands in front of his pursed lips, trying to decide what would be best for Reb. She hadn't wanted to tell Kincaid she was female. It could only cause pain for her to know she had been discovered, especially when Kincaid did not yet acknowledge that he in any way reciprocated Reb's feelings. Blue had warned Kincaid there would be consequences if he hurt Reb heedlessly. He could only conclude it was best to let them work this out on their own.

"No," Blue sighed, resigning the outcome to fate. "I won't tell."

Chapter Thirteen

THE SOUNDS OF CREAKING SADDLE LEATHER AND THE muffled crunch of horses' hooves on the thick layers of dead brown pine needles imposed upon the quiet dignity of the mountains. An occasional warble or chirrup issued from nests hidden in the towering trees. The mournful wail of the wind through the thousands upon thousands of pine branchlets raised goose bumps on Reb's skin that were smoothed by the wafting currents of billowing air that surrounded her like a comforting bath of whirling warm water. She could almost forget that Kincaid followed close on her trail.

A small doe and its dappled fawn paused curiously as she and Kincaid rode by them, but did not flee. It was unusual to find such fearlessness in the forest creatures anymore, and Reb knew that the days of seeing such a rare occurrence were numbered. Even dumb beasts learned quickly that death followed when men invaded their sanctuary.

She and Kincaid had made steady progress since leaving Blue's cabin after lunch and had just emerged from a narrow, shadowy path through a stand of blue spruce into a small, sunny open meadow that sloped sharply downhill. With her eyes receptive to the wonders around her, Reb could not help admiring Kincaid's mount when he rode up beside her.

The glossy, coal-black animal stood seventeen and a half hands high at the withers, so tall that even the willowy Reb had been forced to stand on tiptoe to see over his back when she had brushed him down earlier in the day. Satan had not lived up to his name, quietly tolerating the strokes of the currycomb through his inordinately long mane and tail without biting at her or trying to kick. Nor had he yet this afternoon proved to be the devil on hooves. Kincaid had not had any trouble controlling him. In fact, the two seemed to go together like a pair of well-made buckskin riding gloves.

"That's a beautiful stallion," Reb observed.

"My father bought Satan for me as a gift on my twenty-first birthday," Kincaid replied.

"He's your horse?! I thought the army sent him."

"I've owned Satan for about five years, but I had no chance to ride him during the war. I only started working with him again after I had recovered from my leg wound. Guess my father wanted to surprise me by having him brought out here."

"You could have bought a horse for a lot less than it probably cost your father to do that."

"He can afford it," Kincaid said noncommittally.

Reb had discounted Kincaid's reference to being rich made during his delirium, since he had so obviously appeared to be a soldier. Soldiers weren't rich.

If you were rich, you paid someone to fight in your stead.

Reb had never really considered what her competition would be for Kincaid's attention once they left the mountains. Suddenly it dawned on her that, not only could she not compete with the feminine wiles of the women she felt sure must be attracted to Kincaid's masculine charms, but, as a rancher's daughter, she might not meet the social criteria that a rich man might expect from his wife.

"Are you rich?" she couldn't help asking.

Kincaid cocked his head at the question. "Does it really matter?"

"I'd like to know," Reb replied stubbornly.

"Well then, I have money enough for my needs."

"But are you rich?" Reb insisted.

Kincaid laughed. "Yes. Does it show?"

Reb looked Kincaid over seriously. His black leather boots were standard army issue. He had donned one of Blue's shirts that pulled tightly across the shoulders. He had needed to roll the sleeves up to the elbow to disguise the fact that they were too short, revealing his muscular forearms. He wore no hat and the wind teased the black curls that fell across his tanned brow and down over his collar. The yellow-striped pants seemed indecently snug across his flat belly and along the steel-thewed legs that gripped the huge stallion. No, there was nothing in his appearance to indicate that he was wealthy.

Reb also felt somewhat comforted by the fact Kincaid had never evidenced the pomposity that she automatically associated with the very wealthy. A few of that breed had passed through on the stage, and she had observed their ostentatious displays with an odd

165

mixture of disgust and humor. Never in all the time they had been together, however, had she ever detected the slightest sign of such behavior from Kincaid. It left her reassured as to the unimportance of his wealth in their relationship, however mistaken that impression might be. She had no inkling of how different her behavior had seemed when compared to Kincaid's expectations from the women he knew.

"I guess you don't look rich," she offered finally. What she really meant was that he did not *act* as though he were rich, but of course she couldn't say that aloud.

"I take it that's a compliment?"

"Could be," Reb murmured.

They headed into a copse of pine, and Kincaid fell back to follow Reb's winding path through the trees. It occurred to Kincaid he could now safely inquire about his missing gold pocket watch. He had noticed the loss immediately upon waking in Blue's cabin, but had been constrained by his ruse of amnesia from asking about it.

"Did you by any chance find a gold watch at Standing Buffalo's camp, or in my clothing when you rescued me?"

"Another gift from your father?"

"No. It was a wedding present from Laurie. There's an inscription on the back. It's very special to me."

"Don't you think I would have returned it to you by now if I had found it?" Reb asked icily, bristling at the insinuation that she would have kept the object, but even more upset that Kincaid treasured the gift because it had come from his wife. Then shame washed over Reb for the selfishness that could make her jealous of a dead woman.

"Yes, I guess you would have returned my watch if

you'd had it," Kincaid said, interrupting her self-flagellation. "You've always been so scrupulously honest with me in every way in the past."

Reb blanched at the words that hinted at knowing so much more than they said.

Kincaid had registered Blue's warning about hurting Reb, but there had been nothing in their discussion to dissuade him from making her pose as an unwashed lad as uncomfortable as possible. He thought he knew just the way to set a prickly burr under her saddle for the rest of the ride down the mountain.

"I'm looking forward to seeing your brother, Adam, again," Kincaid said nonchalantly.

"Adam?" Reb swallowed the fear that rose in her throat.

"Sure. From what you and Blue have told me, it sounds as though we have to go right by your ranch to get to my rendezvous. I'd like to thank Adam for his part in my escape from the Sioux. You were planning to stop by and introduce me to the rest of your family anyway, weren't you?"

Reb thought fast. She was horrified at the thought of the humiliation she would suffer if she and Kincaid just rode up to the ranch together and her family greeted her as she knew they would, with questions and comments that would quickly disavow Kincaid of any notions he had that she was a lad. Even if she could somehow get there ahead of Kincaid, she wasn't sure she could convince her whole family to keep her secret. The Old One and Garth would go along. Dillon would, too, if only for the chance to flirt with Kincaid. But not Adam. Adam would probably think it great fun to blab everything. Then, too, Jesse was so young he would likely let the cat out of the bag without knowing it had escaped. Reb was uncertain what her father's reaction would be, but she strongly suspected he would insist she square with Kincaid. It was better not to tempt fate.

"No, I hadn't planned to go by the ranch," she said quickly. "I didn't want to hold you up any longer."

"No problem," Kincaid assured. "I'm anxious to meet everyone, especially your sister, Dillon. Is she pretty?"

"My sister?" Reb said dumbly.

"Now that I'm a widower, I need to keep my eyes open for a suitable new wife."

"A new wife?!" The hairs on the back of Reb's neck stood up in warning, and she turned around in the saddle to watch in astonished silence the performance that followed.

Kincaid wrapped the reins around the saddle horn so he'd have his hands free to emphasize his words. "I'm looking for a petite woman, but with a respectable bosom." Grinning lasciviously, Kincaid gestured crudely with both hands. His idea of "respectable" was clearly larger than what could be considered adequate, and unquestionably more generous than those modest crests with which God had seen fit to bless Reb.

"She should have long, copper-colored hair that curls around her face, like so," he continued, making circular motions at his temples with his forefingers. "Let's see. Green eyes would be nice, and an alabaster complexion. No freckles. Can't *stand* freckles on a woman's face. She should be the kind of woman who needs a man to take care of her. *All* of her, if you get my drift," he said, winking slyly at Reb.

Kincaid had intentionally described a woman as far removed from Reb as possible, thereby suggesting that she was not his type. He watched Reb's face redden in what he expected was embarrassment and was well satisfied with the result of his pointed teasing. If he had been thinking rationally, however, he would have realized that for Reb to be offended, or even more than perturbed, by his graphic presentation, aside from its crudeness, she would first have to be attracted to him herself. Unfortunately, the significance of Reb's blush was lost on Kincaid because he was fighting so hard to deny his own attraction to Reb. Also, unfortunately, he had unknowingly pictured a woman who bore a striking resemblance to Dillon.

Reb felt sick to her stomach. Here she had believed Kincaid so filled with remorse at the loss of Laurie that he could not think of another woman, and he had just lecherously described the kind of feminine pulchritude he had in mind to take his wife's place—her sister, Dillon!

Kincaid's big black stud reached over to nip Reb's mare, Brandy, on the neck for the second time in the space of a few minutes. Brandy whickered in pain and excitement at the stallion's sexual foreplay and danced away from the overbearing animal, so that Reb's leg was crushed against a pine.

"Can't you control that beast!" Reb snapped.

Kincaid reined Satan away from the mare. "He wouldn't be so tempted if you didn't keep putting her pretty tail in his face. We're alike that way. Neither of us can resist an obvious invitation."

Reb turned around quickly enough to catch the mischievous grin that showed off Kincaid's sparkling white teeth, then whipped her head forward when she felt the second furious blush rising in her cheeks in the space of a few minutes. She was grateful that Kincaid was behind her and couldn't see. "That wasn't . . . I didn't . . . I wouldn't . . . Oh!" She was totally tongue-tied. The rider *was* just like his mount, Reb agreed furiously, always trying to prove his superiority by dominating some female! She couldn't understand why she cared at all for such a lop-eared mule of a man. It wouldn't break her heart if she never exchanged another word with that arrogant bully!

Content that he had come away as victor in the badinage, Kincaid peacefully followed Reb's squared shoulders and proud mien down the mountain. With his vision focused on Reb's being, Kincaid's thoughts drifted to her as well. Tonight would probably be his last chance to teach her a good lesson. Then Blue's speech about Reb's unusual upbringing repeated itself to him. Perhaps he was being unfair. He tried to think of a single occasion when Reb had purposely demeaned him and had to admit there was none. On the other hand, he had done his best to humble her at Blue's cabin on at least two occasions that he could remember, and she had cleverly managed to turn the tables on him both times.

Ah! Kincaid, you vain bastard, he thought, as a light dawned. I know what irritates you! That chit of a girl has been able to handle everything you've thrown at her and come up smelling like a rose. Well, she didn't smell *exactly* like a rose, he admitted. His nose wrinkled boyishly at the thought of Reb's pungent buckskins. Her skin was as soft and pink as rose petals though, he admitted to himself. He recalled the velvety smoothness of her small, rounded breasts under his calloused fingertips, and the rosy pink tips of those luscious mounds as they hardened in response to his caress.

Kincaid shifted in the saddle, seeking a way to accommodate his uncomfortable state of arousal. Reb rode blithely before him, totally unaware of his frustration. Damn! She'd done it to him again! He'd be glad to get out of these mountains. Reb was in her element here, more so than he. He wondered whether she had seen the world beyond the Laramie Mountains, beyond her father's ranch.

He tried to picture Reb dancing gracefully in his arms at a grand ball, clothed in an elegant ruby red satin evening gown, her raven black hair perfectly coifed. He felt genuine regret for her hacked-off tresses. What would Reb have looked like with long ebony hair falling forward teasingly over her satin-clad shoulders? He could see Reb in buckskins and he could visualize her naked, but he simply could not imagine her clothed for a role in polite New York society. Kincaid startled Reb when he broke the silence that had reigned for several hours.

"Have you ever been back east?"

Kincaid had pulled abreast of Reb as they moved completely out of the low brush to the beginning of the open grass. Reb hesitated warily before answering, trying to gauge whether Kincaid intended to bring her down a peg once again. She noted the earnest expression in his eyes and decided his question was sincere.

"Only as far as Ft. Laramie," she answered with some trepidation.

"How about south?"

"Adam has been with Daddy to Denver City before, but I've never gone along. Garth's been talking about going to Texas to pick up some longhorns now that the war is over. I've thought about going with him, just to see what it's like, but I've very happily lived my whole life between these mountains and our road ranch."

When Kincaid's brow arched disdainfully, Reb added defensively, "Of course, I've seen pictures in books of New York and Philadelphia. It looks too crowded to me," she sniffed, "people living practically on top of one another. Is it as bad as it seems in pictures?"

"Worse in some places, better in others. New York is never peaceful and quiet like this, that's for sure. It bustles. It hurries. People have places to go, things to do. Everyone's trying to get the most out of life they can."

"Trying to grab what they can from those too weak to protect themselves, you mean."

"Don't start with me, Rebel," Kincaid said abruptly, sitting up straighter in the saddle.

Reb should have been warned, but she couldn't help herself. He was leaving her forever. She needed to hear his voice, to store the timbre of the sound so she could draw upon it when he was gone. Even arguing with him would be better than a return to the quiet ostracism he had practiced for the past few hours.

"You can't tell me they aren't greedy. They want to take away the wilderness. They want to claim it for their damned Yankee train."

"Who is 'they,' Reb?" Kincaid asked antagonistically.

"The Yankees," she answered certainly.

"I'm a Yankee," he said dryly.

"I didn't mean you," she apologized quickly. "I know you're not like that."

Reb's naive trust in him angered Kincaid. Such trust had no place in a world that let brothers fight and kill brothers in a war that just as senselessly took sons from mothers and husbands from wives . . . and wives from husbands. Such faith in the goodness of a man who was a virtual stranger was dangerous. Moreover, it was an anachronism, just like those stupid trusting deer that were going to get shot for somebody's supper if they didn't wise up fast.

"I never told you why I came out here, did I?" he said coldly.

"It isn't important," Reb said. After all, she thought, they weren't even going to be in each other's company very much longer, and what difference could it possibly make now?

"Even if the reason I came was to pave the way for a Yankee train through these mountains?" Kincaid said scathingly.

Kincaid's statement didn't register immediately. When it did, Reb stopped Brandy dead in her tracks. She laid the reins on the left side of Brandy's neck to turn her mount so she faced Kincaid head on. "You haven't! You wouldn't!" Reb gasped, appalled.

"Oh, but I have and I will! Not 'they,' Reb. Me. By the way, while I'm making a clean breast of things, I never lost my memory. I only pretended to have amnesia because I didn't want some unwashed mountain brat interfering with my work for the Union Pacific!"

Reb felt a lump form in her throat. A pain, like a heavy weight, pressed on her chest and her vision blurred with tears that she struggled to restrain. She wavered in the saddle and grabbed the horn with trembling hands to steady herself. Reb forced her next words out in a hoarse whisper.

"You know how I feel about trains . . . and any low-down Yankee who would bring them here where they're not wanted. I trusted you."

Kincaid winced at the ferocity of the quiet statement, and cursed his self-righteous arrogance under his breath. Maybe she had needed to learn to be more cautious with strangers, but there were certainly less cruel ways of making his point. Then he hardened himself to her agony. Not any way so sure, he said to himself. She would not soon forget this betrayal, and if it saved her greater pain later, then it was worth it to him to endure the role of bastard now.

He had learned a lot from his experience with Laurie. His wife had also been innocently sure that no stranger would ever purposely and unjustifiably harm her. He had tried to warn her of the danger of such blind trust, but she had laughingly kissed his concern away, until he had relented to her soft, sweet persuasion. If he had been strong and firm with Laurie when he had had the chance, she might still be alive today.

"Mindless Yankee tenderfoot," Reb said bitterly. "You were neither first nor last of those names, only the most hated one in between." Reb's heart hardened against Kincaid to keep from being crushed by his bitter revelation.

They had reached the base of the mountains, and a bright green rolling plain dotted with sagebrush and wildflowers stretched out endlessly in the distance. There was no shelter, whatsoever. The ball of orange sun was dropping quickly, painting the white clouds along the base of the azure sky in beautiful diagonal stripes of pink. The full moon had already come up and sat incongruously in the bright blue sky. Neither Reb nor Kincaid appreciated the beauty of the sunset.

"We'll make camp here," she announced.

Reb stepped down from the saddle and began efficiently gathering buffalo chips for the fire. By the time she had the fire started, Kincaid had unsaddled both horses and hobbled them nearby. He set the saddles near the fire for future use as pillows and unrolled their blankets to make pallets. Meanwhile, Reb had unwrapped the cold cornbread and jerky she had packed for their dinner. There would be no cooking. The fire was strictly for warmth.

Reb concentrated on the food in her hands and ignored Kincaid. He didn't think he'd ever seen anybody look so tired and desolate as she did now. He leaned back against his saddle with his long legs stretched out before him and gazed pensively into the fire while he slowly masticated the dried beef.

"You know," he said, trying to ease the blow of his confession to Reb, "it isn't a sure thing that the railroad will come through here. In fact, the reason I'm here is to determine whether the tracks should be laid along the base of the Southern Rockies or down Denver City way."

He might as well have been speaking to a stone wall. Reb didn't exhibit the slightest interest in what he was saying, just took a bite of cornbread and stared blankly into the growing dusk beyond the fire. The movement of a large grasshopper caught her eye, and she watched mesmerized as the insect gobbled down small blue wildflowers, chewing furiously as he stuffed each petal into his mouth with his spiny forelegs, and then moved rapidly on to the next.

What Kincaid wanted, without admitting it to himself, was Reb's forgiveness for hurting her. It was a sign of how much he cared that Kincaid contemplated excusing the harshness of his actions by telling Reb the awful truth about how Laurie had died. "You really should be more careful who you take into your confidence," he said hesitantly. "When I first married . . ."

Reb watched the grasshopper stop chewing in midpetal and suddenly take flight. She looked overhead but did not see any sign of a bird or other natural enemy. "Shut up!" she snapped.

Astonished at her brusque interruption, Kincaid was even more bewildered by Reb's next actions. She pitched the rest of her cornbread over her shoulder and laid her hands flat on the ground on either side of her crossed legs to intercept the growing vibrations from the earth. Then she bent sideways to lay her ear next to the ground.

"Damn! Get saddled up quick!" she ordered.

Kincaid obeyed her urgency and something else he'd never heard in Reb's voice—fear. They hastily kicked the fire out and then mounted and galloped north. The moon lit up the plains like daylight, revealing to Kincaid a dark mass closing fast. He could hear a distant rumble that sounded vaguely like thunder, and imagined some sort of prairie tornado descending upon them.

"What is it?" Kincaid shouted across to Reb.

"Buffalo stampede!" she called back. "Ride!"

Kincaid did not understand how the lumbering herd could threaten two riders he believed could easily outrun them on horseback, but he deferred to Reb's superior plains knowledge. He kicked Satan in the ribs and the giant animal surged ahead of the bay mare. Brandy increased her speed to keep up with the racing stallion.

Without warning, Brandy's left foreleg dropped into an unseen hole and at the speed she was moving the momentum snapped the bone like a dry stick. Reb flew over Brandy's head as the horse rolled forward. Reb rose unhurt almost instantaneously. Satan turned of his own volition at the mare's screams and Kincaid moved as one with his steed. Reb stared at Brandy in shock, then sank to her knees to cradle her horse's head in her lap. Brandy quieted as Reb's husky voice crooned comfort to the anguished cowhorse.

Kincaid dismounted in a rush to stand at Reb's side. He too had lost a favorite mount and sympathized with the heartbreak she must be enduring now. He glanced away quickly at the oncoming buffalo, then laid his hand gently on Reb's shoulder.

Reb raised her eyes to Kincaid, pleading for a miracle to save Brandy.

Nothing had prepared him for the gut-wrenching pain he experienced when Reb turned to him for help it was not in his power to give. At that moment, Kincaid gladly would have martyred himself to spare Reb the distress he saw on her face, but he was not a saint, and there was no way he knew to make the mare whole. "Her leg is broken," he said, his voice throaty with emotion. "We have to go."

He reached down to loosen Reb's Colt from her belt. She put her hand over his to keep him from taking the gun, and met his questioning gaze with stone-dry eyes.

"She's my horse. I'll do it."

She gently laid Brandy's head back down on the ground and slid her hand comfortingly down the slick, lathered neck one last time. She leaned over to nuzzle the still-bellowing silky nose, her own nostrils flaring as she inhaled the familiar musky smell of her sweaty horse. Then she slowly rose on her knees, pulled her razor-sharp knife from its beaded sheath and quickly slit Brandy's throat. The mare jerked once before she shuddered and died.

Kincaid held his breath, waiting for Reb to move

away from the dark, red blood that began pooling in rivulets around her, but she remained in her prayerful pose with the knife hanging slack in her hand.

"Rebel."

"Go away," she answered dully.

The buffalo barreled directly toward them and Kincaid knew there was no time to let Reb grieve now. First, they must survive the driving force that threatened to overwhelm them. He grabbed Reb around the waist and pulled her away from the dead animal, twisting the knife from her hand as he rose. Reb fought him like a wild woman, tooth and nail. He suffered her abuse, understanding the loss that precipitated her attack, until at last he manhandled her stomach-first onto Satan's neck.

Over the top of Satan's back he could see the ghostly whites of the giant humped creatures' eyes reflecting the moonlight. Their labored breathing whooshed in and out like the rhythmic straining of a mighty steam engine. With the foreknowledge of certain death if he did not act immediately, Kincaid vaulted into the saddle and yelled a command to his horse. The sound was lost in the deafening roar of thousands of cloven hooves trampling everything in their path. Satan needed no urging. The stallion bolted away from the mystical shadowy shapes pressing down from behind.

If Reb and Kincaid had been caught by such a stampede even ten years before, their hopes of survival would have been slim. In years past, the buffalo had run in herds of tens of thousands, stretching as far as the eye could see across the plains. Trapped in the center of such a maelstrom, there would have been little chance of escape. The white man had systematically killed so many of the beasts, however, that this buffalo herd was not even a thousand strong. It was no wonder that the Sioux, who depended on the buffalo for their livelihood, were bitter and angry. Kincaid was able to move steadily across the herd until he reached the edge of it and safety.

Kincaid dismounted after the last of the buffalo had thundered by, pulling the lifeless Reb down before him. Her legs buckled at the knees when her feet hit the ground. As she started to fall, Kincaid picked her up and held her in his arms like a child. Her glazed eyes stared up at him without seeing him.

Kincaid's heart went out to her.

"My valiant Rebel," he soothed. He clutched her still form to his strong, warm body, then pressed a chaste kiss to her brow, but it was not enough comfort for him or for her. He kissed each side of her mouth, then urgently sought her full, parted lips, driving his tongue between her teeth to the solace deep within.

Reb's soul that had been so chilled, first by Kincaid's bitter betrayal, and then by Brandy's violent death, reached out desperately toward the fiery blaze of Kincaid's love. Reb's eyes fell closed and she entwined her hands in his hair, desperately pulling his mouth down to hers, and battling his tongue with her own.

Their close brush with death had left Kincaid vibrantly alive and Reb's frenzied response inflamed his passion. He laid her down upon the verdant sea of grass. With nothing but the starry, moonlit sky above them, each found in the other's arms a balm for his loss.

Kincaid released Reb's belt and pulled her shirt up from the waist, breaking her hold on him long enough to strip the garment from her. Reb arched her back away from the fringes of cool grass beneath her so that her breasts flattened against Kincaid's rough wool shirt. Her hands groped blindly at the cold, sharp buttons, trying vainly to tear them free. When he heard her cry of frustration, Kincaid ripped the shirt off himself and flung it away. Reb's hands sought his hot flesh, roaming hungrily across his chest, grazing his flat nipples as she felt her way up and across his broad, sinewy shoulders. She raked her nails down his muscular back, demanding closer contact. Her whimper of desire drove Kincaid beyond the bounds of sane consideration for her untried state.

Reb's shoulders gleamed like mother-of-pearl in the moonlight, and Kincaid craved the sight of all of her. He yanked at the thong that held her buckskin leggings in place, then tore it when it would not yield. He freed her long, slender legs and pulled back to look at Reb, who lay panting, wild-eyed beneath him.

"God," he whispered huskily, "you're beautiful."

"Love me," she implored.

Chapter Fourteen

KINCAID FELT AS THOUGH REB'S SOULFUL PLEA TO BE loved had cast a spell upon him, for everything seemed thenceforth to move in slow motion. He was entranced by the sensual fire he saw in Reb's eyes. Her pupils had dilated until the black centers were enormous, and he could not resist their siren's call. He held himself motionless when Reb reached up to trace his lips with the pad of her finger. Her touch was soft as cornsilk.

The wonder of lying beneath Kincaid, awaiting the fulfillment of every fantasy her vivid imagination had conjured over the past weeks with this powerful man left Reb breathless. Her entire body quivered with anticipation.

Kincaid could feel Reb trembling beneath him and attributed her reaction to fear. He sought to calm her, much as he would any frightened thing, with gentle stroking and soft words, but soon he had forgotten why he was touching, aware only of the desperate need to possess this bewitching woman. His hands caressed her ribs and narrow waist. For a time that seemed endless, his fingertips teased the rosy nipples that he'd remembered so vividly from the day at the pond. He marveled at the rounded crests made opalescent by moonbeams when she strained upward toward the tingling stimulation. Kincaid skimmed his hand downward slowly along her silky skin until he reached Reb's inner thigh. She opened herself to him and his caresses moved steadily upward until he met the proof of her innocence. When Reb stiffened, Kincaid withdrew.

"Let me love you," Kincaid breathed in Reb's ear. He pulled back and searched her face, waiting for the answer he must have before he could continue.

Never before had Reb wanted so much to please another. Always before she had carefully run her life to satisfy her own need for independence and control of her destiny. Her eyes slowly closed in surrender to the smoldering passion she saw in Kincaid's darkening, smoky gray eyes, breaking the straining tether on Kincaid's barely leashed desire. Reb knew at last what it meant to give herself up totally to another human being. She shuddered in pleasure as Kincaid's lips pressed hers once possessively in acceptance of her gift, then roamed across the petal soft skin of her shoulders, lingering when they reached the racing pulse at her throat. His mouth and tongue suckled her sweet flesh, while his hands moved downward to grasp her soft buttocks.

Feeling her acquiescence in his arms, Kincaid once again coaxed Reb's thighs open to him and reestablished his intimate contact. He paused when she struggled in his arms, until he realized she was only urging him onward, arching her loins toward his body. He kept himself turned away from her so that she could not incite him to take her before he was sure she was ready for him. When he did bring her close, she bucked against him. Kincaid groaned his delight at the challenge of subduing Reb's writhing body and placing it where he needed it most. He fit his burgeoning need against the nest nature had planned as the place for his spilling seed to be nurtured and grow.

Reb's lips clung to Kincaid's, her mouth seeking more, needing more, the liquid fire inside her eager to join the burning flame with which Kincaid threatened to consume her. The pressure of Kincaid's shaft against her belly intensified what was by now an unsatiated craving. Her hands raced down Kincaid's spine to his strong, muscled flanks, achingly aware that once again cloth separated her from the fiery flesh she sought. As before, she made her dissatisfaction known to Kincaid and he remedied the problem, leaving Reb momentarily bereft while he stripped off pants and boots.

While she lay there naked and panting, the night breeze whirled mysteriously around her, cooling the lover's sweat that covered her from head to foot. Before she could descend from her euphoria to rational thought of how a man who thought her a lad could be providing such delicious torment, Kincaid mantled her chilled body with his own.

He sheathed himself immediately, pressing with certainty beyond the slight impediment to his passage that signaled Reb's virginity. Reb gasped at the surprising but not painful intrusion. Kincaid held his desire in abeyance to be certain her body had accommodated to his size, but knew from the ease of his slippery entry that she had been well prepared for this moment of becoming a woman. Slowly, ever so slowly and deliciously, he began to move in and out.

Reb was delighted with the sensation. She responded with small, throaty animal sounds of pleasure to the crescendo of heat growing within her as Kincaid's thrusting shaft impaled her again and again. Somewhere, just beyond her reach, lurked fulfillment of a need that she could not identify. She instinctively wrapped her legs around Kincaid's waist and grasped with inner muscles to hold him within, soaring ever higher toward the elusive satisfaction that stayed just beyond her reach.

Kincaid suddenly drove his tongue deep into Reb's honeyed mouth. His kiss smothered her anxious cry as she rushed to meet the final savage explosion of passion that threatened to overwhelm them both. Reb felt herself suspended amidst the beauty of moon and stars. She grabbed Kincaid's shoulders and held on tight, not wanting to fall, not wanting to ever come down among mortals again. Someone called to her.

"Lovely Rebel. My beautiful Rebel," a husky voice murmured.

Reb reached out to the voice with all her being and found the fulfillment she had been seeking. Shattering into a million sparkling pieces, she willingly fell from the heavens and drifted languorously back to earth.

Matt Hunter observed through narrowed eyes the angelic halo of pink dawn light encircling his sleeping daughter's head. Stretched out next to her, though wrapped in a separate blanket, an impressively large man slept, the same halo of pink crowning his raven black hair. Reb was obviously naked beneath the wool covering, for Matt could see her buckskins crumpled carelessly near the cold campfire. If he had been an impulsive man, the stranger lying in the dewy grass next to his child with his hand laid possessively across her hip would be dead now, but no one could accuse Matt Hunter of not being fair. It did not make sense that the man was fully dressed down to his boots if he and Reb had spent a night of passion together. He would listen to what this Yankee rogue had to say in defense of himself before he acted.

"Wake him up, Adam," Matt said quietly.

Adam could hear his father's controlled fury in the command, and regretted for the umpteenth time his mischievous decision to leave Reb alone with the stranger. Adam had not been overly concerned at first by Reb's delay in returning home, since Blue had suggested he would wait awhile before returning to his cabin. However, when she still had not shown up after the roundup was completed, Adam had finally admitted to his father his fear that the stranger could have harmed Reb or Blue or both. Matt had sent Garth to drive the cattle back out to pasture, and they had set out to find Reb. Adam vowed he would kill this stranger himself if Reb had suffered at the sleeping man's hands. He kicked Kincaid in the ribs with the toe of his boot a little harder than was truly necessary to wake him.

Neither Matt nor Adam was prepared for Kincaid's attack. Waked from a sound sleep, he reacted with instincts honed sharp by four years of war. He rolled to the left, sweeping Adam off his feet, and slammed his massive fist into Adam's jaw before he heard Matt cock his rifle.

"Hold it right there!" Matt shouted angrily.

"Daddy, stop!" Reb screamed.

All three men froze. Awakened by Kincaid's first movements, Reb stood clutching the blanket draped provocatively across one shoulder and down around her waist like a statue of some goddess. The top of one creamy breast was exposed and her arms and the greatest part of her long legs as well. Her hair fell across her large, frightened mahogany eyes, giving her a vulnerable, wanton look that each man reacted to from his own perspective as father, brother, lover. Both Kincaid and Adam scrambled to their feet. Kincaid froze again when Matt swung the gun up at him.

"No, Daddy!" Reb cried. She reached out to knock the barrel of the rifle down to the ground, causing the blanket to drop so that an entire breast was exposed. At Kincaid's audible intake of breath, Reb scooped up the rough cloth to cover herself, although the blanket did nothing to hide the rosy blush on her face and neck.

"Why aren't you dressed?" Matt questioned severely. One of the first things he'd taught Reb was the need for readiness on the trail. That meant denying oneself the luxury of removing clothing at night for greater comfort. The fact that Reb had disregarded this rule was significant and her state of undress in Kincaid's presence made Matt doubly suspicious.

It was only when her father spoke that Reb realized she was the only one unclothed in the group. Kincaid was fully dressed, as though last night had never happened. Could she have been having some fantastic dream? Her nakedness convinced her otherwise. Reb was not at all cowed by her father's stern face, and would have been tempted to respond less seriously except that she was afraid he would make Kincaid suffer if she did not come up with some plausible excuse for why she was sleeping nude, other than the truth.

"I ran into a polecat. My clothes smelled so rank I couldn't stand to sleep in them," she replied. Her breathlessness was the only sign of her anxiety.

Reb's reason for being unclothed made sense, yet she was known to stretch the facts. Matt would have believed the evidence before his eyes that the two had been intimate if he hadn't known Reb's strong aversion to physical relationships with men. Furthermore, if Kincaid had forced her, there would be no reason for her to say otherwise now. He looked from Reb's proudly defiant stance to Kincaid. The tall man's stony face gave no hint as to what he thought of Reb's explanation, but, to Matt's way of thinking, Kincaid's powerful frame, tensed for action, told a story fraught with guilty knowledge. That, added to the tales Adam had told about Reb's attraction to the stranger, left Matt unconvinced that the situation was as innocent as Reb had suggested.

Matt let his gaze wander up and down the side of Kincaid's Union army britches before he asked Reb sardonically, "It wasn't a yellow-striped polecat you tangled with by any chance, was it?" Out of the corner of his eye he thought he saw the edges of Kincaid's mouth tilt in the whisper of a smile, but it vanished when Matt shifted his position to confront the imposing man.

Reb found herself in a highly uncomfortable situation. What was her father trying to prove? She had half a mind to announce that she and Kincaid had spent the night in reckless passion, just to see what he would do. She was furious with her father for prying into something that was none of his business, and just as furious with Kincaid for taking the whole thing so lightly. She had not missed the telltale hint of a smirk on his face. Her father was a dangerous man when crossed, and Kincaid was foolish to underestimate him. Sometime, somehow Kincaid had obviously discovered she was female. The question was, when? And why hadn't he admitted he had found out her secret? She turned her gaze on Kincaid. How did he feel about her? Was he angry at her deceit? He had lied so cunningly about losing his memory. Had the endearments he had whispered last night also been a lie? Did he care for her, or had she merely been a convenient female body? This time his face did not give her any clues to what he was thinking. She wanted to ask him some pointed questions, but not here and now. That meant curtailing her father's persistent curiosity in a way that would get both her and Kincaid out of this gracefully. When all else fails, she thought, tell the truth—or as much of it as will get the job done.

"This man is Kincaid," she said, using her head to gesture. "I'm sure Adam told you he couldn't remember anything when we found him."

"Adam told me a lot of things about you and your stranger," Matt said insinuatingly.

Reb ignored the provoking statement, but was pleased to see Kincaid squirm. "When he regained his memory, it turned out he's supposed to meet some people at Seth Barker's station," she continued, undeterred. "I was taking him there. Last night a herd of buffalo stampeded and almost caught us. Brandy fell and I was thrown off. Kincaid saved my life."

Matt could picture the stampede, and was so thankful that someone had been there to help that whatever animosity he might have had for Kincaid was immediately dispelled in his relief that Reb had survived the unfortunate incident. He relaxed his hold on his rifle.

"Thanks," he said gruffly to Kincaid. "Where's Brandy now?" he asked Reb.

The pain of that loss was still too new. Reb's eyes misted and she reached up with her free hand to run her fingers agitatedly through her hair, sending it into even wilder disarray. She had to clear her throat before she could answer, and even then there was a strained quality to her voice that she could not control. "Brandy's dead. She broke her leg and I had to kill her. I went a little crazy afterward, I guess. Brandy was Blue's last gift to me when we left the mountains, and when I lost her it was one more part of that life torn from me against my will. If Kincaid hadn't been there, I . . ."

Up to this point Reb had been speaking to her father, but she missed the anguish that darkened Matt's eyes at her troubled admission, because she turned to Kincaid and continued ". . . but we escaped and then we . . . then I was so cold, so cold that . . . and Kincaid . . . my clothes . . ." Reb's voice had drifted off in a whisper. She felt for the first time the shame of having given herself to a man she hardly knew, who had no commitment to her and who had promised nothing. The stricken look on her face evidenced the even more frightening realization that if he came to her again she would not deny him.

Kincaid thought what he saw on Reb's face was fear that her father would deduce from what she had said that they had been lovers, so he made no move toward Reb that would deny her innocence. He knew that if she wanted the events between them disclosed she would do so herself. Therefore he stood immovable as a stone, even though he yearned to give her solace.

189

In fact, what Reb dearly wanted from Kincaid was some sign that he really cared for her, an acknowledgment of the love they had shared. His features betrayed so little emotion they could have been carved in granite. She was shrouded suddenly by the awful foreboding that he had used her body merely for his pleasure, and that she had been no more than a willing receptacle for his passion. Reb's quivering chin fell to her chest and a single tear made its way down her cheek.

Unconsciously, Kincaid took a step toward her, but was drawn up short when Matt angrily jerked his rifle up to aim it at Kincaid's chest. Matt's thankfulness to Kincaid had found its Waterloo in Reb's tears. Adam moved past Kincaid and took Reb in his arms to comfort her, at which point Reb began to sob in earnest. She had not seen that her father had stopped Kincaid, only that it was Adam who held her. Kincaid did not care! The proof lay in the fact that it was Adam's possessive hands on her bare shoulders, not Kincaid's, Adam's chest against which her face lay buried, Adam's strong arms in which she stood protected. She wanted Kincaid! She cried harder.

Kincaid's lips thinned to a grim line and his fists alternately clenched and unclenched in frustration at the turn of events that had not given him the opportunity to talk with Reb about what had happened between them before they were confronted by her father and brother. He should be the one holding her now, not Adam.

No doubt remained in Matt's mind about what had transpired here last night. His eyes hooded in hostile speculation. Kincaid had apparently already rewarded himself handsomely for Reb's rescue, but Matt could not very well kill him for that. Actually, he did not blame either Reb or Kincaid for what had happened. They were both young and had allowed their passions to rule when their minds should have. Nor did he blame Adam, although his son had set this chain of events in motion. No, the real culprit here was Blue. Adam was too inexperienced to know better but Blue, of all people, should have used sounder judgment than to leave Reb alone with a virile young man any longer than was absolutely necessary. Matt swore under his breath, then vowed silently that Blue would never get another chance to interfere with his family. He would make sure Reb didn't visit the mountain man again, even if it meant he had to tell her about Rachel and Blue.

It was just as well Kincaid didn't see the seething hatred on Matt's countenance, but his eyes had never left Reb, so that he was startled when Matt spoke.

"I'll take you wherever it is you're headed, stranger. Adam, you take Reb home."

Matt had expected some sort of rebuttal from Reb, but she continued to stare mutely at Kincaid until Adam picked up her buckskins and handed them to her. She turned her back on the men then to pull on her shirt, and used the blanket to shield herself from view, even though the soreness between her legs reminded her uncomfortably that there was no part of her Kincaid had not seen before. Of course Adam and her father did not know anything for sure, she thought, even though she had fueled their suspicion by putting on such a disgusting show of tears. Devastated though she was by Kincaid's unfeeling actions, she determined not to let him know how much he had hurt her.

A perplexed frown worried Kincaid's brow while he watched Reb dress. Could he let her walk out of his life now, perhaps never to see her again? She was a woman to satisfy a man's every desire, generous with her passion, capable in her caring. Any man would jump at a chance to call such a woman his own. Yet, Kincaid knew he was asking for trouble if he gave his heart to a woman of such boundless independence. He had made that mistake once before, and he always learned from his mistakes. Loving Reb, who spurned danger like some courageous lioness, meant certain heartbreak when some catastrophe befell her, as it would eventually in this wilderness. In this primitive environment she was prey to marauding Indians, to buffalo stampedes, to killing winter storms, even to violent death in childbirth. He wanted her desperately, but *not out here. Not where she wasn't safe.*

When Reb pulled up her buckskin pants, she saw that sometime during the night Kincaid had replaced the broken thong with a piece of rope. That little bit of thoughtfulness took away what little composure she had managed to regain and she could not keep the tears from filling her eyes. "Let's get out of here," she said bitterly to Adam, "before I make an even bigger fool of myself."

"Rebel."

Reb stiffened at Kincaid's call, but did not turn around.

"Sir, I'd like to speak to your daughter alone."

Surprisingly, Matt readily agreed and Kincaid suddenly found himself alone with Reb. Matt and Adam moved just beyond earshot but did not take their eyes off the pair left standing by the cold ashes of the campfire. Kincaid massaged the ache in his wounded thigh as though by doing so he could wipe away the horrible scars the war had left on his leg and on his life. Then he stepped up directly behind Reb, who stood wired taught as a bowstring. When he put his hand on her shoulder, she flinched. He did not try to touch her again.

"Rebel, come away with me," he coaxed softly.

Reb exhaled the deep breath she had been holding. Not "Reb, I love you." Not "Reb, marry me and have my children." Not nearly so much as he had offered Laurie. She could not keep the bitterness from pressing her mouth into a flat line and pinching her eyes at the corners. She closed her eyes and recalled the feel of Kincaid's strong, supple body pressed against her own, the demanding passion of his kiss, and she wanted to say yes anyway. Her pride would not allow it. She deserved a mate who loved and respected her. Desire alone was not enough on which to build a life. She turned to tell Kincaid no, and was brought up short by the unexpected love she saw blazing in his eyes.

"I . . . I . . ."

Encouraged by her hesitation, Kincaid grasped both Reb's hands in his to urgently plead his cause. "You'll love New York, I know you will. It's only because you've never been anywhere but the mountains that you think you won't like it. I'll make it right for you."

Reb's eyes widened in horror. Kincaid just couldn't be asking her to choose between a life with him and a life in the mountains! How could she make such a choice? After everything she'd told him, he must understand how she felt. "I can't!" she cried in panic. She jerked herself from Kincaid's grasp and hissed in fright, "Can't you take the wilderness away fast enough with your damned Yankee train? I'll never leave! Never!"

Frustrated by her intransigence, Kincaid bit out

sarcastically, "Hang on tight to the past, Rebel. You wouldn't want anything as rotten as change to worm its way into your life. But don't expect the world to stand still around you, because it won't! I just spent four years watching half this nation destroy the other half to force them to change their way of life. I won't force you, Rebel. You have to make up your mind that this is right for you. Change is coming, Rebel. You can choose to ride the crest of the tide or be crushed beneath it, but you can't ignore it. Come with me, Rebel!" He held out his open palm to her, asking her to share his life.

So violent was the battle between fear and desire within her breast that Reb began to quake. Kincaid made it sound so easy. Reb need only say yes and she would be absorbed into his regimented world. Yet, leaving the mountains had killed her mother. Reb was terrified, certain that trying to fit in where she did not belong, even for Kincaid, would just as surely kill her. The tug of war went on for breathless moments longer before Reb's fear won. "I can't!" she cried.

"You're a cold-hearted woman, Rebel Hunter!" Kincaid snarled in angry despair at her response. "I hope your precious mountains keep you warm at night, because it's damn certain no man ever will!"

Chapter Fifteen

EVEN IF SHE LIVED TO BE A VERY OLD WOMAN, REB thought, she would never forget that dawn conversation with Kincaid. Often over the past month since she and Kincaid had parted ways, the nightmarish scene had plagued her in her sleep. It replayed vividly in her dreams and, lately, whenever she got to the part where she had refused the handsome Yankee's offer she awoke with a jolt to find hot tears streaming down her face, her balled fists pounding the mattress and her teeth gritting so hard her jaw ached. Then she would roll her head from side to side in agonized frustration before she turned over to stifle her sobs in her soft feather pillow.

Reb's frustration resulted from her inability to curb the emotional free-for-all wreaking havoc with her life. Falling in love with Kincaid had meant putting chinks in the safe wall of rationality behind which she had contained her emotions. Now, she wanted to fill those gaping holes, to keep from feeling anything, but try as she might, the anger and regret and love and fear broke through in torrents.

Regret stood first and foremost among those cascading emotions, and Reb was not coping with it well at all. Within a week after their confrontation, she had decided to go after Kincaid, only to realize in dismay she had no idea how to find him. Then she remembered that he wanted to take her away from the life she knew, and panic rose up to grip her heart. The whole experience was too painful to discuss without crying, so Reb, ashamed to admit her weakness to her family, remained silent.

She spent all of her time outside because she found a balm in having the warm sun upon her face and the stiff breeze cooling the damp hairs on the back of her neck. She rose before dawn each day to ride out and check on the cattle and came back after dark, so tired that she sat in a daze at the supper table. Then she retired to her room, dreading the time that she would have to close her eyes and sleep, for then the real battle began. Unhampered by her conscious will, the love and regret fought the terror, leaving her ravaged when she awoke.

Lying awake in the dark on her narrow bed for fear that when she slept the agonizing decision would need to be made all over again, Reb admitted that saying no to Kincaid had been a terrible mistake. Too much had happened in too short a time and she had acted impulsively, rather than thinking it through. If only she had it all to do over again, she would find a way to convince Kincaid to stay here in the wilderness with her. She conceded the wishfulness of such thinking, but indulged herself because at least it kept the tears at bay for a little while.

In her own bed across the room, Reb's younger

sister Dillon waited for the sounds of distress that had become an almost nightly occurrence. Dillon had garnered enough information from her father and Adam to know that Reb and Kincaid had argued, and that neither was speaking to the other when it was all over. Matt had taken the angry man on to his destination, leaving Reb in Adam's care. Adam had managed to pry most of the story of what had happened at the cabin out of a distraught Reb on the way home. Once home, however, she had retreated inside herself as a turtle crawls inside its shell. Adam was convinced that Reb pined for her stranger, but he could come up with no suggestions as to what he and Dillon could do to help. Reb encouraged no sympathy, hiding her tears under cover of darkness. It was fortunate that Adam had gotten Reb to tell him Kincaid's full name, and that the Yankee worked for the Union Pacific railroad, because that information had put Dillon in a position to offer an end to her sister's misery.

"Reb, I know you're awake," Dillon said hesitantly. "I've been wanting to talk to you about an article in the *Rocky Mountain News* that a passenger on the stage left here about two weeks ago. I kept thinking you'd get over this Yankee, but you're worse now than ever."

Reb pushed her face into the pillow to prevent the sob that arose from getting past the lump in her throat.

"Garth keeps telling Daddy he should have killed Kincaid, but that's just his temper talking. Just yesterday Jesse asked Daddy why your eyes are always so red these days. Daddy told him you're spending too much time eating cattle dust. Daddy's against your ever seeing this Yankee fellow again, but Adam and I think that you and Kincaid should get a chance to work things out." Dillon paused in her chattering and noticed the room was deathly quiet. "Reb, are you listening?"

When Reb didn't answer, Dillon sat up to light the lantern on the small table near her bed. She kept the flame low so that it would not spill over through the small stepladder opening in the pine floor planking at the far end of the room that led down to Matt's bedroom. She didn't want her father waking up and asking what was wrong. The dim light revealed the embracing eaves of the loft bedroom. A window had been cut in the triangular wall at either end of the room to catch the breeze, but no wisp of air relieved the oppressive heat.

As she rose, Dillon automatically checked her appearance in the small, gilt-edged oval mirror that hung at the head of her bed. The sultry look in her green eyes and the kissable pout of her mouth were natural feminine assets that she did not have to practice, but Dillon had spent hours learning the coquettish tilt of her head that she used when she perused herself. Too bad Kincaid hadn't asked her to go away with him. From Adam's description of the man, she wouldn't have hesitated to give the proper answer. Poor Reb had said no once too often, and look where it had gotten her. Dillon nodded determinedly at herself in the mirror when she picked up the muffled sounds from Reb's side of the room. She was going to help Reb get her man if she had to hogtie Kincaid herself to do it!

Dillon marched to the foot of her bed and rummaged through the cedar hope chest that was full of the quilts, tablecloths and embroidered pillowcases she had made, looking forward to the day when she would marry. At the very bottom she found the folded newspaper article she had carefully hidden there. She flounced over and pulled her thin, flowered, cotton nightgown up to her thighs before she sat down cross-legged on the foot of Reb's bed. She leaned back until her elbows rested on Reb's hope chest. The contents of that cedar box testified to how unprepared Reb was for the role of wife, Dillon thought. Instead of the necessities of a frontier home, it contained such memorabilia as the fur of the first beaver Reb had trapped, some stones with fish fossils in them, a switch of hair from Brandy's tail, a blue-and-white beaded Indian parfleche the Old One had made to hold the berries Reb collected on the trail, and a copy of Shakespeare's *The Taming of the Shrew* that their mother had given Reb for her sixteenth birthday. No wonder Reb had given Kincaid the wrong answer!

"I know you're listening, so don't say anything until I'm through," Dillon announced to Reb in a conspiratorial whisper. "How would you like another chance to talk to Kincaid?"

Dillon had no way of knowing she'd caught Reb at a propitiously receptive moment. Reb sat bolt upright, but was cut off before she could answer when Dillon continued, "There's going to be a railroad meeting in Denver City on the Fourth of July. The *Rocky Mountain News* says that officials of the Union Pacific will be meeting with Denver City merchants to discuss the proposed route for the railroad west of Nebraska. It specifically mentions that a Mr. Christopher Kincaid, who's a major stockholder of the railroad by the way, will be there. Here's the part I thought might interest you. The article says, and I quote, 'Mr.

Kincaid is one of the official hosts for a grand ball being sponsored by the railroad at the Broadwell House at 16th and Larimer Streets beginning at eight o'clock on the evening of July Fourth. All of Denver is invited to the ball, which will culminate with a special fireworks display at midnight in front of the hotel.' Well, would you like to go to the ball?"

Before Reb could get a word in edgewise, Dillon added, "If you say no, I will personally smother you with your own feather pillow!"

"Yes, yes, yes!" Reb cried, grabbing Dillon and hugging her. "I do want to see Kincaid and talk to him! But I don't see how I can dance with him at the ball," she added breathlessly.

"Why not?" Dillon thought perhaps Kincaid's limp was worse than she had been led to believe.

"Because I haven't anything to wear!"

"You sound like Cinderella," Dillon giggled in relieved satisfaction. "If that's the only thing stopping you, let me help. I have always wanted to play the fairy godmother, and this looks like the best chance I'll ever get. I have some material that ought to be perfect for a new gown." Dillon hopped off Reb's bed, heading for her own hope chest. Reaching within, Dillon pulled out a length of crimson satin.

Reb gasped at the beauty of the vibrant red cloth. "Where did you ever get anything so magnificent, Dillon?"

"I found it in Mama's things after she died. I know I should have told you about it, but you never seemed very interested in this sort of thing," she said. She laid the satin in Reb's outstretched hands.

Dillon was right, of course. Before Reb had met Kincaid, she couldn't have cared less how she looked in a dress made of satin. The feel of the satin in her hands was wonderfully sensual. "Shall we see how it looks?" Reb suggested somewhat shyly.

When the two girls had stripped Reb's nightgown away and draped her in folds of the cool satin, Dillon pulled Reb over to stand in front of the mirror.

"Look at you. You're gorgeous!" Dillon admitted in surprise.

Reb could hardly believe what she saw in the mirror. The crimson satin heightened the beauty of her opalescent skin and brought out the sparkle in her mahogany eyes. "It is amazing, isn't it?" she questioned Dillon uncertainly.

"Your hair is long enough now for a curling iron to do some good, and a little kohl would emphasize your eyes. We'll use some powder to cover your freckles and, of course, lip rouge."

"I can't believe this is happening," Reb said in a voice that carried her disbelief. "How did you know I wanted to see Kincaid again?"

"When you nearly snapped my head off after I called him a 'dirty bluebelly pig,' I got the hint," Dillon replied, grinning. Neither girl mentioned the nightly tears that had been a dead giveaway, but both girls thought of them. Dillon's features sobered. "Reb, do you think he might have changed his mind about whatever he said that's been making you cry?"

Having been given a second chance, Reb was determined to work things out with Kincaid rationally. "If he hasn't changed his mind, he will," she said quietly.

Dillon sighed. Please, God, let Reb be successful. It wouldn't be easy for her to hogtie someone as big as Kincaid was reported to be, she thought wryly.

"Now we just have to figure out how to get you from here to there, which won't be easy considering the way Daddy feels about letting you anywhere near Kincaid," Dillon warned. "Adam said he'd be willing to help, if we can just come up with a good idea."

Eventually, it was Adam who came up with the plan to convince their father that what Reb needed to bring her back to her old self was a trip somewhere away from the mountains. Dillon refused to be left out, so it was agreed that Adam suggest that he, Reb and Dillon go to Denver City to pick up a hay rake Matt needed. Matt received Adam's suggestion enthusiastically. In fact, he thought it so good an idea that he insisted on coming along himself to observe its success. Garth and Jesse would stay with the Old One to care for the ranch and maintain the duties of the stage station.

Although Matt could never have admitted it to Reb, he was concerned by the unhappiness in his eldest daughter's eyes. It reminded him of a similar look he had seen in Rachel's eyes, but ignored until it was too late. Matt had surmised that it had been more than a moment's passion that bound Reb and Kincaid. He wasn't sure which of the two had denied loving the other, but he knew Reb had taken their separation hard. If Adam thought this trip would heal Reb's wounds, he was more than willing to give it a try. Matt was pleasantly surprised by Reb's acquiescence to the journey, and he proved an easy target for his children's clever manipulation.

Adam and Matt had stayed at the Broadwell House in the past, so it wasn't difficult to get Matt's concurrence to stay there again. Reb and Dillon pushed and prodded their father as much as they dared without making it seem as though they had a reason to hurry. He kept delaying, though, until Adam decided it made more sense to encourage him to attend the

Fourth of July fireworks display, so they would be sure to arrive in Denver City on time. However, because Dillon had waited so long before suggesting the trip to Reb, the foursome did not arrive in Denver City until almost noon on the Fourth of July.

The city had changed some since Matt and Adam had last seen it, but everything was new to Reb and Dillon. Reb was agog at the rows and rows of buildings they passed, many more than she had expected to find. Larimer Street was wide, with hard-packed dirt streets lined with wooden sidewalks on either side. They had to maneuver their wagon among the oxcarts, people on horseback, and coaches that crowded the streets. All of the buildings on the block had been rebuilt in brick after the fire that had destroyed the city in April two years ago. Then, just last May, the Cherry Creek that ran through the city had flooded its banks and made it necessary to restore again.

Among the many structures they passed on Larimer Street, while wending their way toward the hotel, were the Emporium of Fashion, Marx's Bakery, Peabody's Dry Goods and Drug Store, A.E. Cresswell, Photographer, the First Methodist Church and the noisy construction on the Central National Bank. Reb decided that when she and Kincaid had reconciled their differences they would visit the photographer straight-away. She wanted to have a remembrance of her first trip to Denver City.

The red, white and blue pennants hanging across the street evidenced that the Fourth of July celebration was in full swing, and Matt was delighted to discover from numerous posters they passed that there was a horse race scheduled in just an hour or so at the edge of the city. Several dandified gentlemen in fawn trousers and broadcloth coats, sporting low-crowned, round-brimmed felt hats, leaned against the white painted wooden posts that held up the balcony porch of the Broadwell House. Older men, less fashionably dressed in dark trousers and plain white shirts topped by variously hued vests, took their ease in wooden chairs that lined the porch next to the windows. According to the painted sign in the large picture window, the massive two-story Broadwell House, the one wooden structure on the whole street, provided the best hotel accommodations in Denver City.

Reb jumped down from the wagon, while Adam dismounted from his chestnut horse, Ricochet, and helped Dillon down. Reb had worn her buckskins for the trip, insisting that it made no sense to put on a dress to impress the jack rabbits and deer. She could have passed for a young man, and apparently did, for it was not until Dillon stepped up onto the porch in her lace-trimmed, yellow cotton day dress, with her matching parasol perched daintily over her shoulder, that the male whistles of appreciation for feminine face and form began. Seeing the doffed hats and courtly bows for her sister brought a flush to Reb's face. Would she ever learn what it meant to be a woman at all times? How did she expect to make a good wife for Kincaid if she couldn't even manage to wear the proper clothing for the occasion?

Matt and Adam hurried the two girls into the spacious lobby of the hotel where they stood gaping at the appointments in admiration. While Matt registered for two rooms, Reb and Dillon perused the crystal chandelier and examined the gold brocade-covered couches set along the wall. They could hear the tinkling piano and the clink of beer and whiskey glasses from the saloon, that was separated from the lobby by a doorway set with a pair of short, slatted, wooden swinging doors. There was a steady stream of male customers moving through the lobby to the bar.

As Matt signed the register, he spoke over his shoulder. "It appears we made it here in plenty of time for the Independence Day celebration. I think I'd like to take in that race at one, then go see if I can find a hay rake. How about the rest of you?"

The bespectacled clerk handed a key to Matt and one to Reb after he checked the register. "That'll be the last two rooms upstairs on the left at the end of the hall," the diminutive, gray-haired man said.

Adam and Dillon exchanged surreptitious glances. Dillon expected to spend the entire day getting Reb bathed and gussied up to meet with Kincaid. They had prearranged for Adam to keep Matt occupied so there would be no chance of his last-minute interference.

"Reb and I want to freshen up and then go look around the stores," Dillon replied.

"I'd like to go with you, Dad," Adam offered. "Reb and Dillon will be fine on their own. We can all meet here at midnight to watch the fireworks I told you about." Adam turned to Dillon, who quickly agreed.

"Reb and I will probably have dinner at the hotel restaurant, so you two just enjoy yourselves and don't worry about us," Dillon said. Adam had purposely not told his father about the ball, which made Dillon's plans for the evening sound believable.

"Enjoy yourselves then, and Adam and I will see you here at midnight," he confirmed. When Matt turned away from the registration desk, he faced a hulking brute dressed in a filthy green-and-yellow plaid shirt and fringed buckskin trousers. A luxurious raccoon cap topped the trapper's untrimmed, greasy red hair. An enormously long red beard and shaggy mustache covered his face and chin so completely that the only skin visible was a bulbous nose and two wide-set light blue eyes framed by almost white eyelashes. Gargantuan arms circled Matt's chest and the redheaded behemoth began to squeeze.

Matt bent his arms at the elbows to try to get his hands up to save his ribs, but it quickly became evident there was nothing to prevent the redheaded man from cracking Matt like a hazelnut.

At first, Reb thought the aggressive man must be an old friend of her father's, since Matt had not made a sound to ask for help. Then she began to fear that her father's stubborn pride kept him from seeking assistance. Adam seemed unperturbed and, while Dillon shared Reb's agitation, she seemed uninclined to act.

In the next moment, Reb had pulled her bowie and held it at the giant's ribs near his heart.

"Be this yer whelp, Matthew?" the man said calmly.

"Uh," Matt grunted, having no air left to say more.

"Tell 'em I only crush ants 'n' spiders," the burly redhead chortled. As he released Matt, the mountain man whipped an arm down, intending to disarm Reb. Instead, he found an eight-inch slit in his arm, and Reb standing next to her father facing him, knife poised for action.

Reb was astonished when, instead of attacking her, the bear of a man laughed out loud. "Be ye Garth?" he asked Reb.

"This is my *daughter*, Reb," Matt said, grinning. "Garth's at home minding the ranch with his younger brother Jesse."

"Well, I'll be a three-legged buffalo," the man guffawed. The giant pulled the dingy yellow kerchief from around his neck and wrapped it around the cut on his arm. "I'll take her! She'd make a grrreat lassie to have 'rrround in them mountains," he bellowed, rolling his r's with Irish gusto.

Reb reared back when a ham-fisted paw reached out for her.

"Hang on, Breck. This isn't some Sioux squaw you can buy," Matt admonished. "I repeat, this is my daughter, Rebecca."

By now, the piano in the bar had stopped playing and a growing crowd of men and women were gawking at Reb, waiting to see the end of the scene unfolding before them. It was only too apparent to Reb now that Matt knew this unsavory character, and she had foolishly interfered where she didn't belong. More than anything else, Reb was concerned that word of this awful incident would get back to Kincaid. She searched the room for a way out.

At this point, Dillon recognized Reb's plight and generously provided the diversion that allowed Reb to escape, taking the stairs two at a time on her way up to their room.

"Daddy," asked Dillon, "could this possibly be *the* Breck O'Hanlan that saved your life when he killed a grizzly bear with his Green River skinning knife back in '46?"

A murmur ran through the crowd as the famous mountain man acknowledged he was the same. Then, O'Hanlan turned to find the image of Rachel. He stood speechless for a moment gazing at her before he turned back to Matt. When Matt nodded, the repulsively hirsute man walked up to Dillon and worshipfully lifted a copper curl. He watched, mesmerized, as it drifted silkily through his fingertips. Dillon stood motionless, letting the blue-eyed man drink his fill.

"She be real purty, Matthew. Just like Rachel."

"I'd like you to meet my other daughter, Dillon," Matt said. "Standing next to her is my son, Adam."

"Ye look like yer pa, boy."

"Thank you, sir," Adam replied. He was awed by the sight of Breck O'Hanlan because he and his brothers and sisters had grown up with bedtime stories of the legendary mountain man. Somehow there was nothing insulting about having a legend call you boy.

Over the years O'Hanlan had developed his Irish brogue to enhance his mountain mystique, but Matt had known him well when he was a Kentucky farm boy whose Irish parents died of cholera on the way to Oregon. Breck had landed in the mountains where Matt had befriended him. There he'd stayed. Matt had not seen O'Hanlan since just after Garth was born. Although no older than thirty-eight, O'Hanlan had become well-known for his exploits by the age of twenty-five. Breck O'Hanlan was a gambling man. He bet on everything and anything and almost always won. If O'Hanlan bet he could skin a beaver in two minutes flat, then he'd figured out a way somehow to do it. No one could have been more surprised than Matt to find him here in Denver City, until he remembered about the horse race.

"Adam and I are planning to take in the nag race at one o'clock. Care to join us?" Matt asked.

"Need ye ask?" O'Hanlan replied with a grin that showed only in his twinkling eyes. "I heard tell some of these city fellers might have a job fer me to do fer them in the mountains, so I've made up me mind to wager a mite of those earnin's on the outcome of the race. We might's well catch up on old times while I double me money. Boy, did yer pa ever tell ye 'bout the night we was charged by a white buffalo?''

The three men were so engrossed in each other that Dillon was left standing, forgotten, as Rachel also must have been once upon a time. Dillon was not alone long, however, for the men standing at the swinging doors of the saloon recognized beauty when they saw it, and without her male protectors, she seemed like fair game.

The boldest of the bunch quickly made his way forward. His hair was parted in the middle and slicked down to either side with some kind of perfumed oil that wrinkled Dillon's sensitive nose even at a distance. His chocolate brown suit was too wide for his narrow shoulders and his orange checked shirt pulled apart over the rotund belly that preceded him as he advanced across the room. An untrimmed mustache drooped onto crooked, tobacco-stained teeth as the self-important man greeted Dillon with an ingratiating smile.

"Clemens Fremont, at your service, Miss Dillon." The man bowed smoothly, then stood with palm outstretched, waiting for Dillon to supply her hand.

"Excuse me, please, Mr. Fremont," Dillon said primly. "I believe my sister is waiting for me." As she turned toward the stairs, pudgy fingers gripped her arm and turned her around.

"Not so fast, young lady. You haven't allowed me to greet you properly." Fremont held onto Dillon's arm, while he tried to bring her hand up to his lips. Dillon's struggle to free herself was greeted by jeers from the remaining men standing bunched at the saloon door and spilling into the room.

"Hey, Clem," one shouted, "why don't you give her a real big-city welcome right on the mouth!"

"That's good advice Frank give ya', Clem," another echoed.

The ladies of the night employed by the saloon remained aloof, waiting disdainfully to see how the country girl would handle herself.

The hotel clerk pushed his spectacles up his nose agitatedly before he spoke from behind his polished cherry wood counter. "Mr. Fremont, the lady would like to be allowed to proceed to her room."

Fremont hardly gave the timid man a glance. "Back off, Otto. The lady can speak for herself."

"I certainly can. I would appreciate it, sir, if you would kindly let go of my arm," Dillon said firmly.

Her statement was greeted by encouraging shouts from the onlookers. "I think I'll take Frank's advice, instead," Fremont said, leering down into Dillon's face. Over Dillon's shoulder he caught sight of a pearl-studded white shirt and black frock coat, and looked up to see who had had the temerity to intrude on his fun.

Dillon had her sharp-tipped parasol poised and ready to strike where it would do the most good (on his instep, of course), when the disgusting man slightly released his hold.

"I do not believe the young lady desires the pleasure of your company."

The commanding baritone sent shivers down Dillon's spine. It also obviously had an unsettling effect on Clemens Fremont, for the fat man stepped back so hastily that Dillon lost her balance and would have fallen except for the firm hands that caught her around the waist from behind. She could feel the muscled wall of a chest against her back, but was far too amused by the pasty white face of Clemens Fremont to do more than smile in kittenish smugness at his cowardly retreat.

She waited a moment more, expecting the firm hands to release her, but they did not. As the men made way for Fremont, Dillon could see her reflection in the huge mirror that filled the wall on the opposite side of the room. She stared into the mirror at the striking man who was studying her features so carefully in the same glass. He turned Dillon in his arms so she found herself looking up into a pair of sad gray eyes.

Suddenly, Dillon knew the identity of the raven-haired gallant who had rescued her.

Chapter Sixteen

KINCAID COULD NOT HELP SEEING THE IRONY OF THE situation. He had lost the wife he wanted and found the wife he'd dreamed up in his imagination. In his arms stood the very image of the flawless woman he had teased Reb that he would marry, right down to the copper curls, green eyes and full bosom.

He had spent the past month telling himself he could live his life without Reb, but he hadn't been very successful getting the thought of her out of his mind. This encounter was a perfect example. He should be calculating how to entice this young lady into his bed, not remembering that she epitomized a woman with whom he had taunted Reb.

Then a grin broke out on Kincaid's face. He did have one thing to thank Reb for. He no longer reacted to women as a celibate. His thumbs rested just under this wonder's ample breasts and his body had responded with astonishing speed to that simple stimulation. Oh, Reb, where are you when I need you, Kincaid thought. Although the physical evidence of desire was there, the woman he really wanted to bury himself in had short black hair and freckles.

Dillon could see why Reb had gone crazy. This man had to be Kincaid. There couldn't be two men this good-looking in the territory. Imagine letting him get away! What on earth had prompted the silly grin on his face, she wondered. She had just opened her mouth to ask what was so funny when Kincaid dropped his hands as though he'd been holding a hot potato.

"Excuse me, miss. I'm late for a meeting, but can I escort you somewhere?"

"I'm registered here at the hotel. If you'll just walk me as far as the stairs, I'm sure I'll be fine." Dillon linked her arm in Kincaid's and walked the few steps to the winding staircase that led to the second floor. She gave Kincaid her most inviting smile and tilted her head so that she looked upward through feathery eyelashes as she had practiced hour after endless hour in the mirror at home. Kincaid seemed impervious to her charms. In fact, he seemed downright anxious to be rid of her. Dillon had to exert some effort not to be miffed, but then decided the least she could do was make sure for Reb that he planned to attend the ball.

"Are you going to the dance tonight?" she asked, glancing up through demurely lowered eyelashes as she ascended the first step.

"I hadn't planned to, no," Kincaid responded. His father, who was here to speak to the Denver City businessmen, might owe attendance at the ball to the railroad, but he did not. He was here only to make his report.

"Oh." Dillon let her disappointment show. "I thought you . . ." Dillon bit her tongue. She had almost let it slip that she knew Kincaid was a railroad official and, as a sponsor of the ball, had supposed he would attend. It was important to Reb that he be there, so Dillon tried a different tack. "Is there any chance you might change your mind? You see, I have a friend that I think you might like to meet."

Kincaid was intrigued. He had seen enough coquettish flirting to recognize the signs, yet now the girl professed to want him to attend the dance to meet a friend.

"A friend?" he questioned, his eyebrow cocked in tolerant amusement.

"Yes, well, you see her mother died recently and she's been very sad lately, and it seemed to me that seeing you might cheer her up."

"Why is that?" Kincaid asked.

Dillon gulped, crossed her fingers behind her back and launched into a whopper. What else could a fifteen-year-old fairy godmother do if the prince wasn't going to cooperate and come to the ball?

"Right after her mother died, her fiancé was wounded in the war. He looked a lot like you."

Kincaid let his disbelief out in a small smile.

"Except he was shorter. And had lighter hair. And of course his eyes were hazel." Dillon rushed on in spite of Kincaid's skeptical features. "His leg was so devastated that it never healed and he finally died. If you could just take pity on her and be there, I know it would help her to overcome her grief." Dillon really thought she'd overdone it when Kincaid frowned, but she waited patiently while the man who could make her sister happy pondered her fantastic story.

It was the mention of the leg wound that made up Kincaid's mind. Here was one more soul robbed by the war that had so unrelentingly killed so many young men. Kincaid felt a kinship for the girl, whoever she was. Her story was not unlike his own, only he'd lost a wife, not a fiancée. If a simple dance or two would cheer her, why not?

"I think I could manage a waltz," he finally said. "I'll be there at nine tonight. See you then."

Dillon heaved a great sigh of relief, and then had to suppress a whoop of excitement. Wait until Reb hears this, her thoughts shouted. She tucked her parasol under her arm and gathered her skirt in her hands in great bunches to race up the stairs, but was stopped by that familiar baritone voice.

"What's her name?" Kincaid called to Dillon from halfway across the room.

"Rebecca," she replied with a grin. Then Dillon turned and ran up the stairs before he could ask more.

Kincaid briskly crossed the lobby, heading for the private dining room at the back of the hotel restaurant. When he arrived, his father greeted him at the door. Christopher Lyle Kincaid stood several inches shorter than the son he had named after himself, but was no less imposing. The full head of snow-white hair testified to his patriarchal role, but there was nothing old about the lean, hard body inside the dark gray, vested suit. Lyle Kincaid was all business, his rigid stance a clear spokesman for his unyielding nature.

"I'm glad you could make it, son. We've been waiting for you." There was just a trace of irritation in his father's voice. Lyle Kincaid believed in punctuality.

Kincaid turned to the assembly gathered at the

table. He greeted Grenville Dodge with a quick, firm handshake, then eyed the twenty or so Denver businessmen who had assembled to hear his report. They were not going to like what he had to say.

"Gentlemen." He nodded to them as a group. "Shall we eat first?" he inquired of his father.

"Good idea. You may serve now, Mr. Potts," Lyle Kincaid said to the obsequious bald-headed waiter.

They dined on oxtail soup, followed by a thick steak and fried potatoes, and finished up with apple pie for dessert. Strong black coffee accompanied the meal, since Lyle Kincaid believed liquor and business didn't mix. When a second cup of coffee had been poured, and the cigars that Lyle had so graciously provided to his guests had been lit, the entrepreneur gestured to his scion to begin.

"Gentlemen, let's get down to business. We know you want the Union Pacific to run its tracks far enough south to be able to service Denver. However, as much as we would like to accommodate your needs, it is not practical to do so. The grades through the mountains down here are too steep in an east-west direction for the construction to be done without a great deal more time and expense than is justified. There are more gentle grades running east-west about a hundred miles north of here, just across the base of the Laramie Mountains, and that's where I would recommend laying the tracks."

Angry shouts of disagreement came from every direction. All Kincaid could hear in his mind were Reb's pleas to spare her wilderness. It was some time before Kincaid had answered all the arguments against bypassing Denver City, and it was a disgruntled group of merchants who left the room in grumbling pairs and griping trios. Finally, only Kincaid's father and Grenville Dodge remained at the large table.

Lyle Kincaid puffed steadily on his cigar while he evaluated the success of the luncheon. "Do you think they'll go crying to the Republicans in Washington?" he asked Dodge.

"I suspect so, but we've done our homework, lobbied hard. We should have the vote to hold them off. At any rate, I'll start them talking about a spur from Denver directly north to connect with the Union Pacific, and that ought to hold off the worst of the complainers until we finish what we have to do."

Kincaid had wondered how the nondescript Dodge, with his plain features and neatly trimmed, sandy-colored muttonchop whiskers, had worked his way so far up in the army. Now, the general's canny political maneuvering made the answer to that question clear. Dodge convinced Kincaid of his astuteness when he asked, "What do you plan to do about the Sioux, Lyle? You know they've been cheated by the Indian agents and had so many treaties broken that you can expect real problems with your track gangs unless something is done."

"Do you have any suggestions?"

"I allowed General Connor to maintain a campaign against the Sioux at the Powder River this past month, but he has been something less than gloriously successful. I have never accepted the idea anyway that annihilating the problem is a viable solution. That leaves the option of another treaty. Unfortunately, I don't believe the Indians will be willing to listen."

"I think I know someone who may be able to help," Kincaid offered. "When I was recuperating in the mountains, I met a trapper who's a good friend of the chief of the Brulés. Perhaps he could be persuaded to speak on our behalf."

"That sounds like the best bet we have. Are you volunteering to be our emissary to him?" Dodge probed.

"I'd certainly be willing to give it a try." Kincaid could barely contain his enthusiasm for the trip. Blue would know how to convince Reb that she should come back east with him. She might even be there visiting when he arrived.

Their discussion was interrupted when a plate clattered against a cup. "I'll be finished here in a minute. Just clearing the table." The portly waiter had entered through the dark green velour curtains at the far end of the room sometime during their conversation.

"Thank you, Mr. Potts, but you can do that later," Lyle said sharply.

"Certainly, sir. Anything else I can do for you?"

"No, thank you." Lyle Kincaid did not believe in servants listening in on business conversations.

When the waiter had gone, Dodge stood and paced from one end of the long table to the other. "You can be sure the Denver businessmen will know we're concerned about the Indians."

"They can't make the savages any more savage than they already are," Lyle said philosophically.

"They can supply them with guns and bullets. You give them the ammunition, and those Sioux can lift so much hair we won't be able to get a track gang to go near there."

"The Indians won't raise hell if we can promise them enough food and supplies that they don't have to steal to live," Kincaid suggested. "I think a treaty with the Sioux is worth a try."

"I have to agree with you," Dodge said. "Besides, we won't have to placate them long. Once the tracks are laid, there isn't much those heathens can do to stop the natural progress of things."

Kincaid felt a surge of irritation at Dodge's attitude. Then he realized he was seeing the situation with a new awareness, for which Reb was responsible. He recalled her anger at the Yankees who did what they pleased, and the locals be damned. It made him even more determined to pursue the mission. Perhaps he and Blue together could find a way to make progress a little less painful for everyone involved.

"Son, are you sure you're well enough to make this journey? If not, speak up. This mission is too important to jeopardize because of one man's ill health." Lyle Kincaid did not believe in sentimentality.

Kincaid's mother had already told him of how his father had aged ten years when the false news of his death had come, so Kincaid wasn't fooled by the seeming callousness of his father's speech. "I'll be fine, Father," he said reassuringly. "I'd like to leave right away. We'll be expected to provide gifts as a sign of our good faith with the Sioux. Would you make the necessary arrangements, General Dodge, so I can pick up what I need from Miller's Dry Goods here in Denver?"

"I'll be glad to so long as Lyle will open his purse strings for the supplies," Dodge laughed.

"I knew I could count on you to come to the meat of the matter," Lyle responded with a chuckle. "What about the ball tonight, son? A lot of pretty young belles will be there." The last scene in their parlor sitting room before Kincaid had come west flashed across Lyle's mind, and he chastised himself for even mentioning the dance. His son had made it very clear to both his parents that he wanted nothing to do with women after the death of his wife. To his amazement, a sad smile appeared on Kincaid's face.

"As a matter of fact, I think I might indulge in just one waltz."

Reb stood alone next to the wall of the brightly lit ballroom of the hotel while the orchestra played waltz after waltz. Nearby, Dillon entertained an entourage of eligible men who battled to sign her dance card and to bring her a cup of punch between dances.

Kincaid wasn't coming, Reb decided. It was well past the nine o'clock time that he had told Dillon he would attend. In fact, it was nearly ten. Reb had watched the doorway eagerly for an hour, and had rebuffed any male attention so soundly that the young bucks now warned each other away from the "thorny red rose." She felt more like a florid wallflower.

For the past fifteen minutes she had observed a nearby group of gentlemen arguing and she occasionally caught enticing snatches of their discussion. Words like "railroad" and "mountains" spoken in conjunction lured her closer and closer until she stood at the edge of their party.

"There's no mistake, gentlemen," a dignified older man with flinty gray eyes topped by bushy white brows repeated to the assembled group. "The best route for the railroad, the route we will take, is through the Laramie Mountains."

"What if we don't want your railroad in our mountains," Reb startled him and herself by saying.

The gathering parted to locate the source of the husky voice. There was considerable surprise when it turned out to be a poised, elegantly dressed young woman. Dillon had done her job well. Reb's crimson gown revealed soft shoulders and the tops of softly rounded breasts, then tapered to a point in the front at Reb's narrow waist before belling in luxurious folds of ruby satin. Reb's extraordinary intervention in what was so obviously a male conversation impressed the men as much as her loveliness.

"Who's going to prevent us?" Lyle Kincaid challenged, somewhat perturbed that a female, and quite an attractive one at that, would dare to question what he had just convinced the Denver City merchants was an accomplished fact.

"People like me who respect the wilderness the way it is. You have no right to impose your Iron Horse where it isn't wanted!"

"Bravo, miss! That's telling him! You should listen, Father, and believe me when I tell you that there are differences of opinion about the advantages of a railroad."

Reb recognized the timbre of the well-known voice behind her. She watched in bewilderment as a pleasant woman with salt and pepper hair and deep smile lines at the corners of her eyes looped her arm in that of the distinguished man Kincaid had addressed as Father.

"Lyle," she chided, "stop talking business and give these ladies and gentlemen an opportunity to dance."

"Wonderful idea, Mother." Kincaid leaned in to speak softly in Reb's ear. "Shall we?"

Kincaid had been delayed by the need to make additional arrangements for his departure for Blue's cabin the following morning. When he had finally arrived at the ball, he had found the girl he had talked with earlier in the day surrounded by her admirers with no sign of a "friend" anywhere near. Disgusted with himself for being so gullible, Kincaid was about to leave when he noticed the crowd around his father part for a rather tall, raven-haired young woman in crimson satin to confront the older man. There was something vaguely familiar about the woman's proud stance. Kincaid guessed from the increasing aggravation on his father's face that the woman must be disagreeing with him. That he didn't want to miss. Not many people willingly crossed Lyle Kincaid.

Kincaid had surprised himself when he asked the woman to dance, but there was something about the single ebony curl that fell down her neck just an inch or two on the left side that awakened a memory. The woman smelled of roses, and he closed his eyes to absorb the essence at the same time he laid his hand on her smooth shoulder to turn her around. The woman trembled under his fingertips.

Kincaid opened his eyes to a vision. Reb's mahogany eyes, rimmed by thickened black lashes, were cautious. Her sharp white teeth caught her full, rosy red bottom lip in anticipation of Kincaid's reaction. Her raven locks had been curled in soft ringlets that framed her face, one curl falling tantalizingly over her peach-skinned shoulder. He noted that she had carefully concealed her boyish freckles, but smiled in pure pleasure at the enchanting blush that the powder could not obscure. The gown was cut low enough in front for the gentle swells of flesh to titillate Kincaid's imagination. He put one hand firmly on the cool satin that hugged her narrow waist and took her white-gloved palm in his other hand.

"Dance with me."

The mellow richness of the voice flowed over Reb, as welcome as honey on a flapjack. She obeyed willingly, stepping into his arms until the satin-covered tips of her breasts dipped into the silk ruffles of his white evening shirt. They circled the dance floor gracefully, both floating in a heaven of their own. Neither one spoke, unwilling to let reality intrude on the magic of the moment. They did not hear the music stop, nor did they hear it start again, so lost were they in each other.

Kincaid knew Reb must have changed her mind and sought him out. He felt humbled by the sacrifice she was willing to make for him and blessed by the beauty that she offered to him. He danced her through the open French doors to the shadowed balcony, coming to a stop only when they had reached the far end, away from the music and the light streaming through the doors. He brought the gloved hand he held up to his lips, then set it upon his shoulder so that Reb's arms encircled him. He reached with one hand to tip her chin while the other grasped her waist possessively. He used his thumb to brush away the powder on her cheekbones, until he could see a hint of the freckles he had missed so much.

"Oh, Rebel," he breathed. His lips claimed hers gently, asking forgiveness. When her lips parted in response, he eagerly pulled her close. The kiss deepened and Kincaid's hands roved along Reb's satin-clad form. He hardly believed she was real and that he was holding her in his arms, so great was his surprise at finding her in Denver. Reb's satin skirt was gathered so full that it provided a substantial barrier to their touch, and Kincaid's frustration mounted when he was unable to bring her as close as his awakening manhood demanded. Admitting that the dress stood in the way of satisfaction, Kincaid broke the kiss and stepped back to try to draw rein on his rampaging senses.

Reb held on by a thread to the voice of reason that

Kincaid's kiss had direly threatened. "Kincaid, I want to talk to you," she managed to say. "Is there somewhere we can be alone?"

"Come with me." He put his arm around her waist to lead her back to the ballroom.

Reb's naiveté kept her from realizing the devastating effect she had on Kincaid. She was excited, but nowhere near the animalistic state in which Kincaid found himself. She was glad he was willing to discuss their relationship and followed him with alacrity.

As the bright lights lit their faces, Kincaid stopped. "Shall we dance our way back through the businessmen?"

Reb laughed. "I should let Dillon know I'm leaving," she said, "or she'll worry."

"Your sister Dillon is here?"

"You spoke to her just this afternoon. Don't you remember? The girl with a 'friend.' I'm Rebecca." Reb grinned mischievously as Kincaid's eyes widened in comprehension. "Where were you, anyway? You were supposed to be here at nine."

Kincaid had been watching Reb's mouth as she spoke, and was afraid if they did not get off the balcony soon he would take her there. "I'll tell you later. Let's go."

They whirled across the room, Reb safely tucked in close to Kincaid's body so they moved as one when they disappeared out the main ballroom entrance.

"Dillon will worry," Reb protested as Kincaid urged her down the hall toward his room.

"With all the male worship she's enjoying tonight, she'll never know you're gone. We're here. Come in."

Kincaid opened the door to a room that must have been the finest the hotel had to offer. The crisp white sheets had been turned down on the four-poster so that Reb could see only half of the colorful quilt bedspread done in a pattern of blue stars. Dazzling crystal prisms reflected the rosy glow of the cut glass kerosene lamp that sat on a table next to the bed. The jeweled reflections enticed Reb closer and she let her fingers trace the stars and blazes etched into the pink glass at the lamp's base. Reb turned to begin the task of convincing Kincaid to stay. The ferocity of the avid desire in his eyes left her speechless.

Kincaid enfolded Reb in his embrace. He laid his cheek next to hers and let his fingers toy with the single curl that lay against her slender neck.

"Kincaid, we have to talk," Reb murmured dreamily.

"Yes, we do," he agreed. "I love you, Rebel. I want you to be my wife."

Chapter Seventeen

THE WORDS "I LOVE YOU" ROCKETED BACK AND FORTH inside Reb's head, careening off all her carefully planned rational arguments and leaving everything a confused jumble. There was no time to sort things out before Kincaid's lips grazed her cheek on their way to her mouth.

"I love you," he repeated huskily.

The phrase settled as softly on Reb's soul as Kincaid's lips on her own. In that moment Reb underwent a metamorphosis from passivity to aggression that stripped her of her inhibitions as spectacularly as a butterfly shedding its chrysalis.

This time Kincaid did not hold in check the passion she aroused in him. "Turn around," he commanded.

Reb pivoted so that Kincaid could unfasten the crimson gown. It had served its purpose well and she felt no regret when it pooled at her feet. She kicked off her shoes, rolled down her stockings and discarded her bulky underskirt, then spun back to face Kincaid in chemise and pantalets.

"Your turn," she purred with a lusty grin.

She disrobed him, slowly loosening his formal evening coat from his broad shoulders, then freeing the diamond studs from his silk shirt in as tantalizing a manner as she could manage by letting her forefinger drift down his chest until she finally reached the line of black curls on his belly. She sat him down on the bed and relieved him of his boots and socks. Then he obediently stood again while she skinned him out of his trousers. Reb blushed at the burgeoning manhood that saluted her efforts and, in a rush of shyness, kept her eyes averted from Kincaid waiting for him to make the next move.

"I can remember seeing you at the pool that day we walked in the forest as vividly as if I were there right now," he said quietly. "You're beautiful, Rebel. Let me see all of you again." He moved forward and slowly slipped the chemise off her shoulders.

Reb's stupefaction at Kincaid's revelation turned quickly to incensed rage and she punched Kincaid in the stomach as hard as she could.

He emitted a resounding, "Ooof!"

"You knew! You knew I was a woman and you didn't tell me!" she shouted. She alternately assaulted his chest with both her fists and recited the particular incidents for which she punished him in such righteous indignation. "That's for the phony act you put on when you needed your boots off, and that's for the 'Doctor, I need you,' and that's for the description of your perfect wife, you braying mule-headed Romeo! You wolf in sheep's clothing! You faker! Why didn't you tell me you knew I was a girl?!"

Kincaid grabbed both her hands in one of his. "Stop it, Reb!" he yelled.

She used her feet to kick out at him. "Not for one minute!" she flung at him.

"You asked for this," he snapped. He picked her up and threw her over his shoulder, heading for the bed.

"Don't you dare!" she warned.

He threw her on the bed so hard she bounced twice before landing. He ripped the chemise up over her head and pulled the pantalets down over her kicking legs before she had a chance to get away.

When she was naked, Reb scurried to the head of the bed, pulled her knees to her chest and grabbed a pillow to cover as much of her as she could.

"While we're talking about phonies and fakers," he said heatedly from where he stood at the foot of the bed, "what about you? I specifically remember asking you if you were Adam's *brother?*"

"I didn't lie!"

"No, but you didn't tell the truth, either."

"I couldn't!"

"Why the hell not?"

"I was in love with you!"

Kincaid's hands went to his hips in triumph and a huge grin stole across his face.

"You don't have to be so smug," Reb said haughtily. "I didn't *want* to be in love with you."

"Rebel, Rebel," Kincaid said lovingly. When Reb opened her mouth to argue further, Kincaid wagged his finger at her as though she were a naughty child.

She threw the pillow at his head.

"I'm *not* a kid!" she shouted. "I'm a *woman!*"

"Act like a brat, get treated like a brat!" Kincaid responded good-naturedly as he flattened Reb under him on the bed. "Act like a woman, get treated like a woman," he added in a voice that had thickened in passion.

Reb was pinned beneath Kincaid, unable to move, yet it never entered her mind to struggle. She had been waiting for this moment for a long time. She could see the unconcealed desire in the eyes of the man she loved, the man who loved her. Her trader's soul was satisfied. She had given her love and received fair measure in return.

She caressed Kincaid's hips and felt the sinewy muscles tighten under her hands.

Kincaid let his lips wander from Reb's willowy neck across her shoulders and down between her breasts. He kissed each rosy crest once reverently, then lifted himself up to drink the nectar from her lips.

With her hands freed, Reb could satisfy her own need to touch. When their eyes locked, she brought her hands to Kincaid's face and let her thumb brush the scar on his cheek. She splayed her fingers through the errant curls on his forehead, then ran her fingertips across his temple and down behind his ear, finally reaching his corded neck and shoulders, causing him to shiver. Then she brought her hands back to his chest to skim his nipples before aiming her fingertips downward and letting her hands follow where her fingertips led. Kincaid quivered when Reb reached her destination. Her lips curved in an impish smile as she watched the tension increase on Kincaid's face.

"Reb," he said throatily. "Do you know what you're doing?"

"No," she responded saucily. "But that's never stopped me before, and I don't see why it should now."

Kincaid managed a crooked grin. "I'll give you one good reason," he said.

"What's that?" she asked innocently.

"Because turn about is fair play."

Reb gasped when Kincaid made good his word.

They pleasured each other teasingly until their need had heightened beyond what mere teasing could satisfy. Abruptly Kincaid rolled over on his back, bringing Reb with him so that she was now lying on top of him. Heavy-lidded with desire, she pushed herself up to a sitting position so her naked thighs straddled his waist.

"You are so beautiful," he said softly.

Reb shook her head foggily.

"Yes, yes, you are," he argued.

"I wasn't contradicting you," she said with a wry smile. "I just had the feeling for a moment that I had been here before. Of course that isn't possible, is it?" she said, her fingertips smoothing his rising brow. She leaned down to kiss him and he rose with her so that he was seated on the bed with Reb straddling his lap.

"Come, love," he coaxed gently. He lifted Reb enough for her to impale herself on him.

"All for your delight," he said, winking roguishly at her.

Reb blushed wonderfully, but took advantage of the opportunity he had given her to guide their lovemaking. She pushed him back down so he was lying flat once more, then rode him as breathtakingly as the wildest bucking stallion. Kincaid matched her move for move. The rider could not tame the mount, the mount could not shake the rider. The frenzied duel raged, each moment bringing them closer to fulfillment. Reb cried out in ecstasy, then felt the pulsing release of Kincaid's seed within her as he also exclaimed his exultation.

Reb dropped forward to lay panting on Kincaid's

chest in exquisite exhaustion. "You are so warm," she sighed.

He turned sideways so they lay together, side by side in the bed, her head cradled in his shoulder. He kissed her hair and murmured, "It is always so, no matter how cold the weather."

Reb was reminded of Kincaid's parting words at the base of the mountains. She had known the warmth of a man's love. But how long would it last? She was too tired to worry about that right now. Maybe later.

The lovers slept, unaware that the witching hour approached. Kincaid awoke with a start when the first fireworks exploded outside their window, then relaxed when his hand brushed a soft thigh and he was reminded of his pleasant circumstances. He nuzzled Reb's neck lazily, enjoying the recognizable flame of excitement that ignited when he touched her. Reb felt the tightening knot of pleasure that radiated across her loins when Kincaid lowered his mouth and gently suckled her breast. She lay still, pretending to sleep, waiting to see what he would do next.

Kincaid lifted his head to study Reb's face and knew she was awake when her eyelashes flickered against the bombarding lights and sounds from outside their safe haven. "You're missing the celebration," he reminded her lazily as his hand possessively caressed her hip.

"Oh, no!"

Reb instantly pulled free of Kincaid's embrace and scrambled from the bed. She grabbed her crimson gown, yanking it up over her shoulders haphazardly.

"What's wrong?" Kincaid jumped up anxiously and pulled on his trousers to face whatever emergency had propelled Reb out of his arms.

"Dillon and I were supposed to meet my father and

Adam for the fireworks at midnight," she wailed in consternation. "When I'm not there, he'll come looking for me. I have to go."

"When will I see you again?"

"Tomorrow," Reb answered.

"I'm leaving tomorrow for Blue's cabin. I've got another assignment for the railroad," he said hesitantly, unsure of Reb's reaction and unwilling to destroy the peace they'd found.

"That's wonderful!" Reb exclaimed. "I'll meet you here and we can go together." She wasn't any happier about Kincaid's involvement with the railroad, but at least he was not returning to New York right away. She was practical enough to know that they would need some time together to work out their differences.

"No! You can't come! It's out of the question!"

"Why not? What's the matter?" Reb asked, surprised at his vehemence.

"I don't want you exposed to the danger. I'll be asking Blue to take me to Chief Spotted Tail to see if he'll agree to come down and sign a treaty in the spring. It's too dangerous."

Kincaid saw the ominous clouds building on Reb's face and took her in his arms before he continued earnestly, "Reb, I am so pleased you changed your mind and decided to go back east with me. I couldn't bear it if anything happened to you now."

Chills ran up and down Reb's spine.

"I haven't changed my mind," she said icily, tugging herself free from his hold and facing him with hands perched on her hips. "In fact, I came here tonight to convince you to change *your* mind. Even if I *had* changed my mind about going east, I can't change what I *am*."

"Exactly my point," Kincaid interjected. "You're a *woman*, Reb. This is a man's job."

Reb counted to ten, a trick she had taught herself that usually allowed the rational thought to be spoken rather than the emotional one. This time ten was not high enough.

"You know damn well I'm just as capable as you are of taking care of myself in any situation! In fact, I'd even go so far as to say I can take *better* care of myself than you can!" she spat.

"Well, that's something we'll never find out, because you're not going," Kincaid said flatly.

"We'll see what Blue has to say about that!"

"Blue will agree with me," Kincaid shouted angrily.

"See you at the cabin!" Reb threw at him. She jerked open the door and slammed it closed behind her.

He yanked the door open and bellowed at her down the hall. "Reb, come back here! Your dress isn't fastened!"

She pulled the dragging skirt up in her hands and ran faster down the hall.

Kincaid furiously slammed the door.

"Damn! Women!"

Reb hurried to her room, hoping that she was not too late to change her clothes and be downstairs before she was found out. When she opened the door she knew the worst had happened. Her father towered over Dillon, who was still dressed for the ball and who had obviously been in tears for some time.

"Where the hell have you been?" her father demanded.

"Damn, Reb, you're only half dressed!" Adam exclaimed in surprise as he came up behind her.

Reb stood flushed and breathless at the knowledge-able stares of her family, but exhibited no signs of shame at her shocking behavior.

Matt and Adam had returned to the hotel and, when Reb and Dillon did not meet them as planned, Adam was forced to tell his father about the ball that was in progress upstairs. It was there that Matt located his younger daughter surrounded by rogues and rakehells. He had grabbed her wrist and marched her back to her room, demanding to know where Reb was. Dillon had admitted that her sister was supposed to meet Kincaid at the ball, but that she had no idea what had happened to Reb. Worry that some calamity had befallen his elder daughter had keyed Matt to a level of anxiety that made him incautious in the handling of his stubborn child.

"Where have you been?" Matt repeated irritably when Reb remained mute.

"I've been with Kincaid," she answered, un-daunted. "He's leaving Denver City tomorrow on another mission for the Union Pacific. I'm going to Blue's cabin to wait for him."

"You're not going anywhere with that Yankee!" Matt gritted out furiously. "*Especially* not to Blue's cabin!"

"I am too!" Reb replied adamantly.

Matt slammed the fist of one hand into the palm of the other. "That bastard Blue has seen the last of my family!" he muttered. Then he ordered, "Adam, take Dillon to our room. I want to talk to Reb alone."

"If you intend to try to stop Reb from seeing either Blue or Kincaid, Dad, I'm afraid you'll find I'm on Reb's side," Adam said. He stepped up to stand next to Reb. Dillon moved over to join them, presenting a united front.

An expression of frustrated pain flitted across Matt's face before he let his hatred of the mountain man show. His fierce animosity alarmed his children. "I don't want you near that son of a bitch Blue because he can't be trusted," he grated menacingly.

All three children protested his statement vigorously.

"Quiet!" he commanded. "I'm not finished."

Matt took a deep breath before continuing. "Blue violated your mother."

"No. That can't be true," Reb breathed.

Reb's quiet plea for a retraction of the accusation fueled Matt's anger. Couldn't they see through the man? Did he have them all fooled?

"It is," Matt said stonily. In a last desperate attempt to forestall any contact between Reb and the mountain man, Matt let out the secret that had been tearing at his heart for six years, ever since he'd found out.

"I'm not your father, Rebecca. Blue is."

At that moment, a blazing cascade of fireworks exploded violently outside the window, lighting the room like day and bleaching the color from each individual's features. They all stood frozen in horror, like figures in some ghastly wax museum.

Reb took the moment before the room returned to shadowed darkness to let her father's words sink in. No, she thought abstractedly, he wasn't her father, Blue was. How was that possible? Oh, yes. Her mother had been "violated."

"What about the rest of us?" It was a painful question to ask, but Adam had to know.

"You are all my get except Reb."

A poignant sense of loss seized Reb. Precocious Dillon was only her half sister and Adam, dear protective Adam, only her half brother, as were the quiet Garth and the ebullient Jesse. She felt hurt and shut out.

"You see why I don't want you near Blue," Matt said, pleading for understanding. "You're going home."

Reb did not see at all, and her confusion frightened her. In desperation she sought escape. "If you're not my father, you have no right to tell me what I can and can't do," Reb said coldly. She turned to Adam. "May I borrow your horse?" She found her buckskins and hurriedly replaced them for the wilted gown.

Adam looked from his father to Reb. His father looked stunned, Reb shocked. Both were crying inside, but both remained dry-eyed. He knew there must be more to the story than his father had told. There had to be some explanation for what had happened, and if his father's tight-lipped expression was any guide, the only way Reb was going to find out was to ask Blue.

"Ricochet is in the stable. Good luck, Reb."

Reb hugged her brother and sister, but could not bring herself to go near her father. She rubbed the familiar knobby beads on her knife sheath. That simple act had always given her courage because it reminded her of her father's love. Yet he had known, even when he gave her the gift, that she was not his own daughter. Had he meant what he said about loving her, or was it all part of some hideous lie? Reb's eyes sought Matt's with the questions she could not bear to ask. Then she turned quickly and left before he could answer them.

Matt started to follow her, but Adam blocked his way. "She has to go," he said simply.

Matt debated whether to try to get past his son, but

realized that while he might eventually be able to overcome Adam's strength, Reb would have the head start she needed to reach Blue's cabin. Perhaps it was for the best for Reb to have a little time alone with the man who had sired her. If only Rachel were here, maybe she could explain to Reb how such a thing had happened. Matt could not, for he did not understand, himself. He had been a good husband, kept Rachel's bed warm, been a good provider, done everything he knew to make her happy, but evidently it had not been enough. He did not know what he had done wrong. He did not know why his wife had created a child with his best friend.

Matt turned his back on Adam and Dillon to watch the magnificent sparklers through the window. He walked over and leaned his forehead against a cool, clear pane, while his palms pressed against the smoothly painted frame on either side. He closed his eyes to shut out the brilliant light. "Oh, Rachel, *why?*" he cried soundlessly into the blackness.

Dillon let the tears that no one else would shed fall freely from her eyes. She was a proper fairy godmother, all right. She glanced at the crimson gown lying in a wrinkled pool on the floor. It was midnight and everything in Reb's fairy tale had turned into rags and mice and pumpkins.

Chapter Eighteen

BLUE GLANCED OVER HIS SHOULDER TO BE CERTAIN REB and Kincaid still followed. He wouldn't have put it past either one to have done away with the other when he wasn't looking. He had played referee for three days now and his patience was wearing thin. They were nearing the Powder River region, and had reached the beginning of the thick forest that led into the valleys between the Big Horn Mountains on the west and the Black Hills on the east, but he was certain, with all the shouting going on between the two irate lovers, that the Sioux would discover them long before they reached their objective. He only hoped it was Spotted Tail and not Standing Buffalo who sighted them first.

Blue had heard Reb's side of the story, and then Kincaid's. The Yankee had been very persuasive about the inevitability of the railroad coming through the mountains, and Kincaid's proposal for a treaty with the Sioux had sounded intriguing. Blue was not unwilling to try to save some Indian lives if he could. Therefore, he had informed Kincaid that his services as guide and intermediary were available, but only if Reb came along, for he had also concluded that the couple's spat would be resolved only if they stayed together. The Yankee had stormed and sworn but ultimately had had no choice.

Blue began to have doubts about his matchmaking decision the first evening they made camp. Reb had been alternately sullen and sharp with him, and when he had tried to tease her out of her uncharacteristic temper she had burst into tears. Things had gone steadily downhill from there. Reb hadn't spoken two words to him the rest of the trip, but Kincaid's hide must be bleeding in a dozen places from the constant tongue-lashings she'd given her Yankee. Blue grunted disgustedly when he heard the couple begin their childish bickering again.

"You expect me to give up everything to marry you. What are you giving up?" Reb demanded.

"My peace of mind," Kincaid replied sarcastically. Kincaid felt tricked. He would never have admitted to Reb that he loved her if he had had any inkling she was going to pull a stunt like this. Fear squeezed his heart every time the wind rustled the bushes, for his mind's eye saw an arrow headed for Reb. He was furious with himself for caring. He didn't want to love a woman who took the kind of chances with her life that could get her killed. But how did one stop? He couldn't help loving her, but at least he didn't have to marry her if she stayed out here!

"I will not live my life worrying constantly whether my wife is on the brink of some disaster," he said crossly.

"How can you say that?" Reb argued. "I am perfectly capable of taking care of myself."

"God protect me from women who can protect themselves," Kincaid railed derisively. "Laurie said the same thing, and now she's dead! I warned her there might be repercussions because she married a Yankee, even if her Confederate friends didn't know I was a Union army officer, but she wouldn't listen to me. She made the mistake of trusting some Johnny-come-lately who professed undying loyalty to the cause and then took money to set her up for the Union army ambush that killed her. So don't tell me how safe it is to love you, how we can look forward to a long and happy life together if we marry and stay in this godforsaken wilderness!"

"I'm not Laurie," Reb yelled in frustration.

"No, you're a hundred times worse!" he retorted. "I'd have to be crazy to marry a woman who traipses around the mountains looking for an opportunity to get her scalp lifted by some Sioux!"

"You want me to act like something I'm not," Reb charged peevishly.

"I want you to act like a woman," Kincaid corrected.

Reb's face flushed furiously. "Being a woman and being able to handle yourself in any situation are *not* mutually exclusive," Reb grated out. "I have no plans to change my way of life."

"You will if you're married to me."

"Like hell I will!"

"Those are my terms, take them or leave them," Kincaid barked, issuing his ultimatum.

Before Reb could form a sufficiently caustic response, Blue interrupted the wrangling pair.

"Kincaid," Blue called. "I'd like you to ride ahead

a couple of miles and see if you can find a good place for us to bed down for the night. We should be getting pretty close to some of the streams that lead into the Powder River. Find a campsite near the water. Take Trapper with you. He'll help you keep a lookout for the Sioux. If you get captured, be sure to ask to see Spotted Tail," he added sardonically.

Kincaid handed the leads on the seven pack-laden mules to Reb without speaking, and then obeyed Blue. Reb stuck her tongue out at Kincaid's back as he kicked Satan into a lope.

"Reb, I wanted a chance to talk to you alone," Blue began.

"Wanted to give me a little fatherly advice?" Reb snapped at him.

"You could use some," Blue replied testily. "You've been acting like a spoiled brat. Your father should have taken your drawers down and tanned your bottom a long time ago!"

"Why didn't you?" Reb asked flatly.

"Why didn't I what?" Blue asked warily.

Ever since she had learned Blue was her father, Reb had been trying to decide whether and how to broach the subject of his paternity. She was afraid of what she would learn, but desperate to know the truth. She stood at the edge of a high precipice. She took a deep breath and jumped, praying that something would break the fall.

"Why didn't you tan my hide—father?" She turned to see what Blue's reaction to the title would be. His eyes narrowed to slits, and she watched a muscle jerk in his jaw as it tightened.

"What is that supposed to mean?"

Reb agonized before she blurted, "Did you rape my mother?"

Blue yanked back so sharply on the reins in stunned surprise that his horse neighed and reared. He swore vehemently at the animal, and jerked on the bit as he manhandled the horse back under control. When the gelding had steadied, he kicked his mount viciously over to Reb and snatched the reins of her horse near its mouth.

"Get down off that horse!" he commanded angrily.

"NO!"

"Rebecca, get down off that horse by yourself, or by God I swear I'll knock you down!"

Reb clambered off the animal and darted as fast as she could through the thick trees away from the furious man.

Blue swung his leg over the saddle and quickly slid off his mount, rapidly overtaking her. She already had her hand on her knife when he yanked her around, grasped her by both arms and shook her so hard that she was dizzy when he finally threw her away from him. She fought for equilibrium as she reached again for her bowie.

"That knife will only keep you from the truth. Or don't you want to hear the truth?" he grated out fiercely. Blue marveled at how like Matt she was in some ways. Matt had reached for his knife, too.

Reb bowed her head and let her hands fall to her sides in desolate submission. They stood facing each other without moving for some moments before Blue could control his rage enough to speak. Blue had always feared that someday Reb would discover he was her father. On the one hand, he had always been proud of her and would gladly have acknowledged her. On the other hand, it could only be a painful experience for everyone involved. He had had no idea just how painful it would be until now.

"Who told you I raped your mother?" he asked harshly.

"I think 'violated' was the word my fath—Ma—" Reb shuddered and could not speak. What should she call Matt Hunter now? She could not call him father because he was not. She would not call him Matt because she could not. The pain in her chest was a tangible thing. She groaned aloud in distressed uncertainty.

"It's all right. I know what you're trying to say." Blue empathized with the agony that was as great as his own.

"He said you're my father," she said in a whisper.

"It's true. I am your father."

Reb's whole body sagged defeatedly. Deep down she had been hoping against hope that there was some mistake, that this was all some cruel hoax.

"But there was never any force involved. I loved your mother and she loved me."

That possibility was too foreign to everything Reb believed about her mother to go unchallenged.

"You're lying! My mother loved my fath—" Reb pressed the heels of her hands hard against her throbbing temples as her piercing shriek of frustration rent the air. When the eerie echo had died, Reb forced her words out over the huge lump in her throat. "My mother loved the man she was married to."

"At first, yes, she did, and later, afterward, she was a good wife," Blue agreed quietly. "Your father wanted a woman to bear his children, to cook his meals, mend his clothes and keep his backside warm on a cold winter's night. It would be hard to fault him for that. Your mother provided all that and was beautiful, too.

"After she married Matt, your mother missed the world she had left behind in Philadelphia more than she had ever thought she would. Matt could never understand that. Rachel never complained, because she had something to prove to your grandmother and to Matt, too. She did a helluva job of adjusting to what they both expected from her. Your father demanded that she do all the changing, and she did, but she was never happy because of it."

Reb opened her mouth to speak, but Blue's look defied her to interrupt.

"He saw a future that was the same as the past. She saw a future that included everything she had left behind. He didn't want to face the fact that his world was changing. She taught you kids everything she knew in spite of Matt's attitude. He didn't thank her for it," Blue said accusingly. "He thought it was a waste of time. Matt held on tenaciously to the past rather than grow into the future with your mother.

"When he found out about Rachel and me, he could never understand why she had turned to someone else. Matt never realized how lonely she was, how much she needed someone to share her hopes that you children would embrace the changes that were bound to come and her plans for helping you to accept the new ways.

"Our relationship started innocently enough. I visited Matt's cabin frequently because I had no home of my own, and Rachel and I became friends. You see, I knew all about her world, because I came from there, too."

Reb looked up at Blue. She had never thought of him anywhere but in the mountains. Now, he was admitting he had lived another life.

"Gather the horses and the mules and tie them up. Then we can sit and talk," he sighed.

The profusion of fir and pine had provided a soft pillow of needles onto which Blue dropped. Reb hobbled the animals, then returned and squatted across from him on her haunches and picked up a pine branchlet, pulling it apart in agitation. When she had torn each needle away, she picked up another to give her nervous hands something to do. Blue picked up a perfectly formed pine cone and tossed it up in the air and caught it several times, letting the prickly points lend a stab of reality to the nightmare in which he found himself. Neither one really wanted to begin the distressing discussion again, but Reb finally broke the silence.

"What's your real name?" she asked.

"Cabell Ashton. It's a good Virginia name. I was born and raised there and went to the university at Charlottesville. My father and I had a falling-out over the matter of whether men should own other men and he disinherited me," he said, reminiscing. "It has been a bitter comfort to me that the North has finally settled the question in my favor. Your mother and I talked about our pasts a lot, about that other world back east. Our friendship deepened and we fell in love." There was a long pause before he added, "You were the result of that love."

Reb stood and walked away a few steps to put some distance between herself and Blue. She could not bear the tears that had risen in the intense mahogany eyes of the invincible mountain man sitting across from her.

"I begged your mother to come away with me," Blue continued softly. "She wouldn't take Adam and Garth away from their father. Once she had made up her mind that she wasn't ever going to leave Matt, she wouldn't see me alone anymore. She decided that Matt deserved better, that so long as he was her husband she owed him her love and respect. She kept that promise to be faithful to Matt until the day she died," Blue said bitterly.

Reb whirled and spat disbelievingly, "Then how did my—how did he find out?"

Blue rose to confront her sadly. "Sometimes the fates are not kind. I wrote a note to your mother when you were born, telling her how happy I was. Apparently she saved it." He paused and remembered that joyous time so long ago, and Reb could see the bittersweetness of that memory on his face. "Matt found the note six years ago."

"That's when we left the mountains," Reb exclaimed, putting two and two together and coming up with four. She felt a sharp stab of pain in her chest when she thought what such a discovery must have been like for her father. "You were his partner. He trusted you. How could you and my mother betray him like that?!" Reb charged uncomprehendingly.

"Betrayal is a pretty strong word," Blue defended. "When you're in love, you don't always do the 'right' thing. Sometimes the need to be with each other is so strong it takes over. We made the mistake of letting our love rule our actions," he said hesitantly, his brow furrowed in torment. "Haven't you ever done anything that seemed so right at the moment, and then regretted it later?" Blue asked, distressed at her intolerance. His voice rose angrily. "Your mother stayed with Matt because he needed her, and she had vowed 'to love, honor and obey till death us do part.' She knew a few things about what it means to love someone that you could stand to learn," Blue snarled savagely. Without pausing, he challenged, "Do you love Kincaid?"

"Of course!"

"Enough to change for him? Enough to try to be more like what he wants you to be?"

"If he loved me, he'd take me as I am!" Reb countered.

"No, Reb," Blue contradicted with a harsh laugh. "The truth is both of you have to give a little bit. It's called compromise. One person can't give everything like Rachel did. It cuts the heart away," he said, begging her to understand what he was trying to tell her. "If you love Kincaid, you'll give a little, and if he loves you, he'll know when you've given all you can, and he'll give the rest of what it takes for you both to be happy."

Kincaid galloped his horse up to the two people faced off against each other in the wilderness and vaulted from the saddle on the run. Trapper almost bowled Blue over in his excitement at the frenzied pace of their return.

"I heard Reb's scream. What happened?"

Reb flew into Kincaid's arms and grabbed him desperately around the waist, burying her face in his shirt, hiding from the suffering Blue had let her see.

"What happened?" Kincaid repeated anxiously. He was pleased that Reb, who had been fighting with him constantly for four days, suddenly clung to him for dear life, but he wanted to know who or what had threatened the woman he loved.

"You'll have to ask Reb," Blue said curtly. "Take her as far as the river and set up camp. As much noise as you two have been making, it's a wonder we aren't already surrounded by Indians. I'm going to see if I can locate Spotted Tail before Standing Buffalo finds us. If I'm not back by morning, stay headed northeast and keep your eyes peeled for trouble. Come on, Trapper," he called to the large dog.

After Blue had galloped off, Kincaid pried Reb's hold loose and stepped back.

"What happened, Rebel?" he questioned tenderly.

"It's about Blue and me. Blue is my . . . He's my . . . My father isn't . . . My mother . . ." Reb said incoherently.

"It's all right, Rebel," Kincaid said, kissing her softly on the mouth. "I can wait." He walked over to the mules and unhobbled them, then took the lead to the animals and mounted Satan, waiting patiently for Reb to mount.

Reb felt dead inside. She grabbed the reins of her horse and mounted stiffly. Then she and Kincaid followed Blue's faint path through the thick forest.

Blue had barely ridden out of Reb and Kincaid's sight when he backtracked around the couple and picked up the trail they had previously traveled. He found a comfortable spot where he could remain concealed and waited. Now that Matt had told Reb that Blue was her father, it was a safe guess that he was somewhere behind them, waiting to see the results of his stick in the anthill. Blue had given Reb the best advice he knew, and now he intended to see that she had the time to think over that advice, and to act on it without Matt's interference.

Sure enough, in less than two hours Blue heard the telltale sounds of shod hooves on rock and the crunchy jangle of horses trying to chew grass around a bit. Blue moved his horse into the path of the oncoming riders and waited.

Matt and Adam both saw Blue at the same time.

Matt reached to pull his rifle from its leather case on the saddle and Adam caught his hand.

"He's Reb's father," was all Adam said.

Matt let the rifle slide back down in its boot and kicked his mount to urge it closer to Blue. The air bristled and popped with the tension that streaked between the two men.

"Where's Reb?" Matt asked.

"With Kincaid."

"Where are they?" Matt persisted.

"Ahead. It was a cruel thing you did, telling her." The only sign Blue had that Matt acknowledged the criticism was the slight narrowing of Matt's eyes. "Only you left out some of the facts," Blue added coldly.

"I told her what she needed to know," Matt countered angrily. "I've come to take her home."

"I'm afraid I can't let you do that," Blue said. "Reb has finally found a man she can love. He's a good man, a strong man, as strong as she is. They need some time alone to work out their differences and I intend to see they get it."

"Just how the hell do you propose to stop me?" Matt reached for his rifle again, but Blue kneed his horse to reveal the loaded Spencer he had aimed at Matt and Adam.

"Reb and Kincaid are headed for Spotted Tail's camp. We're going to take a short cut and meet them there. I have some talking to do with Spotted Tail before Kincaid arrives, anyway. You can come along peaceably, or I can make the trip very unpleasant. It's your choice."

Matt scowled, but Adam was not at all displeased.

"Dad," Adam said quietly, laying his hand on his father's shoulder comfortingly, "I don't pretend to know how you feel right now. I only know that if there is any chance at all for Reb and Kincaid to come to an understanding, they deserve to have it. There will be plenty of time for you and Blue to kill each other later," he finished sardonically.

Matt gazed over at the son who could find humor even in this tense situation, then back to Blue. "We'll go with you, but she damn well better arrive at Spotted Tail's camp in one piece!"

Secretly, Blue acknowledged that Matt's concern bore merit. There were risks that Reb and Kincaid would run into trouble if left to themselves. However, when he weighed those risks, even the risk of death, against a lifetime of happiness together, Blue had no difficulty making his decision.

"Don't worry," Blue reassured. "Reb can take care of herself, and I don't doubt Kincaid will have a care for her as well."

Reb and Kincaid had lost Blue's trail but were continuing northeast through the sun-speckled forest when, without warning, they were startled by the screeching, war-painted Indians that dropped onto them from an outcropping of rock. The weight of one attacking brave knocked Reb from her horse. Once on the ground she was quickly overwhelmed when two Sioux appeared from the underbrush and joined the first. Meanwhile, Kincaid had been the victim of the same kind of surprise attack. The two Sioux who had leaped from the cliff above him, together with two others who had joined them from their hiding place in the heavy thicket along the trail, sat on his extremities while he swore vigorously but fruitlessly at his captors. Concern for Reb was foremost in his mind, since he could not see past the four Sioux who surrounded him.

"Rebel, are you all right?" he shouted.

"Kincaid!"

The fear in Reb's voice galvanized Kincaid into action and with superhuman effort he managed to free one arm. He swung his huge fist savagely at the nearest Sioux and broke the warrior's cheekbone. Kincaid heard a gutteral command from somewhere behind him, and the wounded Sioux was replaced by two more. He struggled vainly against the increased restraint.

"Reb? Reb?" he called anxiously. He got no answer.

Reb had been gagged with rawhide after she had severely bitten one of her attackers. Her hands had been pulled back viciously and tied behind her. A brave, naked except for breechclout, moccasins and a war vest of bone and feathers, rode up before the pair. He gestured authoritatively and Reb was jerked up on her feet and a rawhide rope placed around her neck. The lead was handed to the arrogant Indian.

Kincaid had been so concerned about Reb that he had not paid attention to his own plight. Each wrist had been secured with a long rawhide thong, and the thongs handed to mounted Indians on opposite sides of him. Another noose of rawhide had been forced over his head and down around his neck, and the end of it had been handed to the same vividly war-painted buck who held Reb's line and who appeared to be the leader of the war party.

The two Indians holding the rawhide that bound each of Kincaid's arms simultaneously applied pressure. The pull in opposite directions yanked him to his feet, stretching his arms out and wrenching the sockets. A younger brave made the mistake of coming too close and Kincaid lashed out with a booted foot, catching the foolish man in the groin. The other Indians ridiculed the unfortunate victim, for he had previously been warned of the caliber of his enemy.

The line around Kincaid's neck snapped taut and the band started homeward with their prizes, not the least of which was Kincaid's magnificent black stallion, Satan. The lead around Reb's neck was longer, so she ran about ten paces behind Kincaid. When she stumbled over a rotting log, she was dragged by the neck for a few paces before a passing Indian snagged her excruciatingly by the crook of her elbow and dropped her back on her feet. Kincaid looked over his shoulder and met her eyes, willing her to stand. She staggered for a few steps, and then managed to keep up with the spotted pony trotting ahead of them.

The Indians laughed among themselves, speculating how much they could get in barter for the goods on the confiscated mules, and wagering their share of the loot on whether the smaller captive, whose face already showed the first bloody scrapes from the trail, would survive the forced march back to the camp.

Reb watched Kincaid jogging ahead of her, his arms stretched out painfully on either side, one occasionally jerked backward or forward when the available space between the trees narrowed so that the Indian riding on one side could not keep pace with the one on the other. She could tell by Kincaid's darkened features when he turned around to check on her that he was not happy about the situation. Reb knew the extent of her love's ire when he started ranting furiously at their predicament.

"Dammit, Reb! I warned you something like this

might happen! You better, by God, do your damnedest to stay alive until I can get us out of this mess!" he yelled at her in frustrated helplessness. Kincaid clung to his anger desperately because it left no room for the fear and despair that clutched at him with fierce talons. He forced his mind away from the pictures that rose before him when he imagined what would happen when the Sioux discovered Reb was female. Where the hell was Blue when he needed him? he raged.

Reb formed an appropriate retort in her mind but could not transmit it to Kincaid because of the gag. None of this was her fault! He was supposed to be watching out for Indians! She had no intention of rolling over and playing dead, either! She would prove to him that wilderness women were raised to survive anything that man or nature threw at them!

Standing Buffalo turned back proudly to gaze on his two captives. The Great Spirit had given back not only Too-Big-For-Horses but also one of the two trappers who had set him free. He would not be cheated again of the vengeance owed for the death of his brother, and all in the village of Spotted Tail would be witness to how well Too-Big-For-Horses met his death.

Chapter Nineteen

REB LAY FACE DOWN ON THE ROCKY GROUND, HER
hands still tied behind her back. The gag had been
removed the previous night, so that the Indians could
tease her with the promise of water that was not
delivered. Her tongue lay swollen in her mouth as
though it did not belong there. The red rims of her
eyes burned, and her eyeballs screamed their disap-
proval when she raised her shielding eyelids. She
could hear the gutteral bark of shouted commands but
could not seem to make her body obey her will. It was
the morning of the third day of their captivity, and she
had had no food or water and very little rest for two
days. A vicious kick in the ribs rolled her over on her
back and she squinted her eyes at the very ugly Indian
blocking her view of a partially overcast gray sky.
Only a mother could love a face like that, she thought
cynically. She grunted as the brave leveled another
kick that brought tears to the corners of her eyes.
Beauty is as beauty does, she remonstrated silently,

and that kind of conduct isn't going to improve your appearance any.

"Get up, Reb," she heard Kincaid plead.

She turned her head and saw that two Indians were working on the knots that had tied him stretched out between two pines during the night. How her life had been changed since that first felicitous meeting, when she and Adam had found Kincaid tied spread-eagled in the forest as he was now. Would some passing stranger rescue them? she wondered. She snorted to herself at the poor odds she would give to the sucker who bet on that. She realized then just how fortuitous it had been that she and Adam had found Kincaid. She smiled beatifically at the thought that, thanks to Kincaid, at least she was not going to die a virgin. The smile split the skin on her lower lip, and a trickle of blood spilled down her chin.

Kincaid was sure Reb's mind had gone when he saw her grinning like a Cheshire cat, but he said nothing because whatever she was thinking about had started her moving.

Reb called on her cramped stomach muscles to pull her into a sitting position and, though they screamed in agony, she rose. She felt sure she must have at least one broken rib. She pulled her bruised knees up and laid her forehead on them, trying to gather the courage to face another day. There was no part of her aching body that did not protest its soreness. Her shoulders and wrists throbbed. The smell of urine on her clothes bespoke the most wounded part of all— her pride. For she had been forced to wet herself like a child and then endure the Indians' mocking laughter at her shamed embarrassment.

Reb lifted her head and rolled onto her knees, preparatory to rising. The same ugly Indian put a foot on her buttocks and pushed her back down on her face with a croaking laugh. Reb wanted to cry when he replaced the awful gag, and she lay there unmoving after he was done.

"You Red Devil son of a bitch! Do you want her up or not?!" Kincaid shouted hoarsely. "Dammit, Reb, get up or I'll kick you up myself!"

Reb's resentment at Kincaid's threat provoked her to rise unsteadily on her feet to confront him. She wanted to shout that it wasn't fair. Kincaid had not had so much as a finger laid on him since he'd been captured. The Sioux all seemed to keep their distance from him as though he were some special kind of demon. This respect had increased after one of the braves had tried to ride Satan and had been thrown and trampled to death. She, on the other hand, had been the brunt of every cruel trick or unsporting joke the fiendish Sioux bullies could think up. Sure, he could stand there and shout "get up" without a mark on his body! She'd like to put him in her moccasins and see just how well he'd fare. Reb's eyes shot sparks at Kincaid from a face that was a patchwork of bloody scrapes and scratches, before her tether jerked her away.

In the blindness of her own pain, Reb could not see the agony Kincaid stoically endured. The scarred muscle in his thigh had tightened over the past three days, and the excruciating ache in the old wound caused him to limp badly. It had become a hellish struggle to pick the leg up and put it down again. Kincaid also suspected that sometime during the journey he had torn the muscles in the recently knitted flesh of his left shoulder, for the jerking pull of the rawhide thongs had become a throbbing torture, and he had no other explanation for the kaleidoscope of black-and-blue discoloration. Worst of all, he had been reduced to shallow panting, for he could not take a deep breath without encountering the damnable constriction in his chest that visited him each time he thought of losing Reb.

Kincaid struggled painfully with all the ferocious strength of his sinewy back and shoulders against the rawhide thongs that bound him. He was not unaware that Reb bore the brunt of the Indians' vindictiveness. If he could have brought their fury down on himself and spared Reb, he would have done so, but nothing he did seemed to provoke the Indians to grapple with him. He vented his frustration by raining imprecations down upon the heads of the Sioux.

Throughout the early morning, Reb dragged at the end of her tether in exhaustion. The terrain had become rockier. The majesty of the tall peaks all around them would have been breathtaking if she had only had the strength to lift her head to view them. Those among the band who had bet that Reb would not complete the journey contributed to her labor, for they frequently tripped her, then struck her meanly when she was down or cuffed her roughly when prodding her to rise. Each time Reb fell, Kincaid alternately murmured cajoling words of encouragement and threatened dire punishment if she did not succeed in getting up. Kincaid was heartened that, after all they had been through, Reb was somehow still doggedly on her feet. Still alive. And that meant there was still hope.

Some of that hope vanished when he detected the distant cacophony of barking dogs and playing children that indicated they had reached the Indian village. He realized then that he had been counting on Blue to rescue them before they were ensconced among the Sioux. There was still the remote chance Kincaid would be able to find someone to get a message to Spotted Tail. Blue had explained, however, that there were numerous tribes camped in the Powder River region, and Kincaid had no way of knowing which one had captured them.

The Indian camp was nestled in a grassy valley in the shelter of two enormous rocky bluffs that projected upward on either side. A rushing stream wound in and out among the tepees pitched on either side of the ribbon of water. Wooded thickets rimmed the edges of the bluffs, hemming in the camp.

The Indian women stopped their work cooking, tanning hides, and crushing dried buffalo meat for pemmican. The children dropped their hoop and pole game, and all came from the tepees, stuck here and there as far as the eye could see down the valley, to congregate around the renegade leader and his two captives as the band arrived with their booty at the center of the Indian camp.

"Stand back!" Standing Buffalo warned. "Lest Too-Big-For-Horses send you to the Happy Hunting Ground before your time."

The awed faces of the children bore mute testimony to the stories that had already been told about the fierce white warrior.

The Indians bound Kincaid as securely as a duck on a roasting stick to a stake at one side of the main circle of tepees, and he was left strictly alone. Reb, on the other hand, was a hub of unwelcome attention. She hunched her face to her chest and curled herself into a ball on the ground to avoid the blows aimed at her by the women and children.

It was Standing Buffalo's intention to wait for the return of Spotted Tail, who had gone to powwow with the Oglala Sioux in another village, before he began his test of Kincaid's merit. There was no reason, though, to delay their torture of the other captive.

"Let us make an example of this trapper," Standing Buffalo ordered curtly. "Strip him."

Someone produced a knife and Reb's bonds were cut. Then the women and children tore at her, ripping her buckskin shirt away. Gales of crowing laughter and pointing fingers revealed the fact that Reb's sex had been discovered.

Kincaid's eyes closed and he swallowed convulsively.

Reb blessed the Indian who had cut the gag from her mouth, even while using her now freed tongue to revile the rest. She hugged her arms to her breasts to hide herself from view, welcoming the million pinpricks in her arms and shoulders that signaled the returning flow of blood to her numbed limbs. She felt herself being yanked again to her feet. She could not help shivering at the threatening voices of the Indian braves, who pulled her hands away to reveal her femininity to all.

Standing Buffalo observed Reb with more than a little admiration. Of course, the woman had been gagged so she could not cry out, but he had been witness to her travail on the journey, and the bruises on her chest and ribs evidenced the hardship she had endured and had still kept going. When he remembered that this female had also been instrumental in the initial escape of Too-Big-For-Horses, he acknowledged her medicine must be very powerful. Such a woman would breed very strong, brave sons. He reached out to run a forefinger appraisingly down her cheek.

Even though Reb knew she was making a mistake,

it was too good an opportunity to pass up. When Standing Buffalo's hand neared her mouth she snapped her teeth down hard on the fleshy part of his palm, near his thumb. The renegade chief howled in surprise and tried to shake Reb off. She held on like a bulldog and had drawn blood before he freed his hand by cuffing her in the head with his other fist so she lost consciousness.

"She be a wild she-cat all right!"

The Indians parted like the red sea for the burly mountain legend.

"Ah, girl, I had not expected to see so much of ye again so soon," Breck O'Hanlan chuckled to the unconscious form. "Too bad yer pa is me friend," the redheaded giant added, tsking his regret as he looked her up and down appreciatively. "But I guess since he is, I'd better see what I can do to get ye out of this."

"I have captured a very bold woman," Standing Buffalo boasted to the mountain man in the Sioux tongue. "She will make an excellent second wife when she is tamed." He gestured to several of the women and gave instructions that Reb be carried to his tepee, which was next to the Council tepee in the center of the camp, and given all the care befitting the wife of a warrior.

Kincaid had watched Reb attack the Sioux and watched her knocked unconscious with equal parts of pride and terror. When he saw the redheaded behemoth appear, a portion of hope was added to the other two emotions. His features darkened when he saw Reb carried to an Indian tepee and Standing Buffalo follow her inside, after depositing his shield and weapons on a tripod outside the doorway.

Breck calmly made his way to the trussed-up man, the cogs turning furiously in his mind for some way to save Reb from the fate Standing Buffalo had planned. So far no bright idea had emerged. Judging from the man's size, for there could not be many in the territory to match it, this must be the Yankee that Matt had told Breck he'd found with his daughter. How had the two gotten back together again? He was sure Matt had told him the lad had left for parts unknown. "Why be ye travelin' with the colleen?" he demanded sternly.

"She wouldn't stay home where she belonged!" Kincaid snapped.

Breck let go with a great belly laugh. "That fits me first impression of the girl," he agreed. "That there brawny buck Standin' Buffalo be wantin' her to wife," Breck drawled teasingly.

"Standing Buffalo?! Never!" Kincaid raged. The confirmation that their captor was Standing Buffalo left him with mixed feelings. The Sioux was a renegade who had a reason to want revenge, but they were obviously also in the right place to contact Spotted Tail.

"Calm down, lad. Ye'll get yer chance to fight soon enough. What be the young miss to ye?"

"I love her," Kincaid conceded angrily.

Breck pondered this admission with great interest. Perhaps there was a way to rescue the she-cat and save the Yankee, too. "Be ye willin' to marry the colleen?"

"Marry her?" Kincaid snorted incredulously. "Here? Now?"

"Aye, unless ye be wantin' to give her to Standin' Buffalo for his second bride. He figures he'll breed hisself brave sons with a she-cat like her."

"You're not making it sound as though I have much of a choice," Kincaid said, giving the redheaded man a withering look.

"No, lad. No, I'm not. So then, you agree?"

"I agree," Kincaid said reluctantly.

"Good. Now, here's me plan."

After discussing with Kincaid what he would have to do, Breck made his way to Standing Buffalo's tepee. He entered and waited at the opening to the buffalo hide dwelling for an invitation to join Standing Buffalo, who was sitting cross-legged facing the doorway. When Standing Buffalo welcomed him in, Breck was careful not to cross between his host and the fire burning on the ground in the center of the circular space. He seated himself on Standing Buffalo's left as an honored male guest. Breck asked in the Sioux tongue to be allowed to speak to Reb, and received Standing Buffalo's permission.

Reb had been completely stripped and was lying naked on a huge buffalo robe. Her head was cushioned on a fox skin stuffed with grass. She had been carefully washed, her ribs strapped with lengths of deerskin, and her cuts and scrapes bathed with a soothing salve. Reb's need for water had been met with the supply kept in the rawhide water pail in the tepee, but her stomach rumbled her hunger. A kettle of buffalo meat stew sat warming on the fire, that any who were hungry should be able to fill their bellies at will, and the smell had set Reb's saliva to flowing. She stared up at the small opening that vented the smoke from the fire, feeling as impotent as an animal caught in a steel trap. She did not attempt to hide her nakedness when Breck squatted next to her to speak. The mountain man could not restrain his wandering gaze, and he ogled the long-legged form greedily. He brought his mind back to the business at hand when Standing Buffalo grunted in displeasure.

"How feel ye 'bout an Indian husband, girl? Standin' Buffalo has a mind to claim the spoils of war as his second wife."

"I'll choose my own husband!" Reb spat, rising painfully to a sitting position and knocking away the woman's hand that tended her.

"That's the fightin' spirit!" Breck licked his lips, and thought with woe of the rising tumescence that was not going to be satisfied by this spitfire. "I spoke to the man ye came here with, and he says he be willin' to take ye for wife hisself."

"That's very generous of Kincaid," Reb said sarcastically.

"Kincaid, is it then? Of the railroad Kincaids?" Breck asked in surprise.

"Yes, blast his hide," Reb snapped.

"What be ye doin' up here?"

"Kincaid plans to talk to Spotted Tail on behalf of the Union Pacific about a treaty with the Sioux."

"Mary, Joseph and Moses," Breck said, crossing himself. "Did Spotted Tail know ye were comin' fer that purpose? From the looks of this reception, I'd guess not," Breck said, answering his own question. "All them rifles I brung from Denver City," he muttered to himself, then said, "Well, let's get one problem settled before we look fer more. Ye must tell Standin' Buffalo that Kincaid has also asked ye to be his wife. Do it where his braves will hear yer words. I'll be there to translate. Say that ye'll take whichever man proves stronger in combat."

"That means Kincaid will have to fight!"

"Of course, girl. What did ye expect?"

Standing Buffalo had not been able to resist showing off his prize, and later the same afternoon had paraded Reb around the village dressed in a light fawn-colored buckskin dress decorated with an intricate blue-and-white beaded design. Breck was on hand to translate when she made her announcement.

"I am already promised in marriage to this man, Kincaid," Reb said, when they were within a few feet of the white captive.

"Too-Big-For-Horses is my prisoner," Standing Buffalo replied.

"You have stolen my woman as you stole the gifts I brought to Spotted Tail," Kincaid accused.

A murmur of alarm ran through the assembled Indians when Breck translated this message, and the group of onlookers began to grow.

Standing Buffalo had frequently challenged Spotted Tail's authority, but ultimately had always submitted to the chief's supremacy rather than leave the tribe. He was unpleasantly surprised to discover he had apparently committed a blunder by claiming the pack-laden mules of this tall man. If the gifts were really intended for Spotted Tail, then he would have to give up his booty. He might be allowed to keep the black stallion, but that was little comfort because it was death to ride the animal. Now, the woman contended she belonged to Too-Big-For-Horses as well. Standing Buffalo's temper flared. It looked as though he would come away empty-handed.

He was also confused. Hadn't the Great Spirit placed Too-Big-For-Horses in his power so that he could wreak vengeance for Smaller Bear's death? Could he have so totally misjudged the Great Spirit's intent?

Breck saw the furious indecision that plagued Standing Buffalo, and used his knowledge of this particular Sioux, who shared his love of wagering, to take advantage of the situation.

"If the gifts belong to Too-Big-For-Horses until he presents them to Spotted Tail, then he can wager them if you have a contest."

"That is true," Standing Buffalo mused.

"Ye could insist the she-cat be part of the bargain as well," he continued.

"I could only honor as my husband he who has proved himself strongest in combat," Reb said on cue.

Standing Buffalo crossed his arms pensively. He could see all sorts of advantages to a competition with his captive. He believed the white man had been worn down sufficiently by the journey to be easily defeated, especially if the contest took place soon, before the powerful adversary had a chance to regain his strength. It would only enhance his image among his people to have conquered this mythical enemy in battle. If the white warrior wagered the pack-laden mules and Standing Buffalo won them from him, no demands for the gifts could be made by Spotted Tail. Perhaps, in defeating his enemy, he would also learn the secret to mastery of the great black devil stallion. Most important, when he had vanquished Too-Big-For-Horses, he would be able to claim the white woman, who would bear him strong sons, and perhaps that was what the Great Spirit had intended all along, he convinced himself.

"I will fight Too-Big-For-Horses," Standing Buffalo proclaimed. "If he wins, he may have his freedom, the mules and packs, his black devil horse and the white woman, and there will be a tepee for his lodging until Spotted Tail returns. If I win, the woman and all else will be mine and Too-Big-For-Horses forfeits everything, including his life, in payment for the life of Smaller Bear."

The crowd shifted uncomfortably. The stakes were very high.

"I accept the challenge of Standing Buffalo," Kincaid said gravely.

"We will fight before the sun leaves the sky!" Standing Buffalo shouted exultantly.

Reb waited alone in the darkening tepee stuck away in a thicket in a corner of the valley, so hidden that one might pass within a few yards without seeing it. She had been moved there while Standing Buffalo danced himself into a fighting frenzy. The thudding drums and the wailing howls of the chanting Indians thrummed on her nerves, and her senses had been heightened to fever pitch when she heard a noise at the opening to the tepee.

"Shhh. Do not be afraid," a soft, delicately accented voice called to her.

Reb watched a lovely Indian girl come forward into the flickering firelight. The tiny child could not have been more than ten or eleven, Reb guessed. She had long black hair held in place by a rawhide band at her brow and plaited in two long braids that reached to her waist.

"You speak English!" Reb exclaimed.

"Shh," the girl warned again. She came around the fire and sat next to Reb. "I am Morning Dove. The guard's back was turned so I sneaked in. I was curious to see the white woman captive. You are not so beautiful," she said matter-of-factly.

"I've never thought so," Reb answered honestly.

"But two brave warriors will fight each other to see which will claim you as wife."

"That's true," Reb replied, her heart lurching with fear for Kincaid. "I wish it were not so."

"I do not like Standing Buffalo. He would not be a kind husband."

"Then perhaps you would do a favor for me," Reb asked. "Do you know whether they have given the white man any food or water?"

"I do not know. I do not think so, though. Everyone is afraid to go near him."

"Are you afraid?"

"Me?" The child's eyes were as big as saucers, and it dawned on Reb suddenly that they were as blue as Dresden china. "I'm not afraid of anything!" the girl said with false bravado.

Reb located a buffalo calf's-head skin filled with water and handed it to the maiden. "Then I ask you as a friend to be sure the white man gets some water before he must fight. Will you do that for me?"

The child looked troubled, then seemed to make up her mind. "I will have to find a way to be tall enough to reach his mouth, but I am smart. I will think of something," she said confidently. The audacious sprite left as quickly as she had come.

Only moments later, moving cautiously from between two closely pitched tepees, Morning Dove urged Satan closer to the post where the white warrior stood tied. The pounding of the drums and the frenzied dancing of Standing Buffalo at the center of the circle kept the Indians entranced. They had left a wide berth for Kincaid, and by stealth the Indian maiden maneuvered the horse so that she was partially hidden in the heavy thicket directly behind the tall man.

Kincaid felt cool hands tip his stubbled chin up and then force his mouth open to dribble in some warm water. His mouth opened wider and he craned his neck toward the refreshing liquid like a baby bird seeking worms from its mother.

"Not too fast," a girl's voice whispered.

Abruptly, Kincaid stopped drinking and turned his head in astonishment to peruse the tiny child sitting bareback astride his huge black stallion.

"Satan has never let anyone on his back except me!" Kincaid said in amazement.

"Do not worry. All animals are my friends," the girl reassured. "The white captive woman sent you this water."

"And you were not afraid to bring it," he added, his brow rising speculatively.

"Only a little," she responded in a small voice. "Now I can see, though, that you are not a devil, only a man. For would a devil straight from the fires of hell really crave water?" she asked.

"Your logic is impeccable," Kincaid said, smiling through cracked lips at the precocious child.

"What is 'impeccable'?" she asked.

"It means 'without fault,'" he answered.

"That is not a good word to describe anything I do."

"Why not?"

"Because I am always causing trouble," she answered frankly.

"I can believe that," Kincaid said with a grin.

The imp frowned at the incomprehensible man. Why did he smile at one who admitted to being a worrisome burden to her master?

"May I have some more water?"

The girl complied with Kincaid's request, but broke off hastily when the drums stopped beating. "They will come now." The child ran a small, inquisitive hand timorously over Kincaid's muscular biceps, then up the taut, steely sinews that ran across his shoulders. "I do not think you will need it," she said when her examination was complete, "but I wish you good luck."

In the awesome silence that had descended on the Indian camp, Reb rose and paced the hazy, smoke-filled tepee nervously. Damn Breck O'Hanlan and his bright ideas, she thought. Imagine two men butting heads over her like rutting stags. Reb shivered in fear and excitement. Soon Kincaid and Standing Buffalo would fight for the right to claim her. No matter which man won, tonight she would be a wife.

Chapter Twenty

WITH THE TWO RIVALS STANDING BEFORE HER IN THE center of the camp at twilight, Standing Buffalo dressed in breechclout and Kincaid stripped down to his buckskin pants, Reb was almost willing to admit that she had been wrong to come along on this journey. It was the first time since their capture that she had taken stock of Kincaid's condition, and she was horrified by what she discovered. His naked chest revealed the rainbow of bruises on his shoulder. She saw the tight lines of pain around his mouth each time he took a hitching step. She had no way of knowing whether he had received the water, but his lips looked parched and his face showed the gaunt signs of hunger.

"You don't have to do this for my sake," Reb offered miserably.

"What would you suggest as an alternative, Rebel," Kincaid replied grimly.

Reb remained mute, but her mind was working

furiously. She just might prefer life as an Indian bride to marriage with Kincaid under these forced circumstances. Assuming he won.

Virtually the whole tribe, women and children included, surrounded the pair that was poised to fight. Some held torches in the event the contest extended into darkness.

"The object of the competition is merely to prove yer superior prowess," Breck explained, working with both hands to try to loosen the muscles on Kincaid's scarred thigh. "In order to win, ye must force Standin' Buffalo to yield. There'll be a single knife and, if ye can get possession of it, ye can use it to defend yerself, but not to kill. Understand?"

Reb tied one end of a six-foot rawhide thong to Standing Buffalo's left wrist as Breck instructed her to, and then knotted the other end of the thong around Kincaid's wrist. A single knife had been stuck in the ground about ten feet behind the two combatants. When Reb stepped back, the contest began. The Sioux yelped their encouragement to Standing Buffalo, who had been a participant in many such contests in the past, and had always come away the winner.

As he watched his opponent warily, Kincaid massaged the muscle of his leg, but it was still stiff enough to hamper his mobility. His enforced three-day fast had left him lightheaded, and he knew his reactions would be slow, so he played for time, giving his shrieking joints and sinews a chance to loosen and his adrenaline a chance to flow. When Standing Buffalo leaned all of his weight against the thong and then let go, Kincaid seemed to lose his balance and he stumbled backward to the ground.

Reb kept her features absolutely blank, even though her heart had leaped to her throat.

Standing Buffalo grabbed the knife from the ground and grinned lecherously as he strode toward Kincaid's inert form. This fight is going to be over almost before it has begun, he thought. He stepped up confidently to claim his victory and paid for his carelessness when Kincaid jerked his feet out from under him.

"Let's see how you fare when your enemy's hands aren't tied," Kincaid muttered under his breath. He barreled his right fist into the stocky Indian's gut.

Standing Buffalo stabbed reflexively with the knife when Kincaid hit him, and was pleased to see the gash left by the blade.

Reb watched the line of red grow and begin to drip freely down Kincaid's iron-thewed arm. She tried to convince herself that Kincaid would have had to fight even if she hadn't come along, but knew she was only making excuses to assuage her conscience.

After measuring the mettle of the man, Breck had wagered heavily on the Yankee to win this battle against the many braves who believed the extensive scar on Kincaid's thigh would hold him back. The legendary Irishman had been mildly irritated when Kincaid seemed to fall like a green farm boy for Standing Buffalo's first trick, then gloated when he saw the tables turned. Breck vigilantly watched the two strong men exchange blows for a few minutes. For a thickset man, Standing Buffalo was amazingly agile, but Breck decided that Kincaid's devastating right fist was doing at least as much damage as the Indian's slashing knife.

Kincaid could tell he was tiring and took a chance he would not otherwise have taken. He kicked out suddenly with his unreliable scarred leg, disarming the

Sioux renegade. Kincaid had no time to enjoy the astonishment on Standing Buffalo's face at the attack that had come from such a totally unexpected source. He merely took advantage of his longer reach to catch the Sioux in a stranglehold around the neck. His bulging muscles strained with the effort of holding the squat, struggling Indian, whose short arms could not get to any part of Kincaid to enforce his resistance.

"Yield," Kincaid commanded.

With a chortling laugh at all the furs he was going to win, Breck translated Kincaid's demand.

"I-will-not-yield," Standing Buffalo rasped. He could see all the prizes and glory he had possessed, when he had so proudly ridden into camp earlier in the day, flowing through his fingers like so much sand. Desperate, he kicked backward with his right heel, catching Kincaid square in the middle of his old wound.

Kincaid yelled out loud and saw stars for a moment, until the pain became bearable. Before the renegade could repeat the very effective attack, Kincaid tightened his grasp, cutting off the Indian's supply of air until the limp body of the Sioux marked his capitulation.

Kincaid stepped over Standing Buffalo's still body and took Reb's hand possessively in his own. He turned to face the deathly quiet crowd of awed Indians that observed in fear and dread the invincible white warrior who had defeated their champion.

"I have defeated Standing Buffalo and have won my right to this woman. I claim her as my wife." Kincaid turned a stony visage to Reb and waited.

She looked to Breck and he nodded insistently.

"I accept this man as my husband," she announced.

"I will stay in the village of Spotted Tail and await his return. I offer my hand in friendship to any who will take it," Kincaid vowed.

Such an unprecedented turn of events took the Sioux aback, and Breck's translation was greeted with utter silence. "I think they be afeard of ye, lad," Breck said quietly.

"I am not afraid."

The crowd parted and Morning Dove walked slowly and surely forward. When the tiny girl stood before the tall man, she held out her hand to him. He clasped it firmly, then leaned down to kiss her on the cheek.

"Thank you," he whispered gratefully.

"See. He will not eat you," Morning Dove called with a burbling laugh to the dumbstruck Brulés that surrounded them. She shot Kincaid an impish grin.

Several of the older braves slowly approached, offering their friendship to Kincaid. Among those who sought him out was the ugly brave who had so viciously mistreated Reb. Apparently the brave was willing to let bygones be bygones. Kincaid had not really thought of that eventuality, and he hesitated momentarily before offering his hand to the Sioux. Breck translated as the Indian spoke.

"A woman so brave must bring honor to your lodge. May she give you many fine sons."

When Kincaid embraced the grotesque, soft-spoken man warmly in friendship, so many others rushed to follow suit that Breck finally had to shout at them to stand back.

When she was certain that Kincaid's welcome was secure, Morning Dove joined Standing Buffalo's wife in reviving the fallen braggart. Standing Buffalo awoke to find Kincaid being touted as friend by all around him. He took his ill temper out on the nearest object, slapping Morning Dove vindictively.

Kincaid heard the distinctive sound and turned to locate the source. He discovered Morning Dove on the ground next to the sullen Indian.

"Why do you mistreat this child?" Kincaid asked menacingly.

Standing Buffalo jumped to his feet furiously. "I need no excuse to punish this girl. She belongs to me."

Kincaid waited for Breck to translate, then said, "Come here, girl."

Morning Dove looked fearfully from Kincaid to Standing Buffalo and back again, but did not move.

"Ye can't just take the girl," Breck protested.

"Then I'll make a wager for her," Kincaid said, smiling cold-bloodedly. "Tell Standing Buffalo that I dare him to ride Satan. If he can stay atop the horse, he wins all the mules and the packs. If he can't, I get the girl."

Breck translated the challenge.

A cold sweat broke out on Standing Buffalo's forehead. He had seen the bloody pulp the devil horse had made of the foolish brave who had attempted to ride him. He was not stupid. He was certain the white warrior had the same fate in store for him. If he refused the challenge, it would mean a loss of face. Yet what choice did he have? The white man had tricked him, and he saw only one way out.

"It is not necessary for us to make such a wager. If you want her so badly, I will make a gift of the girl to you."

Kincaid did not let his triumph show in any part of his body, but the sprite was not so discreet.

"You are a coward, Standing Buffalo," the child taunted, as she skipped over to Kincaid.

Standing Buffalo's fist caught the girl behind the ear and she went flying.

Kincaid engulfed Standing Buffalo's fist in his own and stepped up close to the squat Sioux.

"Breck, come here. I want you to translate this so there's no mistake," Kincaid said with a feral growl. "Tell him that if he ever so much as lays a finger on Rebel or that girl, either one, ever again, I'll kill him."

Kincaid waited until Standing Buffalo's slitted eyes revealed he had gotten the message, and then turned his back contemptuously on the defeated bully. He gathered Reb and the girl, and allowed the excitedly chattering tribe to escort them through the stand of timber along the creek to the secluded tepee hidden in a deep thicket, where Reb had waited before the fight. Kincaid held the flapped doorway decorated with porcupine-quill designs open for Reb and the girl to enter and then followed them in himself, shutting the village out behind them.

He walked past Reb and the tiny girl, then turned around to the two expectant faces. Kincaid let the fury he had been hiding show in his flashing eyes and rigid jaw and in his aggressive spread-legged stance. He wanted to grab Reb and shake her and tell her what a fool she'd been to come along, so that he had been forced to marry her. He was married to Reb! The realization hit him in the stomach like a vicious punch, and he wavered slightly on his feet. All of his swearing and promises had come to nothing in the end. He determined to get her the hell out of there at his first opportunity, to move her as quickly as possible to somewhere really safe.

Yet, hadn't Reb done everything she had said she could do in the wilderness? Hadn't she stayed alive in the most brutal circumstances imaginable? He studied the patchwork of scratches on the beloved face and felt a surge of pride in what she had accomplished. She had done even more. Though a captive herself, had she not thought of his agony of thirst and sent the girl to bring him lifesaving water?

Kincaid could not deny he wanted Reb physically. Just thinking about caressing her rounded breasts, skimming his hands down her slim hips and thighs, touching her in places where he knew no man had been before him, awakened his body so that a hardened ridge was visible along the buckskin leggings. Having let his thoughts get so far out of hand, his eyes slipped to the small child who stood between his desires and action. His sense of humor rescued him from irritability. It was going to be a very crowded honeymoon, he thought wryly.

The fierceness of Kincaid's glower when he had entered the tepee had rocked Reb's confidence. What if, in retaliation for the forced marriage, he would not touch her? She watched him waver unsteadily and wanted to reach out to him, to hold him and love him, but she stood her ground warily, waiting. She would not beg him to love her. She had her pride. Then she detected the avid gaze that raked her body and the rising need that followed it, and she knew a fear greater than the first. What if he did take her and there was no love in his touch? She could not help shuddering.

Kincaid perceived her shudder and believed Reb had caught a chill from the night air. His sexual desire vanished at the advent of his concern.

"Are you all right?" Kincaid questioned anxiously.

When she nodded slowly, he crossed to put his arm around her shoulders. Reb's trembling increased.

"Hand me that pail of water near your feet," he said abruptly to Morning Dove. The girl fetched the rawhide pail, and Kincaid held it while Reb drank, then quickly drank most of the rest himself. Then he barked orders to the girl. "We will need more water to drink and some food; a broth, nothing solid. Can you take care of that?"

Anxious to be of help to her savior, Morning Dove grabbed another pail and raced from the tepee to get more water and to procure the herbs she would need for the broth. When she had gone, Kincaid turned again to Reb.

He suddenly felt a desperate need to claim her body, to make her totally his, but was horrified that he could even consider such a thing when she was not well. Self-consciously he dropped his arm and stepped back, breathing deeply to stem his rising desire.

"I'm glad you're safe," he said inanely, unable to direct his mind to any kind of intelligent conversation.

I love you, Rebel, he thought, searching her eyes to see if she felt the same way.

"You're hurt. Let me see to your cuts," Reb responded.

I love you, Kincaid, she thought, avoiding his glance, afraid that the love she felt would not be mirrored there, and concentrating instead on the blood mixing with dirt and sweat that streamed from a dozen places on Kincaid's body.

"There's one slash on my side that I think may need stitches, but the rest don't seem to be serious."

Reb's heart was in her eyes when she finally looked up sideways under her long, inky lashes and said, "Go lie down over there on the buffalo robe and I will take a look."

Relieved at having found in her unknowingly adoring gaze the love for which he had searched, Kincaid obeyed her, feeling suddenly enervated in the aftermath of the forced march without food or water, and the fight with Standing Buffalo. After he lay down, he closed his eyes for just a moment.

"Kincaid!" Reb cried anxiously, kneeling down beside him.

His eyelashes fluttered open.

"Oh," she said sheepishly. "I was afraid you were hurt worse than you said and were hiding it from me."

"I'm only very tired, love," he said tenderly in reply to her concern.

Reb's heart skipped a beat at the endearment, but her voice was steady when she urged, "Then rest. I will take care of you."

Kincaid closed his eyes again, thinking, as he allowed sleep to provide a surcease to his pain, how pleasant it was to be married to a woman so capable and caring.

By the time Reb sat down next to Kincaid with the rest of the pail of water and a cloth to wash him, Kincaid's regular breathing signaled that he was asleep. The blood had dried on the cut he had asked her to check, and she decided, after looking closely at it, that it did not require stitching after all. When she had removed as many of the signs of the previous days' hardship from his body as would come off with a cloth and water, Reb laid her head down next to Kincaid's on the buffalo skin for just a moment to wait for the return of Morning Dove.

When the Indian girl entered the tepee, she found

the couple sleeping contentedly. Knowing that they would both be hungry and thirsty when they woke, she continued her preparations for the liquid meal.

Several hours later Kincaid tried to turn on his side and rolled onto Reb.

"No more! No more!" Reb screamed, waking Kincaid.

"Wake up, love! You're dreaming! It's all over!"

Reb awoke to find Kincaid's concerned gray eyes watching her anxiously.

"I thought I was tied up again and that someone was kicking me," she cried, letting the tears fall freely.

"It's over now, Rebel. You're safe. We're together, and I'll keep you safe from now on," he vowed ardently, damning again the cruelty of Standing Buffalo's band of renegades.

"I'll try to stay out of trouble, Kincaid," Reb promised, hiccupping as she tried to halt the tears.

"I don't know if that's humanly possible for you," he sighed quietly, "but yes, by all means, Reb, do try."

He kissed the tears from her eyelids, then followed the wet paths down her cheeks to her mouth. He let his hands roam down her silhouette, curving in at the waist and back out again at the hips. Then he pulled the fringed buckskin skirt up to expose Reb's long legs to his exploring touch. She cried out once, when even the weight of his hand was too much for a bruised area on her hip, and he lifted himself up to gently soothe the tender spot with a kiss.

A giggle from the other side of the room made them both sit up in alarm.

"I have water and food for you," Morning Dove

said. "Unless you have other needs to attend to first," the urchin added, too knowingly for a child her age.

Reb was surprised and then amused to see Kincaid blush.

He frowned at Reb's smirk and cleared his throat, as though to erase the uncomfortable knowledge that their prior amorous activity had been observed by the child.

"We'll eat now," he said gruffly.

It was amazing how refreshed they both felt after the rest, and after consuming as much water as they could drink and broth as they could swallow.

"I feel as stuffed as a chick with caterpillars," Kincaid said when he set his empty bowl down. "Thank you for the delicious meal," he said, praising Morning Dove.

"You never complimented my broth," Reb said archly.

"I think I'll give my leg some exercise. Would you like to come along with me?" he asked, ignoring the jibe.

"I'd love to," Reb and Morning Dove both answered together.

For a child who had seemed all knowing half an hour ago, Morning Dove now appeared to be totally undiscerning of any desire on the part of the newlywed couple to be alone. It was insane for Reb to be jealous of a ten-year-old girl, but she wasn't sure what other term accurately described her feelings at that moment.

Kincaid gave Reb a helpless shrug when Morning Dove's back was turned and mouthed the word, "Later."

Reb had to be satisfied with that promise, as the

three stepped from the tepee for a stroll by moonlight through the quiet Indian village. Morning Dove turned out to be pleasant company, acting as a guide and explaining the unusual sights, such as the strips of buffalo meat hung up to dry high out of the village dogs' reach on long poles held up by wooden scaffolds. They reached the stream that ran through the village and sat down on the bank to skip stones into the moonlit water.

"How did you learn to speak English," Reb asked the girl.

"My mother taught me." At Reb's inquiring gaze, Morning Dove explained. "I have not always belonged to Standing Buffalo. My mother is the wife of an Oglala Sioux. My father's name is Silent Water," she said proudly.

"Does your mother also have blue eyes?" Reb asked.

"Oh, yes," Morning Dove agreed. "And yellow hair."

Reb and Kincaid each acknowledged to the other the significance of that statement. Morning Dove was at least half white.

"My father treats my mother well," the girl continued. "Nor did he beat me. Unless I was bad and deserved it," she added as an afterthought.

"Last summer Standing Buffalo visited in our village. He saw me playing and asked my father if he could have me as his wife when I came of age. My mother begged Silent Water not to consent to such a thing when I was so young, to wait at least until I was grown. My father agreed. But Standing Buffalo was cunning. He played a gambling game with Silent Water until my father had nothing left to wager. Standing Buffalo urged him to wager more, and when my father did, he lost. Then he had nothing left to pay with except me. Silent Water was ashamed of what he had done, but there was nothing he could do. To save my father's honor, I was forced to come to the lodge of Standing Buffalo. Now I belong to you," she said to Kincaid. "Does that mean when it is time you will take me as wife?" she asked innocently.

Kincaid turned to Reb in consternation before he spun the small girl to face him, took her shoulders in his hands, and spoke in as paternal a voice as he could muster.

"It is the custom of my people to take only one wife. I have chosen my woman." Kincaid saw the crestfallen posture of the child and looked to Reb for some sort of suggestion as to what he should say next.

Reb put her hand on the girl's shoulder comfortingly. "I have several brothers," she offered, "who will also be your brothers and who will protect you until the time comes for you to choose your mate."

"I too will always be your protector should you ever need my help," Kincaid assured her.

With the fickleness of youth, Morning Dove accepted the lost opportunity to have Kincaid as her spouse, but asked, "Will you still let me ride your horse if I am not your wife?"

Kincaid laughed out loud in relief. "Of course, if you will ask permission first, and if you promise to be careful!"

"That's wonderful! I will go and see him now and tell him what good friends we will be!"

"She is a delightful child," Reb said when Morning Dove had gone.

"But too much for me to handle," Kincaid said. "Especially since I already have my hands full." He let his actions suit his words, unlacing the buckskin dress and cupping Reb's breasts gently in his palms. He let his hands drift lower and encountered the strapping that bound Reb's ribs.

"Are any broken?"

"Just cracked, I think," Reb answered lightly.

"You were very brave," he said solemnly. It was as close as he could come to admitting that maybe Reb could take care of herself in the wilderness.

"I didn't want to die," she answered simply. She ran her fingers through his wavy locks, and caressed his cheek with the back of her hand. "I love you, Kincaid," she said. Blue's words went caroming through her mind. Enough to change? Enough to be more like what he wants you to be? "I will try to be the kind of wife you want," she whispered. She saw the acceptance of her offer in Kincaid's eyes as he moved his lips to capture hers. Reb gasped when Kincaid ran his thumbs across her nipples, and shivered when he put his lips to the pulse point behind her ear. They both groaned when they heard Morning Dove's approaching footsteps.

"Come quickly," she called. "Spotted Tail has returned!"

Chapter Twenty-one

BRECK HAD MADE A GOOD DEAL WHEN HE PURCHASED the new model Sharps rifles and ammunition that he had been paid by the Denver City merchants to bring to the Sioux. Those "peace-loving" businessmen hoped to make it possible for the Indians to undermine the Union Pacific's attempts at a northern route. Breck had just traded his own Henry rifle to Standing Buffalo and kept the last of the batch of new Sharps for himself. He and Standing Buffalo could hear the commotion start at the edge of camp and work its way toward the center. They stepped outside at the same moment Spotted Tail rode past. When Breck saw who rode beside the Indian chief, he crossed himself and said, "Mary, Joseph and Moses, it's time fer me to take a little trip." He turned to make a hasty exit, but was stopped by a harsh voice.

"Breck O'Hanlan, you conniving Irishman! Where are they?!"

"Now Matt, don't be blamin' me fer any of this. I only did what I could to help."

"Where are they?" he roared.

"Honeymoonin'!" Breck answered, with a roguish grin.

Matt turned to Blue, who rode beside him. "See the result of your meddling?"

"I don't know," Blue said sardonically. "It sounds to me as though everything turned out all right."

"I think it's great!" Adam said, beaming his approval.

Blue, Matt and Adam had reached the Indian village, discovered both Spotted Tail and Standing Buffalo gone and located the Brulé chief with the Oglala, all in the time it had taken Reb and Kincaid to make their forced march back to the village. Matt had spent the past few days with his heart in his throat because no one knew exactly where Standing Buffalo was, and O'Hanlan's flip answer had not done much to assuage his fear.

At that moment, the couple in question appeared. Reb looked from one to the other of the two men who had both been her father. It was an awkward moment. She nodded in greeting to Matt, then to Blue. At last she flashed them both a grin and quipped, "It's about time you showed up! Two fathers and neither one here to give away the bride!"

Both men were still too furious with each other to realize that Reb had made her own peace with the fact they both claimed fatherhood. Matt eyed the patchwork of scabs on Reb's face, and the red welt that the thong had left on her neck. Blue made the same survey, and the two eyeballed each other with enmity. It did not take much imagination to surmise why Reb and Kincaid had not reached the camp before Blue and Matt. The marks on Reb's face and neck spoke for themselves. Breck's presence helped explain why the couple were no longer held captive. Each man blamed the other for the harm that had come to Reb.

Matt thought that Blue had no business taking Reb along on such a dangerous journey in the first place.

Blue thought that if Matt hadn't come along he would have been with the couple, and they would have avoided capture.

Both men glared at each other until Spotted Tail interrupted the unspoken hostilities.

"I am Spotted Tail," the Indian announced to Kincaid in English. "You wish to speak with the Council?"

"Yes. I've brought gifts on behalf of a group of men who want to build an iron road for a great Iron Horse on a ribbon of land south of here. We want to do this peacefully with Spotted Tail's help."

"My friend Blue has already spoken to me of your desire. Now, it is late. Let us rest tonight and tomorrow we will speak more."

Blue accepted an invitation to enjoy Spotted Tail's hospitality, and Matt and Adam accepted a similar invitation from Breck, leaving Reb and Kincaid alone —except for Morning Dove—who volunteered to make one last trip to the stream for more water.

Standing Buffalo watched the departing white men with gritted teeth. He should have killed Too-Big-For-Horses when he had the chance! Spotted Tail was always too ready to believe the white man when he offered gifts and promised peace. If the white warrior convinced the Brulé chief to sign a treaty, in the end they would only be cheated again, just as he had been denied his vengeance against Too-Big-For-Horses. He would not be robbed by the white man any longer.

Standing Buffalo formulated a very simple plan. He would take the white woman and deal with the tall warrior when he came to get her back. But how was he going to get the woman away from Too-Big-For-Horses?

Just then, Morning Dove passed him on her way to the stream.

Standing Buffalo stepped boldly into the path of the Indian girl.

"What do you want of me?" she asked, confident that the Indian would not touch her while she was under the protection of Too-Big-For-Horses, but nonetheless leaning away from him cautiously.

"Tell Too-Big-For-Horses that, since he has betrayed the Sioux with his talk of a treaty with the white man, I take back my gift and will touch you as I please." With that, Standing Buffalo slapped Morning Dove, knocking her down, so that one of the sharp stones along the bank cut her cheek. He turned and left, smiling triumphantly as he assessed the certain success of his plan.

Morning Dove picked herself up and filled the water pail before she returned to the tepee. She had tried to staunch the flow of blood on her face, but, when she entered the tepee, Kincaid noticed immediately that she had been hurt.

"What happened?" he questioned. He took her face in his hand to turn it into the firelight to see the cut.

"Standing Buffalo . . ."

"Did he do this to you?" Kincaid raged.

"Wait!" Morning Dove said. "I do not want to make trouble. He said he is taking back his gift. I must go back to him."

"You stay right here. I'll settle this with Standing Buffalo once and for all," Kincaid said coldly. "Reb, you take care of Morning Dove, and stay out of trouble!"

Reb caught her lower lip in her teeth to avoid hurling a childish retort. She had made up her mind to try to be more like Kincaid wanted her to be. If he said stay, she would stay. At least for a little while.

Kincaid had been gone only a moment when Standing Buffalo stepped inside the tepee. He reached for the girl close to the door and put a knife to her throat.

"Tell the white woman that I will kill you if she makes a sound."

As soon as Reb heard the first gutteral word, she reached for the knife she had been using by the fire and turned with it in her hand, ready to attack. The sight of Standing Buffalo with his blade pricking the skin on Morning Dove's neck brought her up short.

"He says he will kill me if you make a noise," the terrified child said. There was more gutteral barking from the squat Sioux and the tiny girl translated. "He says to drop your knife and come with him quietly. He says there will not be a second chance to obey."

The Indian's eyes gleamed wickedly as he pressed the point just a little deeper into Morning Dove's flesh. Reb dropped her knife as though it had caught fire.

"Tell him I will do as he asks."

Standing Buffalo gestured for Reb to go ahead of him and followed with Morning Dove still in his possession. His plan was working perfectly. He would have the white woman as bait, and the girl to serve his needs while he waited for Too-Big-For-Horses to come to meet his fate.

Standing Buffalo escorted the two women out of the village on foot to a spot where he had hidden two horses. He pulled Morning Dove up in front of him while indicating that Reb should mount the other horse.

Reb had felt helpless when tied and gagged, but it was nothing to the feeling of powerlessness she had now. Nothing kept her from speaking, nothing kept her from saving herself, except the certainty that if she made one wrong move Standing Buffalo would kill the small girl.

Standing Buffalo took the lead on Reb's horse and headed for the craggy mountain bluff that was closest to the village. He did nothing to soften the imprint left by the horses' hooves on the mossy rocks. He made no effort whatsoever to hide his trail, for he wanted the white warrior to be able to find him.

Meanwhile, Kincaid had searched the entire Indian village for Standing Buffalo and, when he could not locate him, decided that the cowardly Sioux must have thought better of his precipitous action and absented himself from the village. As Kincaid returned to the tepee, he was worrying about how he was going to get enough privacy with Reb to have a proper honeymoon without hurting Morning Dove's feelings. By the time he arrived back at the tepee, he had made up his mind that he didn't care about the child's feelings.

He lifted the decorated tent flap and entered. His mouth was open to speak, but no words came out. Nothing inside was disturbed. All was as he had left it. Reb's knife lay on the cutting stone beside the kettle slung over the fire, but the tent was empty! After he'd told them both to stay put! Kincaid rued the day he had fallen in love with his hellcat in buckskins.

"All right Rebel," he gritted out through clenched teeth. "Where are you?"

Standing Buffalo stopped the horses when they reached a small stone cave set into the side of the mountain.

"Get off your horse," he ordered Reb. Morning Dove translated.

"Now you, girl, take this rope and tie her hands securely," Standing Buffalo said to Morning Dove. He replaced his knife in its sheath and took in his hands the Henry rifle he had just bought from Breck. He hefted it slightly and then cocked it.

Morning Dove worked quickly. When she had finished, Standing Buffalo checked the knots. "Now, go inside," he ordered. He turned slightly to watch Reb and at that moment Morning Dove shoved him as hard as she could and ran. The stocky Indian was off balance momentarily, but recovered quickly, and swung the rifle up to sight on the fleeing girl. Just as he pulled the trigger, Reb flung herself into him, knocking him to the ground, where their momentum rolled them over together several times.

Reb gasped with the pain that assaulted her already bruised and battered body, but strained her shoulders up off the ground to see if Morning Dove was all right. Nothing moved in the darkness.

"She is dead!" Standing Buffalo said maliciously to the uncomprehending Reb. "I saw her fall. You will pay for your stupid action," he threatened, "after I kill Too-Big-For-Horses." He pulled Reb up and dragged her into the cave after him.

Kincaid had waited a half hour for Reb and Morning Dove to return, and then had decided that he would have no peace of mind until he knew what they were doing. The etiquette that forced him to wait for permission to enter Spotted Tail's tepee tried Kincaid's patience. He could see Spotted Tail, with Blue on his left, still seated before the fire, talking. Exiled from the tepee, but guarding the doorway, Trapper thumped his tail on the ground in welcome to Kincaid.

When Kincaid finally entered, Spotted Tail was coldly polite.

"I have said I will discuss the treaty tomorrow. What brings you here?"

Kincaid was furious with Reb for the embarrassing position in which he found himself. "I'm looking for my wife," he said in chagrin. "I thought she might have come here to see Blue."

"I haven't seen her," Blue answered with an amused smile. "Perhaps she went to visit Matt and Adam."

Kincaid remembered what Reb had said about her brothers being Morning Dove's brothers, too, and thought that she had probably had some brilliant idea of getting Morning Dove and Adam together tonight. He would kill her when he found her.

"You're probably right," he answered ruefully. "I'll go check there. I'm sorry to have broken your peace," he said to Spotted Tail.

"She is a new wife," Spotted Tail said sympathetically. "Be patient, and make your wishes known to her, and she will learn to please you."

Kincaid only wished it were that easy. Feeling more foolish with every step he took, the angry newlywed made his way to Breck's lodging. The mountain man had set up a tent of sorts, which was really no more than a piece of hide to keep the sun off during the day. There were no sides to the shelter, and Kincaid could see as he neared that Reb and Morning Dove were not there. Then where the hell were they? he thought in exasperation.

When Kincaid approached the three men it was anxiety, not embarrassment, that beset him. "Have you seen Reb?"

"Lost her already, have ye, lad?" Breck chuckled mirthfully.

"Standing Buffalo attacked Morning Dove, so I went looking for him to make good my promise. I never found him, but when I got back to the tepee Reb and Morning Dove were gone. I thought they might have come here."

"We haven't seen them," Adam said.

All four men heard the distant echo of a single shot, and each one knew with a chill of certainty that Standing Buffalo had Reb and Morning Dove. Each man searched the others' faces for the answer to the same question. Which one had been shot?

"Rebel," Kincaid whispered. The name floated on the night air, drifting toward the craggy bluffs from which the bullet's echo had come.

"Ye won't be able to see yer way to follow him tonight and, even if ye find the trail, he'll be waitin' fer ye somewhere in the dark," Breck intoned.

"We have to try!" Adam urged.

Kincaid put his hand on Adam's shoulder. "I agree. I'll get Satan."

"It's yer funeral," Breck cautioned. "Ye'll be needin' a weapon. Here's me good new Sharps rifle," he said, offering Kincaid the spanking new gun. "It's loaded and ready to go. I'll join ye at daybreak when there's more light."

"I'll get Blue. We'll need all the help we can get," Matt said.

Matt and Blue joined Kincaid and Adam and the four men headed toward the closest mountain, each one using all his skill to search the ground for signs that would tell them which way Standing Buffalo had gone. It was Blue who first saw the hoofprints that let them know they were on the right track. They followed the trail slowly for another half hour before Matt raised his hand for all to be still. Then they all heard the noise. Something was coming through the undergrowth. The men dismounted and spread out behind whatever cover they could find to await whoever was proceeding so hurriedly and noisily toward them. The tension mounted as the crash of broken branches drew closer.

Adam saw the black braided hair and buckskin shirt and attacked, bowling over and subduing his struggling victim with a minimum of effort. That achievement had put his hands in contact with two mounds on his opponent's chest.

"It's a girl," he shouted in amazement. "And she's hurt," he added when his hand came away from the girl's arm sticky with blood.

"Morning Dove?" Kincaid knelt beside the girl, who still lay between Adam's knees.

"Yes," the girl cried in relief.

"How badly are you hurt?"

"Only shot a little," she answered Kincaid. "Standing Buffalo has taken your woman prisoner. They are at the cave a little way up the mountain. He means to kill you, and her, too, I think. I will take you there," she said, trying to get up. She did not have much success because Adam had not moved from his position straddling her.

Kincaid put his hand on her shoulder to lay her back down. "You've done enough. We'll do the rest.

Adam, will you take Morning Dove back to the village? Adam?"

Adam was entranced by the large luminous eyes in the perfect heart-shaped face revealed by the moonlight. He hitched his knee over the girl so he knelt to one side, then lifted her easily into his arms. She was so tiny!

"I can walk," Morning Dove murmured. She had been caught by Adam's intense gaze, and held her breath waiting for him to speak.

Adam stood up, then shook his head as though to clear it. He handed Morning Dove to Kincaid. "Hold her until I mount Ricochet, then hand her up to me."

When Adam had settled in the saddle, Kincaid passed the girl up into the bewildered man's arms. Adam cradled the girl as though she were a small child and, indeed, he thought, she was not much larger.

"Good luck," he said to the other three men as they all mounted up. "I'll see you back in the village."

Kincaid heaved a sigh of relief that Reb had not been shot, but, thinking back on Morning Dove's words, a shiver ran down his spine. The one thing that had kept him sane was the belief that Standing Buffalo did not want to kill Reb, that he wanted her for himself. Morning Dove had suggested that the Indian wanted to kill them both. He considered calling Adam back to question the girl further, but realized he would have his answers soon enough. Arguing voices brought his attention back to the immediate situation.

"You had no business letting Reb come on this trip," Matt railed at Blue. "She would have been safe at home now, if it hadn't been for you."

"You never learn, do you?" Blue countered. "You don't understand Reb any better than you did Rachel."

"Don't you dare bring Rachel's name into this!" Matt said savagely. "I should have killed you six years ago, and I would have, too, if you weren't Reb's father!"

Kincaid digested that juicy tidbit of information, and felt his stomach roll with the punch of it. So that's what Blue had told Reb, and that she hadn't been able to talk about. No wonder the concerned faces of Reb and Blue that had greeted him when he'd opened his eyes in Blue's cabin had borne such identical features! Blue was Reb's natural father!

"If Spotted Tail hadn't come along and found me where you left me, I would have been dead," Blue retorted. "Matt, you were my friend. I didn't mean to fall in love with Rachel, it just happened. I'm sorry you were hurt. I've been sorry for a long time. But I have no regrets about Reb! I love her like a daughter. She's as wild and as free as the mountains she was raised in. Believe me, when I say you can't tie her down. You just have to learn to swallow your fear and love her as she is!"

The speech could have been aimed at the tall Yankee, and perhaps it was, but neither Matt nor Kincaid had a chance to reply, because at that moment the silence was shattered by an otherworldly scream.

Chapter Twenty-two

FOR SOME REASON, STANDING BUFFALO HAD NOT TIED Reb's feet or gagged her. He had merely gestured to Reb to sit in a back corner of the dark cave. She would have obeyed the rifle in his hands no matter the condition of the cave floor, but she was glad to discover when she sat that the ground was dry, and it did not crunch with little bugs or scurry with little animals. Standing Buffalo lit a fire with flint and tinder he had brought in his rawhide bag-for-all-possible-things and the cave began to reflect the cheery light. The Indian continued talking to himself in his gutteral tongue, eyeing Reb every once in a while. He seemed to be working himself up to something and, from the lascivious leers that were frequently visited upon her, Reb could make a pretty good guess of the particular activity he had in mind.

Reb had thought for a while now that, if there were just some distraction, she might be able to get past

Standing Buffalo and run for safety. She had decided to create her own diversion, when she heard the voices arguing in English and knew that help was on its way. Unfortunately, Standing Buffalo heard them, too, and walked to the front of the cave to look out. Reb cursed the stupidity of the lumpkins who would take the time and trouble to rescue her and then botch it by letting their presence be known in such a clumsy way. Well, as long as they were close enough for her to hear them, the reverse was also true. Reb let go with an earsplitting shriek and charged Standing Buffalo like a billy goat. The Indian was caught unawares and sent twirling by Reb's butting shove. She was in the open air in moments and running.

"I'm here!" Reb yelled at the top of her lungs. "Help me!"

The three men urged their horses dangerously fast in the darkness toward Reb's voice.

"I see her!" Matt yelled. Just then, he identified Standing Buffalo's silhouette in the firelight at the entrance to the cave taking aim on Reb. At the instant Standing Buffalo fired, Reb tripped and fell.

"She's down!" Matt threw himself off his horse and ran to Reb, who rose unsteadily.

"I just fell," she mumbled breathlessly. "I'm not hurt."

Matt pulled her into his arms and rocked her back and forth as tears of relief streamed down his face.

Seeing that Reb was with Matt, Kincaid let Satan thunder on directly toward the Sioux renegade. He shouldered the Sharps rifle Breck had given him, but, when he tried to fire the gun, it jammed.

Standing Buffalo saw Too-Big-For-Horses on his devil steed barreling directly toward him, and he leveled his gun at the big man's heart. Then he thought how much better his revenge if the white man should be robbed first of that which was dear to him.

Kincaid watched in horror as the Indian turned the gun on Reb.

"NO! Rebel!" he screamed. He yanked hard to turn the black stallion into the path of the Sioux's fire, knowing as he did so that there was no way he could get there in time. His eyes were riveted on Reb, expecting to see a repetition of the tragedy he had experienced once before.

Both Matt and Blue heard Kincaid's warning yell, but it was Blue who acted first. He grasped Reb so that she was sandwiched between the two men who had raised her and loved her and who had both been her father.

Kincaid jerked when he saw Blue take the bullet that was intended for Reb, then cling to his daughter, guarding her from further harm.

Standing Buffalo screeched his rage at Blue's interference and pumped two more shots into the white man. Out of the corner of his eye, the enraged Indian perceived a streak of gray fur. He wheeled and barely had time to fire his gun before Trapper crashed into him with a yelp of pain. The weight of the dying animal bowled the Sioux over, and the Henry clattered away across the stony ground out of his reach. Standing Buffalo threw off the carcass just as Kincaid launched himself from Satan's back.

The two enemies rolled from the force of Kincaid's thrust, but it was Standing Buffalo who came out on top with his knife poised to kill the white devil who had so plagued him. A ghoulish leer had frozen on the Sioux's face as he anticipated his moment of glory.

Standing Buffalo had underestimated the fury of his adversary. It was the last mistake he ever made.

Kincaid grabbed Standing Buffalo's wrists, and the muscles of the two men bulged with the strain as Kincaid slowly but surely turned the blade up to the savage's heart and then inexorably pressed it home. Kincaid pushed the hated body away and rose to stand over the fallen Sioux. Standing Buffalo's eyes glazed and a trickle of blood ran from his mouth.

"I always keep my promises," Kincaid growled ferally to the dying Indian. He turned and staggered back to the huddle around Blue. The mountain man was stretched out on the ground with his head cradled in Reb's lap.

"How is he?" Kincaid rasped breathlessly.

"Don't talk as though I'm not here," Blue said irritably. Blue grabbed his chest with his hand as though to stop his life's blood from pouring out, but soon it seeped through his fingers. "Rachel and I will finally be together for the first time without causing pain to anyone else." Blue did not realize he had spoken aloud.

Reb watched Matt reach for Blue's other hand and take it in his own, then saw the forgiveness in her father's eyes as he held on tight to his dying friend.

Blue coughed and his lips tightened from the pain. "Damn, that hurts," he rasped. "Remember what I said," he admonished Reb. "I meant it."

"I will," Reb answered, smoothing the silver-streaked black hair back from his cool forehead.

"I will," Kincaid answered.

Blue looked at Kincaid and smiled. His voice had weakened, so Kincaid had to lean in to hear him. "I thought you might get the message. I'm glad you did." Kincaid could hear Blue's expiring breath, and he reached over to close the lifeless mahogany eyes. Then he stood up.

"I'm sorry, Reb," Matt said in a voice thick with grief. "I never had the courage to tell you when I first found out he was your father. I was so jealous of the love Rachel gave to him, and I was afraid of losing yours, too."

"I will never stop loving you, Daddy," Reb whispered. She leaned across Blue to kiss her father on the cheek.

Matt cleared his throat, then stood. "I'll take Blue back to his cabin to bury him."

"Take Trapper, too, Daddy, and bury him next to Blue," Reb said quietly.

Matt nodded his agreement, then asked Kincaid, "Will I see you when your business here is finished?"

"Of course. Reb and I will come to visit you before we go . . ." Kincaid stopped in midsentence and glanced down at Blue, whose head still lay cradled in Reb's lap. Kincaid saw that, for the second time, Reb bore her loss dry-eyed. ". . . before we make our final plans," he finished his original sentence.

Reb helped Kincaid and Matt place her father across his horse and tie him down, with Trapper alongside him, then mounted her own animal and waited while Kincaid strapped the Indian down in similar fashion.

It was a sadly pensive party that made its way back toward the Indian village. When they arrived, Reb went directly to their tepee, where she found Morning Dove and Adam.

"Blue is dead," she said dully. "So is Standing Buffalo."

Adam took his sister in his arms to comfort her. Kincaid entered the dwelling and walked over to tap Adam on the shoulder. Adam nodded and stepped back to let Kincaid take his place.

"We'd like to be alone," Kincaid said. "Adam, do you think you could find a place for Morning Dove to spend the night?"

"The girl can stay with me." Adam took Morning Dove by the hand and led her from the tepee.

When they were alone, Kincaid walked Reb over to the buffalo robe and made her lie down. He lay down beside her and took her in his embrace, laying his cheek against hers.

"I'm sorry, Rebel. Blue was a good man."

The words were the catalyst that released Reb's tears. She buried her face in Kincaid's chest and cried and cried until finally sleep overtook her. Kincaid was careful not to hold her too tight for fear of hurting her bruises, but soon he, too, lost the battle with fatigue and slept.

They woke to the cheerful voice of Morning Dove, who was trying to convince Adam that the couple would be grateful to have a hot breakfast and not mind the intrusion at all.

"She's right, Adam," Kincaid called from his pallet.

"Ooooh!" Reb groaned as she raised herself up. "I'm so sore."

"Me, too!" Kincaid agreed, giving Reb a light kiss on the nose. "The sooner my business is done, the sooner we can be out of here and on our way home."

Reb chewed on her lower lip to keep from asking where Kincaid thought home was. She reminded herself of Blue's sacrifice, and her mother's, and determined that her love was at least as strong as theirs. So she decided to say nothing.

"You are looking well this morning," Kincaid said to Morning Dove as the girl entered the tepee.

"The bullet only scratched my arm. This man," she gestured to Adam, "took good care of me."

"This is Adam, one of my woman's brothers she told you about, who will be your brother also until you choose a mate," Kincaid explained.

Adam looked confused. "What's this about my being her brother until she chooses a mate? The girl's just a child!"

"That shows what you know," Morning Dove sniffed. "I have passed fourteen summers."

"Fourteen!!" Adam, Reb and Kincaid all exclaimed together.

Kincaid turned to Adam ominously. "Where did you two spend the night?"

"By the stream, but you can just forget whatever you're thinking. She's a kid!"

"A kid who knocked you off your skids the first time you saw her!"

"I was just surprised because she was so tiny and because . . . because . . ."

"Yes?" Kincaid asked aggressively.

"Because she had breasts!" Adam blurted. A blush spread up his cheeks at the admission.

"Damn!" Kincaid muttered. "Where Reb and I are going, we can't take any extra responsibilities. So you'll take this . . . this . . . tiny child with breasts home with you and take care of her like the good *brother* Reb promised you'd be. Understand?"

"I already have two sisters," Adam said sullenly.

"Well, now you have three," Kincaid said with finality.

They had completely forgotten that Morning Dove was listening to every word they said.

"I will not go where I am not wanted," she spat at

Adam. "Besides, I would not like to have a brother with green eyes like a cat and a broken nose!"

"Last night you told me that my eyes reminded you of the prairie grass in summer, and that my broken nose made my face look strong!" Adam contradicted.

Kincaid and Reb exchanged amused glances.

"Well, maybe I was wrong!" Morning Dove shouted. She scooted out the door before Adam could answer, and he raced out after her.

Reb again resisted the urge to ask where it was they were going that they couldn't take extra responsibilities. They sat down to the breakfast Morning Dove had brought, and it was shortly thereafter that Kincaid was called to meet with the Council.

Kincaid entered the Council lodge with some trepidation, since he was not sure what Spotted Tail's reaction would be to the death of Standing Buffalo. If he had known what an irritant the renegade had been to the chief, he would not have been so concerned. As it was, he knew the answer to his question when he was seated at Spotted Tail's immediate left as an honored guest. No word was spoken of the Indian's death, as they smoked the ceremonial pipe that was passed to the left from man to man.

"Tell us of your iron road," Spotted Tail finally invited.

"It will change the face of the mountains near the Platte," Kincaid explained. "We cannot know what the future will be, but it is possible for both our peoples to share in the good things the Iron Horse can bring along the iron road. It will join this nation east and west together, and that is a good thing after the strife of the years past. In peace, your people and mine can learn much from one another. Will you join me at Ft. Laramie in the spring to decide the terms of a treaty?"

There was some discussion of whether Too-Big-For-Horses could be trusted, but Spotted Tail was supportive and reminded that his friend Blue had also been in favor of sitting down to talk with the white man. Spotted Tail turned to the circled Council and they took a vote.

"We will come," he said.

Kincaid left the Council meeting feeling satisfied with the results of his mission and very thankful to Blue for the ease with which the Indians had concurred with his suggestion. Anxious to spend some time alone with Reb, he was unpleasantly surprised when he arrived back at the tepee to discover they had company. Kincaid sat down next to Reb and made it clear from the glare he gave Breck O'Hanlan that the Irishman was not welcome.

"I just came to give me condolences to Reb and to bring ye a little weddin' present," Breck said. The burly mountain man fished around in his pocket and came up with Kincaid's gold pocket watch.

Reb watched anxiously to see how Kincaid would react to the vivid reminder of Laurie.

"Where did you get this?" Kincaid asked, smoothing the engraving on the back with his thumb nervously.

"I gave Standin' Buffalo me Henry rifle and he gave me that. I saw yer name etched in gold and thought ye might like to have it back."

"Thank you, yes. It meant a lot to me," Kincaid said. Kincaid looked up at Reb with all the love he felt for her in his heart as he said, "I thought I would never be as happy again as I was when I received this gift the first time. I will always carry it now, remembering that the gift has been given again."

Reb nodded imperceptibly, yet Kincaid saw her gesture and acknowledged it by bringing the golden symbol to his lips.

"I was sorry to hear 'bout Blue," the mountain man said, oblivious to what had passed between the couple. "I heard ye done in Standin' Buffalo with his own knife."

It took Kincaid a moment to focus on what the redheaded man had said. Then he let out some of his anger over the tragedy of the previous night. "If your damned Sharps had fired, I could have saved Blue! When I checked it this morning, I discovered that it has a defective firing mechanism."

"Mary, Joseph and Moses," Breck muttered, crossing himself. "Be ye sure?"

Kincaid nodded solemnly.

No wonder the Sharps had been so cheap! Breck wondered just how many of the rifles he'd been trading were faulty. He sure didn't want to give up any of those prime pelts he'd acquired. "I think I'll check the lay of the land out west over Ft. Bridger way," the burly man said. "Good luck, girl," he said after he had risen. "Take care of yerself," he cautioned Kincaid. "If ye ever get out to Ft. Bridger, come see me."

"We just might do that," Kincaid said.

Reb glanced at Kincaid. When were they ever going to be as far west as Ft. Bridger? That was on the other side of the Rocky Mountains. Weren't they going back east to New York?

When Breck left, Kincaid turned back to Reb with a grin. "Now that we're alone, how about a walk?"

"A walk?"

"I have in mind a place with a little more privacy." Kincaid led Reb to the stream and they strolled north along the bank for several minutes. As they meandered past the rushing water Kincaid said, "When I was in Denver City, my father offered me a job."

Reb's first thought was that they were going to be leaving the wilderness, and a ration of fear rose up to choke her. She managed to ask, "Did you accept?"

"Not at the time, but I'm going to."

In panic, she wondered how long she had before he wanted to leave. "When will you start?"

"Right away," he answered. "He needs someone to survey the rest of the Union Pacific route west, and then to act as an advance man for the track gangs."

Reb caught Kincaid's gaze and her eyes widened in disbelief. "You're not going back to New York!" Then she bubbled with laughter, and began to leap and dance in a circle around him. "You're going *west!*"

"We're going west." Kincaid opened his arms to her and she threw herself into them. He swung her in a circle until they were both dizzy and giddy with joy. Blue had been right. She was special, and wild and free. He swallowed the lump of fear in his throat and hugged her tighter.

"It sounds like a wonderful job," Reb whispered in Kincaid's ear.

They had reached a point where the creek widened and deepened into a pond that was surrounded by stone cliffs on three sides and rimmed in cat-o'-nine-tails. A stream of water glistened along one wall, and green moss had grown out along either side of the slick wetness. Kincaid released Reb, and she immediately began unlacing her dress. She let it fall, then strode boldly into the cool water. Reb whirled to confront Kincaid, who still stood on the bank watching her.

"Come in. The water is refreshing," she called.

Kincaid unlaced his buckskin shirt and carefully pulled it off over his sore muscles, then slipped out of the buckskin pants as well. Reb waited patiently for him to walk the few paces into the water to her.

"Hold me," she said quietly.

Kincaid gently embraced Reb. She encircled his waist with her arms. The feel of flesh against flesh in the soothing water left them strangely contented.

Reb turned her face up to Kincaid and bathed in the love that radiated from his eyes. He brought his mouth down to gently cover hers and sipped delicately of the nectar that was Reb.

Reb leaned forward to touch her lips to Kincaid's chest, which tasted distinctly salty. Then she twirled her tongue around each of his nipples, noticing with delight that they hardened into buds as hers also had in mere anticipation of Kincaid's touch.

"You're asking for trouble, Reb," Kincaid growled low, when Reb kept up the teasing titillation.

"When have I ever run from trouble?" Reb taunted. "Besides, you'll drown if you try to kiss me like this!" she laughed, referring to the fact that her breasts were under water.

"We'll see about that," he said.

When Kincaid took a deep breath as though he

were going to dive under water, Reb lunged back and splashed furiously away from him.

"Catch me if you can!" she shouted merrily.

Kincaid swam powerfully toward her, then disappeared underwater. Reb turned in circles, searching for the telltale ripples that would reveal his presence, but the pool remained so calm that a green dragonfly lit on the surface nearby. Just as Reb was beginning to worry, Kincaid burst upward with Reb cradled in his arms so that her rosy crests were accessible to his mouth. He smacked kisses noisily across her face and neck.

"Now, what was that about drowning?" he asked smugly, threatening to drop Reb. She screamed and grabbed his bruised shoulder for support. Kincaid yelped at the sharp pain and flinched away, losing his balance so that they both went under. Reb shot up, breaking the surface with a surge of excitement, then hunted for Kincaid. She felt his kiss on her navel moments before he appeared before her. Kincaid lifted Reb up out of the water by her waist flicking the crystal drops from her breasts with the tip of his tongue, then working his way up her neck to her mouth, as he slowly lowered her into the water. The touch of lip to lip caused them both to shiver in pleasure. They let the world pass unnoticed as they loved playfully, tugging on just an upper lip or just a lower lip, or running tantalizing tongues along the edges of lips, each learning what most pleased the other.

Reb ran her hands through the wet curls at Kincaid's nape, then traced the line of his strong jaw and the familiar angled planes of his face. "I love the feel of your skin," she murmured.

"I feel your touch in my heart, Rebel. It warms

me, it soothes me and I am content." He hugged her to him, reveling in the way their bodies molded together.

Reb stood in the sparkling water with her arms around Kincaid and her head leaned quietly against his chest so that his voice rumbled in her ear when he said, "You're getting all wrinkled."

"I just wanted proof that you'll still love me when I'm old," she whispered against his flesh.

"I will love you forever, Rebel," he said. He lifted her chin with a forefinger and sealed the promise by touching his lips to hers.

"Are you two going to stay in there all day?" an irritated voice called from the bank. Adam paced back and forth nervously. "It's Morning Dove. She's run away. I need your help to find her."

Reb looked up mischievously at Kincaid. "He should have known better than to try to boss her around," she said. "We'll be right there," she called to Adam.

"I'll be right there," he corrected. "Humor me," he said when she opened her mouth to retort.

She smiled sweetly at him, then dashed a huge scoop of water into his face. "Hurry back!" she said, grinning broadly, "and maybe I'll give you a chance to get even."

Kincaid snatched a quick wet kiss before he splashed from the water. He pulled on his buckskins while Adam ranted and explained to a very understanding Kincaid how Morning Dove had been impossible to talk to.

"I'll be back soon," Kincaid shouted to Reb. "Go back to the tepee and wait for me and stay out of trouble!"

A LOVING DEFIANCE

When the two men had left, Reb stepped slowly from the pool, letting the rivulets of water cascade down her sleek form. Reb felt so loved she could have purred in contented she-cat satisfaction. She would go back to the tepee and wait for Kincaid's return, and she would do her best to be good and to stay out of trouble as he had asked. At least for a little while.

HISTORICAL ROMANCES

POCKET BOOKS

Home delivery from Pocket Books